Black Art Publishing Limited

THE SCARLET TESSERA

JULIAN LORR

Copyright © Julian Lorr 2012

The moral rights of the author of this work have been asserted by him in accordance with the Copyright Designs and Patents Act of 1988

All rights reserved

This novel is entirely a work of fiction. The names, characters, incidents and places portrayed in it, other than those clearly in the public domain, are the work of the author's imagination and not to be construed as real. Any resemblance to actual persons, living or dead, events or localities, is entirely co-incidental.

For Nicola…

For everything.

"And I thought the dead who are already dead more fortunate than the living who are still alive"

Ecclesiastes 4:8

July 1st

01

6.04pm

He drew on his cigarette, eyes tracing her outline against the world around her. Perhaps he might cut her out as if she were no more than a picture in a magazine. Stick her in his mental scrapbook. Show her to the world the way she should be seen. Stripped bare and pure.

The waiter flitted hurriedly between the handful of tables, squeezing through the gap between his customers and the river of people passing by. She exchanged a few words with him, smiling and laughing, and then she was up, collecting her things. Moving on.

He pulled his jacket on and followed her into the mass of people. She walked self-assuredly. Seemingly in no hurry; But he knew this was no woman of leisure. She didn't go home each night to a husband or to children. She went home alone and focused on her studies. She drank coke and high-caffeine drinks and ate chocolate to keep herself awake in her study of the dead. She laughed her way through flirty text messages whilst trying to memorise formaldehyde procedures, and slept with her on-off boyfriend amongst the books she left open at the pages on human dissection. Perhaps she even called that love. And then, in the morning, she would paint herself another face, gather up her books, and do it all again.

To the outside world she was a beauty with brains. A butterfly too clever to be caught; but when he looked at her he saw the truth. Tiny hooks, thrown out into the world.

Tiny little scarlet tessera, promising entrance to her theatre, for these are the things of Man: Sex, Lust, and Death.

She crossed the road leading to Farringdon Tube Station. He quickened his pace and followed her to the station opening. He was only a few feet from her now. He watched the sway of her body as she turned into the station and started down the steps. He watched her tuck her hair behind her ear as she looked down to her ticket, passing through the turnstile and into the line of bodies, filtering like sand through a timer, down to the trains.

The southbound platform heaved as if alive. Lines of people three to four deep stretched away down the concrete curve. He squeezed his way through, moving closer, close enough to touch her now if he wanted to. The tunnel at the far end of the platform rumbled as the train made its way through.

And then it was powering toward them.

People began to push forward.

"Mind the gap" he said, close enough to her ear for her hair to touch his cheek.

"Wha - ?"

And then, in one swift and almost imperceptible movement in the mass of people, he pushed her forward.

July 2nd

02

2.32am

Detective Chief Inspector Claire McMullen toyed with her rosary.
Click-clack. Click–clack.
The sound echoed through the sterile corridor, fading into the endless tunnel of strip-lights.

She had waited a long time to be here. Nineteen years in all; Every day of every month of every year feeling longer and more unbearable than the last.

It wasn't true what they said: Things did not get easier as time went on. Well, not this, at least.

The door opposite bore the words "No Unauthorised Personnel". She found it hard to believe anyone would want to be down here , by choice, unauthorised or otherwise, in what amounted to nothing more than a place of indignity. A place of death and detachment. A place where the body came, long after its soul had gone. Each time she came to these places she felt the sickness of death in the pit of her stomach. The kind of emotional revulsion at the base of herself that made her want to vomit up her core; throw up the horror before she choked on it. *And God knows*, she thought, *I've been to these places enough times...*

She spun the rosary around her finger, catching it as it hit her palm. Then she spun it back the other way, catching it again as it lashed itself over the back of her hand. She did it again. And again.

Click-clack. Click-clack.

All the while she stared at the door, listening to the sound of the rosary echoing through the emptiness.

"Hail Mary, full of grace" she said, her words leaping out into the stillness like demons from Pandora's Box, "The Lord is with thee".

She continued with the rest of the prayer, her voice eventually falling into a whisper as she repeated the phrases over and over, hypnotic in their cycle. "Pray for us sinners, now and at the hour of our death". She held the rosary loosely in her hand, pushing the beads around in a circle with her fingers.

"Now and at the hour of our death" she repeated.

The echo of her voice died, and the silence returned.

Fate is such a terrible thing, she thought. When Death comes for us there is no turning back. The Greatest Leveller. Rich man, poor man. Beggar man, thief. All the same… in the hour of their death. Resistant in the greatness of their ego, and ultimately desperate in the weakness of their grief.

The door opened in front of her. A tired looking man in a green surgeons gown emerged, face mask hanging around his neck. He looked up and down the corridor and frowned before turning his attention to her. "Detective Chief Inspector McMullen?" he asked. "Claire McMullen?"

"That's me" she said, flipping the rosary into her coat pocket as she got to her feet.

"Is anyone with you?" he continued.

"No. Why? Should there be?"

He took a deep breath, seeming to give his body some kind of welcome relief. "It's a very strange sight, that's all" he said. "You may benefit from a colleague being present, or….", he trailed off, cut short by the look on her face.

"I'm a big girl now", she said, adding "Dr. Vanner" after glancing at the ID card clipped to his chest.

"Very well". He stepped aside and gestured for her to enter the examination lab.

The periphery of the room was in semi-darkness, cast into shadow by the large strip lights above the steel table in the centre of the room. She paused by the door, waiting for him to join her.

"Thank you for letting me see her so soon" she said. "It's possible that this woman was killed by someone who has been on the run for a very long time. We need every head start we can get".

"Yes, I heard about the general view from Detective Inspector Webber. Nice chap, very friendly. He did, however, impress upon me the urgency of the situation in no uncertain terms".

She noted the comments. *Webber. Nice chap.*

He moved round the table to the opposite side. They faced each other, divided only by the corpse under the white sheet on the cold steel.

"We have found some striking similarities" he said, removing the sheet. "In fact, as I will show you, it seems that this is identical in all respects to the original killings, as I understand them. You will appreciate that the urgency with which I have been asked to work on this means that although I have read the file, I am by no means able to give, at this stage, an in depth analysis".

McMullen was staring at the woman's face. "No, that's fine" she said distractedly, her voice softer than usual. "I'm not expecting miracles, I just needed to….." She forced herself to look up at him; To focus. "I just needed to see it for myself" she said purposefully.

He drew another deep breath. "Indeed. Well…" he moved to the head of the table. "As you can see, the victim's head has been shaved completely. What is interesting is that it is without a cut, nick or graze. To shave a head with such precision there must be co-operation, or, I would say, sedation".

He moved to the side of the table again, before continuing. "This theory of sedation, however, does not seem to fit the facial mutilation. You see how the victim's lips have been cut off. The cuts are serrated and jagged. They are not clean. They are carried out as if under extreme resistance. Extreme distress".

She stared at the woman's head. The absence of the lips gave the victim a skull like appearance. With no hair and nothing to soften the edges it became a sickening hybrid of the living and the dead. Mutilated just enough to be horrific, but in no way enough to be the cause of death.

"What else?" she said slowly, her voice cracking slightly as she spoke. "What about the cause of death".

Dr Vanner pointed to the marks on the woman's wrists and neck. "There are no other lesions" he said. "The poor girl was bled to death"

"Then she wasn't killed at the scene" said McMullen. "There was no blood at the scene. Just the body".

She ran both her hands through her hair, a single blonde strand coming away in her fingers. "What about the markings?"

"Right in front of you" he said. "Top of the left thigh, just as before".

She took a step toward the body, and stared down at the tattoo. It stood out like a dark shadow on white snow against the girl's pallid, blood drained, alabaster skin. Three symbols, written in a vertical line, followed by one Roman numeral.

"Number 8" said McMullen, quietly.

"Indeed" said Dr Vanner, reaching for the sheet and starting to cover the body.

"When will the toxicology reports be ready?" she asked.

"Oh, some time tomorrow morning I should think. The samples have been couriered as you requested".

She glanced up at the clock. 3am. "Some time *this* morning, you mean" she said, attempting to shift her focus back toward reality.

"Well, Detective Chief Inspector. I intend to sleep whilst I still can. So far as I am concerned toxicology will be dealt with tomorrow". He half smiled. She wondered what he really thought, being collected from his home in the middle of the night by a police driver and a phone call from the Commissioner. All of that just to meet with her and let her see what she could have seen at any time. Any reasonable time, at least.

She moved toward the door as he finished covering the body. "Toxicology won't show anything" she said.

"I wouldn't be so sure" he replied, finishing up and returning the body to the vast steel container that kept it in stasis. "I did mention the possibility of sedation".

McMullen snorted. "There was no sedation Dr Vanner, I can assure you of that".

He slammed the main door shut and bolted top and bottom. He picked up his coat and made for the door where she stood. "Why so sure?" he said, reaching into his pocket for his keys.

"Because I saw the victim alive right before she died. The first uniformed officers on the scene found that body at 7am yesterday morning. By the time they had cleared the location, circulated information, and by the time I had even left Manchester to get to London, an anonymous man delivered a DVD to a local nick. It shows that girl alive right before she died, and I can assure you, Dr Vanner, there was no sedation. None at all".

He stared at her for a moment, unsure of what to say.

She stood to one side, opening the door for him as she did so. He locked up, and they walked in silence through the sterile corridors. The only sound beyond their footsteps being the incessant *click-clack, click-clack* of the rosary in DCI McMullen's hand.

Pray for us sinners…
Now, and at the hour of our death.

03

9.07am

"I'm so glad you called" said McMullen. "I'm sorry I missed you. You know how it is".

"Work" said Sally McMullen, flatly, from the edge of the college car park. "Don't worry, I know exactly how it is. Dad always used to explain it to me on your behalf".

"Don't be like that" said McMullen defensively. "I am in London now. I thought we could get together".

There was a silence, then "I needed you when I phoned".

"Sally, I have said I am sorry. It was – "

"Yeah. You said. Work".

"What did you need me for?"

Another long silence. Then, "Something happened on the tube, that's all. I was waiting for a train and when it arrived I honestly felt like someone pushed me. I was scared, that's all. I just needed to speak to you".

And there it was. The one thing McMullen had always had in her emotional baggage compartment, and for which she always paid the surcharge for carrying because it was too heavy to take on board: Her daughter wanted so little from her, and she couldn't even give her that tiny morsel because work with a capital "W" had always, somehow, managed to produce a crisis right at the crucial moment and push the family aside. It was the reason for her divorce, and it was the reason for her disastrous, piecemeal relationship with her daughter. Her brilliant, intelligent, high-achieving daughter who was so much the product of her, if only she knew it.

"There are cameras on the underground, we can – "

"No thanks. I needed my mum, not a police officer".

Another long silence. "We can get together, though, right?" offered McMullen. "You know how much I want to. How much I *always* want to?"

"I have to go, Mum. I've got a lecture to go to. Text me, when you get the chance. If they let you go then, yes, I would like to see you, but… you know. That stuff gets in the way, doesn't it". It was a statement, not a question.

"I will make sure it doesn't"

"You mean to, I know you do, but I have to live my life too. I am glad you're in Town. I have a few things I can show you this end of the country, you know. Manchester is great, don't get me wrong, but it's not London".

McMullen laughed. "Spoken like a true Londoner! When was the last time you were in Manchester?"

Neither of them answered the question. Like so often in life, harmless banter had led them to the truth. The last time Sally had been in Manchester was when McMullen's matrimonial lawyer had thought it a good idea to insist on a change of court venue for the custody hearing during her divorce proceedings. This had forced her ex-husband and her then thirteen year old daughter out of their London comfort zone and into what turned out to be a legal blood-bath that McMullen, ultimately, lost. Forgiveness was still a long way off, even now, ten years down the line.

"Just text me, okay? I am sure we can find the time if we both want to".

"Okay. And if you need me, just call. Even if I can't take the call I always, always phone you back, don't I?". There was a hint of emotion in her voice that was not lost on her daughter.

"You do, Mum. I know you do. I'll speak to you later".
"Okay. Speak soon. I love you".
"I love you too".
The line went dead.

McMullen took the phone slowly from her ear and stared at the screen for a long time before ending the connection. This was not the life she had planned for them both. She was proud of Sally, more proud than Sally would ever know, and as a trainee pathologist she always wondered if one day she would be walking into a case to find herself working alongside her own daughter… but Sally's post-graduate studies would take several years more yet, and McMullen was an established DCI with her own unit in Manchester….

So what are you doing here……

She put the phone away and tried to push the baggage to one side again.

She picked up a manilla file and did her best to look nonplussed as she exited her office.

"Is everything ready, Joe" she said, distractedly.

Detective Inspector Joseph Webber held on to the passport sized picture of his wife and child between his fingers. His wife, Sarah, was smiling. His daughter, Chloe, touching her mother's face, like nothing had ever happened. It was a small, innocent, snapshot that he kept in his wallet, like all things of value, but it carried the awful, portentous air that old photographs do – when no-one in the picture could ever have foreseen the horrors that would befall them hurtling so quickly toward them. His daughter's eyes stared up at him, happy. If there was any consolation anywhere it was in the fact they had, at some point at least, known true happiness.

He wiped his eyes quickly, not wanting her to see.
"Erm… yes. Yes, it's all ready".

He stuffed the picture back into his wallet and got up from his seat, keeping his back to her as he briefly checked each desk, but she seemed to stand alongside him too quickly. He couldn't hide the red-rims of his eyes.

"I was sorry to hear about the accident", she said. "I am not going to pretend to know what to say, or to know what it must have been like. I have a daughter of my own, Sally. She's twenty-three now. She's a post-graduate pathology student at King's College".

He nodded, but said nothing. She immediately regretted what she had said. *Too much information* she thought angrily to herself. *His daughter was only six for fuck's sake.*

"How long has it been?" she asked.

"Since the accident, or since I came back to work?" He continued placing files on the various desks as they spoke.

"Both" she said.

"Seven and a half months since the accident. Six weeks since I've been back at work".

She nodded but didn't press him further. Being divorced, she knew what it was like to come home to an empty house that used to be so much more, but divorce was something else. DI Webber's loss was in a different league; A different league altogether. Rumour had it that he blamed himself for the accident that killed them, but fact confirmed that he hadn't been anywhere near the scene. He had been fifteen miles away working a case that had just come in. Rumour also stated that this was why he had crumbled and been unable to function after it happened: He shouldn't have been working that job. He was supposed to be on leave. He had only cancelled it because he needed to keep leave back for later on; for a family holiday in Disneyland Florida. McMullen figured that this took them to right about now, and instead of being on the trip of a lifetime with his wife and six year old daughter, he was six months down the line from having buried them and now working an unsolved multiple-murder case that seemed to be alive again.

The door at the end of the room banged open. The first member of the team to arrive strode in, take-away coffee in hand. "Guv" he said, and then, more respectfully after glancing up at the tall, blonde-haired woman at the end of the room dressed all in black, "Ma'am".

"Try and leave the door on its hinges" said Webber, regaining his composure.

McMullen acknowledged him with an almost imperceptible nod. She was not familiar with many of these people. There were a few remembered faces about the place; a few people whom she had known from the early days who now rode high on the badge of honour that was the Murder Investigation Team, but in the main most had moved on. And methods were different too, it seemed. The Metropolitan Force was a different animal to the Murder Investigation Team she worked with in Manchester. She was rapidly finding out that all forces were not the same.

The rest of the team filed slowly in. Sometimes in pairs, chatting. Sometimes alone and jovial. Some kept their own counsel, giving nothing but a smile or a quiet acknowledgement. By the time they were gathered in full strength before her, she felt distinctly like a stranger. All she could hope was that she would not prove to be an unwelcome one.

"Good morning everyone" said Webber, making his way to the front of the room. There were muffled and indiscriminate noises in response. He smiled as he turned to face them. "Nice to see you're all your usual hospitable selves, even in company". He glanced at DCI McMullen who was studying the team. "This is Detective Chief Inspector Claire McMullen from Manchester Police. She will be heading up this investigation. If you have any questions as to why then you can direct them to her after this briefing. I know that recent events have meant rumours are rife, but DCI McMullen's arrival has nothing to do with my own personal difficulties. I thank all of you for the support you have shown me over the last few months, but DCI McMullen is, for this investigation only, the officer in charge. Both you, and I, will give full co-operation in that regard".

   He looked from McMullen to the team and paused to re-enforce his point. "OK, let's start from the beginning" he said. "A railway maintenance engineer was working on a broken signal in the early hours of yesterday morning on the small stretch of Circle Line track that passes overground between Gloucester Road and High Street Kensington tube stations. This was between the hours of approximately 2am and 4am. He says he neither saw nor heard anything at the time that appeared out of the ordinary. He left the site believing the problem was fixed. He was recalled by his line manager at 6.00am to go back and deal with a further signal failure on exactly the same circuit. He was therefore back on site at around 6.30am. He says he was working on the problem for no more than ten minutes or so before he spotted the body. This puts the first reported sighting at around 6.50am Monday morning. We cannot rule out the fact that his initial call-out may have indicated activity in the area several hours earlier. We need to keep that in mind for later when we decide when and how we appeal for witnesses. However, at this stage, we are keeping a press blackout. The reason for that is simple: We need more time to work out who and what we are dealing with, and we don't need political or press interference right now whilst we are trying to do that".

He stepped to the side of the board and directed the teams' attention to the photographs.

"The full autopsy will be dealt with as soon as possible, although an initial examination has shown that the victim died from blood loss. The general view is that this occurred at a different location to the one where the body was found. Forensics are still collating and cataloguing information gathered from the scene at present. We are unlikely therefore to get any further useful information from them or the body itself for another 48 hours, but the toxicology report is expected today. Firstly, though, we need to identify this girl as our number one priority. Although the face has been disfigured by the lips being cut off, and the head has been shaved removing all hair, there is still enough recognisable material for an ID to be made. I know some of you have been carrying out a trawl of all missing persons, female, in their early twenties but so far we have drawn a blank. Someone must have known this girl and someone must have missed her".

He pointed to the photographs. "I have already mentioned the cause of death was blood loss. See the deep lacerations on her wrists and neck. There was not enough blood at the scene to suggest she was killed there. We are therefore working initially on the theory that she was killed somewhere else, so be aware of all reports to uniform countrywide over the last five to ten days of domestic style incidents with uncharacteristic qualities – you know the kind of thing: neighbour reports sounds of screaming etc but when officers attend it is something and nothing, or no-one can be found at all"

"Now I want to say a few words about the scene" he continued, "and particularly the positioning of the body".

He took a step back from the board, still facing the row of photographs displayed across it. "It could not be seen from above. You would have to have been down there to have found it. The killer could have simply dumped it and let a Circle Line train plough into it. With a train full of Joe Public getting off to have a look we could have had a gawper's paradise. Instead, the body appeared to have been placed, as opposed to thrown or dumped, and it is likely that this has meaning – that the murderer wanted the body to be collected quietly – hence the interference with the signal, which was clearly deliberate, being the main source alerting people to the corpse. The point is that it would not have been easy getting that body to where it was found. It would have been easier to leave it somewhere on display and cause mass panic. Instead the body was left in a complicated location that involves risk, and risk for no apparent benefit.

The appearance of the face is also important. You will all be aware by now that the removal of lips and hair from the head has linked this killing with a series of unsolved murders from around 19 years ago. DCI Claire McMullen of Manchester Police is here because she was involved in the initial investigation when these trade marks first appeared. She has an intricate knowledge of what went on at that time, so she will now brief you. The only thing I need to add is that the killer left a DVD showing the victim still alive. For those of you who have not yet seen it DCI McMullen and I will show it at the end of this meeting. For those of you who have seen it there is certainly no requirement to sit through it a second time. I appreciate that once is enough for anyone".

He turned away from the board. "Any questions?"

No-one spoke, but furtive glances were exchanged between many. The few who had seen the DVD looked down.

"Good. I shall now hand you over to DCI McMullen. She will be taking charge of this investigation as of now. She has a great deal of knowledge to share with you so listen and take notes. What you learn here will move you all forward and possibly begin to help us understand who this killer is and why they have resurfaced. We are not ruling out a copycat, but the similarities are so striking that we are starting from the premise that it's the original killer, or at least someone operating at his direction".

McMullen got to her feet and looked around the room, taking in the faces.

"Good Morning everyone" she said. "I will obviously get the chance to speak to you all individually during the course of the day, and I am already known to some of you from my days in the Met. For those of you who don't know me, I was a WPC when this killer first became active. I was the liaison officer assigned to work with a woman called Maria Blakemore. Miss Blakemore was, and is so far as we are aware, the only known surviving victim of this killer".

There were murmurs from everyone.

"The purpose of this briefing" she continued, "is for me to impart my knowledge of the person who carried out yesterday's attack".

She turned sideways to the team so she could look over the photos on the board behind her. Webber's collection of brutal images dominated the room.

"Firstly, I should say I am here because I have been involved with this attacker before, and I believe I can help. Admittedly, I could perhaps have done that remotely from Manchester, but, if I am right and this attacker is the same man, then I have information and experience to offer this investigation that cannot be given by anyone else. That knowledge and experience was gained from all the hours I spent counselling, interviewing and befriending Miss Blakemore. She was abducted by this man nineteen years ago, and whereas six other women abducted before her were found killed in this identical manner, she was released. The two of us came to know each other, and to trust each other".

She gestured toward the blown up pictures of the face and head of the victim.

"In every case back then the exact same disfigurement had occurred. The lips had been cut off, not with something sharp and precise like a scalpel, but with something more crude. That was the part that troubled us at the time because it was the clear violent part of the attack – done with anger we thought, or in a frenzy. Everything else was more planned and more purposeful. The shaving of the head must have been done either voluntarily, which we doubted, or, more likely, whilst the victim was drugged, or perhaps dead, or perhaps dying and unable to move or resist. It has no tiny nicks or cuts that you would expect if this were done against resistance."

She moved along slightly to point to the magnified pictures of the wrists and throat.

"This is the same here as it was back then. The cause of death was blood loss. The main arteries in the wrists have been cut. This would of course have amounted to exceptional volumes of blood being deposited not only around the body but upon the actual location from which the body was discovered". She pointed to the photo showing the body itself. "There was no blood on the ground or on the route taken down to the location where it was left. This woman therefore must have been killed elsewhere and then brought to the scene".

She turned back to face the team. "Which brings me to the location itself. This was an area that is part of the Circle Line. This is how it was with the previous killings. Each victim was found at a different Circle Line station. Six stations in all were used. As DI Webber has already said, this latest victim was placed at a complicated location, difficult and risky to get to, and for no apparent benefit. I believe there was real purpose in this, because we had to shut the tube service for several hours in order to recover the body. It is a statement. It says I am back. It is also a new location on the line. He has never used the same station twice".

"You have a file in front of you. This is the overview file. It is for information purposes only. The actual files are being delivered here later today and I will go through them with you at that point. For now, could I please ask you to turn to the back of the file here".

She picked up a spare file and took out a picture from the last few pages. She placed it on the board in the bottom left hand corner. It was a facial portrait of a woman, jet black hair hanging in curls around her modelesque face. Her eyes a deep and rich brown, almost black. She was smiling, a pure and brilliant white smile.

McMullen turned to face everyone again.

"This is a picture of Maria Blakemore as she was when I knew her. She is not known by that name now and she is nineteen years older than the picture you see here. In this picture she was nineteen, and had just started working as a model in London when she was abducted, attacked, and ultimately released by the killer. This is what makes this particular case so confusing. Her release was not characteristic of this man's M.O. All of the women that had been attacked had, ultimately, been killed. The lead-up is the same though. All the women were abducted between two and three months prior to their bodies being discovered. Maria was no exception. She had been missing for thirteen weeks before she was found, naked and unconscious, on wasteland on the outskirts of Newcastle. The location, we decided at the time, was a red-herring. The murders had taken place in London, the abductions had taken place in London, and we had no reason to believe that the women, once abducted, had not been held in London, as opposed to Newcastle or anywhere else. Some weight was given to this argument when Maria told us that she had been transferred to a van shortly before she was released, and that she believed she had been in the van for some time before she gained her freedom. That said, you will see from the files when they arrive that she actually believed she had been in the van for several days although her perception of time by that point was unreliable. Either way, she was not released from the place where she had been held. She had been released at a different location.

"She was, however, able to give us some insight into where she had been held and we believe this was not only the location where the women were detained but also the location where the murders took place before the bodies where removed and displayed. Unfortunately, other than a description of a warehouse or outbuilding she was unable to go further. She had been secured by shackles to a stone wall. The killer had spoken to her from behind what she believed was a searchlight, or a bank of powerful spotlights, so she never saw his face until her release, but it was always a male voice, and on her evidence we concluded this man was working alone. Food and drink was left for her and she urinated and defecated in a bucket that was changed daily. This man had both the time and resources to do this. She was passed a bucket of warm water each day and was allowed to wash herself whilst remaining shackled. The area had some kind of electric fan heating that was used periodically. This man obviously wanted his victims to remain healthy and free from illness. He wanted them to remain as they were when he abducted them. We understand that punishments or pain only resulted from refusing to eat, drink or wash. Regrettably, this was all she could tell us, save for the conversations she had with him. The transcripts of those conversations will be in the files when they arrive later on. I would urge you to read them in small doses. Maria obviously did not recall them word for word, but you will get the general picture as you go through them. These were followed by a series of letters from the killer to Maria after her release. Again, the transcripts are in the files. You will need to familiarise yourself with them. On a personal note, I believe that after-shocks are a trait of his. The event itself is not enough for him. When Maria was released, he wrote to her repeatedly. This latest victim was filmed and the DVD sent to us after we found the corpse. We could not fail to find the corpse – he gave it to us on a plate by interfering with the tube train signals. It is for that reason that I give such weight to the DVD. The body was the statement. The DVD was the reason for that statement".

She removed some more photographs from the file on the table and placed them next to the others on the board.

"I want you to look at these closely" she said. "Look at what is different about each one".

Those who could not see clearly shuffled forward.

"Each of the first six victims had the same symbols tattooed on their bodies. So did Maria Blakemore. The only symbol that differs is the roman numeral. It took some time but we eventually identified the meanings of the recurring symbols".

She pointed to the first one.

"This is a symbol representing the two phases of the moon – waxing and waning. This is the two phases, divided by the full moon. The waxing period ends with a full moon, and the waning period ends with the moon not being visible at all. The symbol is a representation of the two phases".

She pointed to the second symbol:

"This is an ancient alchemist symbol. It means purification. The only connection or relevance of this so far as we are concerned is that it probably relates to the method of killing – blood loss. There appears to be no other reason for it to be given such credence by the killer, but we obviously have nothing to connect the symbol to the removal of the lips and hair of the victims. Is that part of the purification? Is there some kind of purification ritual? We don't know".

She moved to the third symbol. "This took some time to decipher as it appears to be two symbols in one":

"The inner symbol is obvious. It is the representation of the female gender. We have concluded it simply represents a woman or women in general. The symbol that surrounds it presented more difficulty. It is predominantly a male symbol and it is known as Saturn. Eventually, our researchers made the link that seemed most relevant. The planet Saturn is often associated with Death and this seemed the most obvious reason for its inclusion".

She went back to the main photo display behind her. "If these symbols are read together they probably mean something like a Moon Cycle, or a Moon God, bringing purification to a woman, or women, through death. This is only our best guest based on the most obvious meaning. These symbols are clearly of exceptional importance to the killer as he has taken the time to tattoo them on the victim's bodies. This means that the message, whatever it is, is permanent. When you see the DVD you will see that it ends with a message. The killer speaks of a moon cycle, something known as the Metonic cycle. Although the moon often appears to be in the same place from time to time, the actual length of time it takes for the moon to appear in the same place twice is nineteen years. The killer cites this as part of the reason for his return. He is following his own Metonic cycle, returning to the same place after 19 years. I wouldn't ordinarily give this any relevance, but the recurring symbol of the Moon God on the bodies shows it does have relevance, to him at least."

"And what about the numbers?" said an officer from the back of the room. "The roman numerals".

McMullen glanced over the spread of photographs. "We don't know", she said solemnly. "Perhaps nothing more than ego – an increasing body count. A taunting of the police. Something intended to depersonalise the victims, or perhaps the opposite – something designed to give them greater relevance, greater importance. Perhaps nothing more than a mechanism to inflict further pain on the relatives who grieve for these women".

"And Maria Blakemore" said the same officer. "Where is she now?"

McMullen glanced at DI Webber. There was a long pause before she said, "We don't know. As the weeks and months passed after her release, and as our investigation produced no suspects and no leads, her confidence in us and her belief that her nightmare would end began to die. I had many unhappy conversations with her as it became evident we were losing the trail and were becoming less and less likely to catch him. I tried to keep her on board, but you have to understand what she was going through. This man could have, and based on his M.O. should have, killed her. He let her go for a reason and no-one knew what that reason was. When the letters started arriving for her it was too much. Nothing we did made any difference. We had nothing to go on. We ended up looking like clowns in the face of a man who was doing nothing but taunting his last victim and slowly driving her insane. In order to protect her long term we placed her into a witness protection programme. She was then the responsibility of The Met". She looked over at Joe who was already getting to his feet.

"As you are all aware", he said, "we had a new piece of legislation come into force a few years ago. After the Serious Organised Crime And Police Act all witnesses who were under any scheme of protection had to be reviewed, and a risk assessment made as to whether we felt they were still at risk. Only if there was a sufficient risk to them could the protection be continued". He glanced at McMullen. "Given the length of time since Maria's attack, and the fact that she had lived openly, albeit under her new identity, in comparative safety, it was considered that the risk to her life was negligible". He turned to face the team. "For several years now she has been outside of our protection. We did have a last known address but we have been there and she is no longer resident. It was a rented flat in Chelsea. Uniform are doing door to door for the sake of being thorough, but the Witness Protection Records suggest she may have left England for Italy. Details have already been circulated to Interpol. Although the Italian authorities would have been made aware of her situation by us, whether they chose to do anything with that information would have been up to them. Maybe they kept updating Interpol, maybe they didn't. We don't know yet. However, we have other lines of enquiry. As part of her new identity she was given a new National Insurance number. She wouldn't have been able to change that and we have some Civil Service bodies giving it the once over as we speak. You know the type of thing, checking for benefit payments, and benefit office locations if such payments are being collected or posted; NI contributions being made, if any, and if so from which employer etcetera".

McMullen had begun pacing up and down behind him. He considered the faces of the team briefly. "We are working on the premise that this is the same killer. From the DVD we are making the assumption that Maria Blakemore, if she is in this country, is at risk. These are our only absolutes. The wider reality is that all women are at risk, and we need to use these crucial first days to get a strong hold on what leads we push our resources at. For now we are going to maintain the press blackout, but we all know what the reality is". He paused, before adding, "We are as much at his mercy right now as the next potential victim. A press blackout will only hold all the while the bodies are not displayed publicly. Personally, I want to locate Maria, to bring her into protective custody again, and once I am satisfied on that we can deal with the Press at that point. If nothing else, it gives us an early upper hand, by making us look like we were on it from the very first minute. What we can't afford is for news to break and Maria to be out there in the wilderness somewhere".

McMullen stopped pacing and stood next to him. "And if it is anything like last time" she said, eyes flitting from one team member to another, "then when this does reach the newspapers they will have a field day. I am sensitive to the Press for obvious reasons, but I am particularly sensitive to how coverage of this latest killing might be handled as it was the Press who created a persona for this man last time round. During the original investigation a journalist who was covering the case published his own interpretation of the evidence showing that each of the killings had taken place during a waning moon period. This is that time of the month between the full moon and the point where the moon disappears. It had no relevance at the time and I do not believe it should have any now, but because of the connection between the Circle Line being a continuous cycle, and the fact that the killings appeared to have a common time in another continuous cycle, that of the moon, the press started calling this attacker The Horologist. For those of you who don't know, an Horologist is someone who deals with clocks, watches and time pieces in general. Horology is the study of time itself. The name caught on, and became widespread amongst all the newspapers at the time".

She raised her hand to draw attention to the photographs behind her on the board. "It's all a very pretty idea but it didn't have any bearing on the fact that this man, whatever he was called, was a very sick man who was killing in some kind of ritualistic fashion. The first six victims are a matter of historical record. Maria Blakemore was tattooed as number seven. This latest victim is number eight. When this gets out we will have a media frenzy and public outcry on our hands, of that you can be sure".

"Before we take a look at this DVD" she continued, "I need to draw your attention to this". She pointed to a photograph of a necklace. "This was delivered along with the DVD. It is currently at Forensics for analysis but it appears to be a small piece of stone with a hole drilled in it, through which a long shoelace has been passed to make a necklace. When you see the DVD you will see the victim is wearing something similar. It appears to be the same one, but tests will no doubt confirm. You will see it is reddish in colour. It also has specks of blood on it. We are waiting for Forensics to confirm if it matches the DNA of the victim and whether there is any other unidentified or non-victim derived DNA on it".

She picked up the file in front of her, and indicated to Webber to start the DVD. "I want us to look at the DVD now, so we understand what we are dealing with. If you have already seen it, you are not expected to watch it a second time".

Two officers were setting up a large television screen that sat on a wheeled trolley. They toyed with the cables at the back, none of them speaking. This would be the first time that the whole team had viewed the DVD. The handful who had already seen it didn't move. No-one was minded to take McMullen up on her offer. It seemed they would stand or fall together.

Webber stood by McMullen against the side wall, saying quietly "Once we have this out of the way, what do you plan to do with the DVD?"

"When we have all seen the content I am sending it for analysis. We can get the frames isolated to see if there is anything shown that might identify the location. The audio can be slowed and analysed. There is no telling what might be on there, inadvertently, that could help us".

"I don't suppose there's any way they can tell what type of camera it was, do you think? Anything unique or specific about the model, where it might be bought from, that kind of stuff?"

"Who knows. My money would be on mass produced generic stuff. The tattoo kit might be a different story. They're not exactly high street goods. Final pathology reports will be a few more days yet though. Like all these things, Joe, we just have to hope that we get lucky somewhere".

"All set up, Ma'am", said one of the officers returning to his seat.

"Thank you" said McMullen. She turned over the thin black DVD case in her hands. "All I will say is that we need to watch this to ensure we have not missed any vital piece of evidence that might be on it. If you wish to leave the room at any point, please feel free to do so. No-one will think any the less of you for it. And remember the open invitation to use the counsellors. No-one needs to be a hero over this stuff these days. Dealing with the dead is one thing. Seeing the victims alive is something else".

She looked from one face to another, and then another. No-one spoke.

"Right then" she said purposefully. "Let's do it. Joe, can you do the honours please"

Webber took the DVD case from her. The screen came to life. A black hole staring out at them with a DVD logo flickering in the corner.

The low whirr of the DVD tray sliding out, and then in, heralded the shocking display that burst onto the screen.

"Jesus!" blurted Webber, reaching for the remote control to turn the volume down.

The screaming filled the room, flooding out of the speakers. The screen was filled with a close up of a woman's face. Tears streamed down her cheeks. Her head had been shaved and her face and been mutilated – her lips cut away leaving her teeth baring out like some living skull. On each side of her face they could just make out the hands of someone holding her head in place for the camera.

"SAY IT!" shouted a male voice over her screaming. "SAY IT!"

In amongst the sobs, and the inability to form any meaningful words without her lips, the woman tried to say what the man demanded of her.

"Ah – eee – ah" came the sound, over and over in desperation. "Ah – eee – ah… Ah –eee- ah"

Then one of the hands, that they could now see was gloved – a thin surgical rubber glove – seemed to be grinding something into the wounds. The woman's eyes were at first screwed tightly shut, then open wide with fear and pain. Mucus ran from her nose and she screamed hard and shrill. They could not see what he was doing to her out of shot, but she was uncontrollable now. Hardly able to breathe as he wrenched her head toward the camera, shouting all the while "SAY IT! SAY IT!"

"AH – EEE – AH!" she screamed, frantic and pleading. "AH – EEE – AH! AH – EEE – AH!"

Then his gloved fingers were shoved into her mouth and part of his body came into shot as he fought to hold her head still. "Say it properly you unclean bitch before I rip your fucking tongue out!"

He took his fingers away as she sobbed. Her head suddenly rolling out of shot before being pulled back in as a clear plastic bag went over her head. Her breathing pushed the bag in and out, in and out as he wound it, taut, behind her, moulding it to her face. The inside quickly smeared with moisture and blood. "Now you say what I fucking tell you to say you filthy whore!"

He pulled the bag from her face. "AH – EEE – AH" she screamed. "AH – EEE – AH" and then fell into uncontrollable sobs as her head rolled out of shot again.

And then the screen went dead, plunging them all into nothing but the hiss of white noise and the crackling madness of the black and white television snow. The woman's face had gone. The screaming had stopped.

Then the screen flickered into life again. This time the lens seemed to take several moments to adjust to what seemed to be a bank of vertical spotlights shining into the camera. There was a man's voice, calmer now, and disguised through some sort of amplifier. The team stared intently at the screen.

"Behold! A light in the darkness!"

There was silence for a few seconds, and then "Hear how she screams… but it is not the screaming you must listen to. It is the name she screams. Did you hear it? Did you hear the name on the wind? You must ask her, when you find her. You must ask her about her tattoo. Ask her how she sees her tattoo."

McMullen glanced over the faces of the team as they listened.

"The moon never appears in the same place twice until nineteen years have passed. It is called the Metonic cycle. I am your Metonic cycle. I will appear in the same place in your world every nineteen years, conducting my work. Continuing my work. Think back then to my last appearance. Think back to my last celestial location. Remember that date. On its' recurrence, you will lose me again, but before that time, my work continues".

The lights went out. The screen went black. The voice fell silent.

Joe let it run for a few seconds more, then pressed fast-forward on the DVD, but there was nothing further.

He pressed "stop" and moved solemnly toward the television screen to turn it off.

McMullen took up her place at the front of the room. "He asks about the name we hear. I believe that woman was being made to say the name Maria. He says that we must ask her, when we find her, how she sees her tattoo. He also talks about a date when he will disappear again". She picked up the file in front of her and held it up. "I have checked and re-checked the dates in the old files. The last letter to Maria was dated 27th July nineteen years ago. After that, he was never heard from again. The victim we have just seen was found dead yesterday, the 1st July". She dropped the file back on the table in front of her. "Basically, we've got three weeks to catch him before we lose him again". She looked intently at the faces before her. "I lost him once. There is no fucking way on God's earth I am going to lose him a second time".

The door at the far end of the room opened. A uniformed PC entered and gestured at Webber.

"Let's call it a day there" she said, breaking up the meeting. "We all have plenty to be getting on with".

04

4.34pm

The woman fought for breath in her panic. The tape across her mouth forced her to breathe through her nose and she struggled against her own heaving chest to try and get enough air. Her arms were taped to the chair in which she sat, wrists facing upward in a forced supplicatory pose. Her legs were bound in the same manner, and she had been placed in the middle of the room.

Her attacker scrolled down through the numbers on the woman's mobile phone. "Ah", he said at last. "Here we are". He glanced up at her. "One of the benefits of having an affair with a work colleague is no doubt the ability to hide their name in amongst all the other work colleagues. How many of the people listed here do you actually phone, I wonder?"

He looked down at the name on the screen. "David Sachs" he said aloud. "A fairly unemotive description for the man who has, for so many years, been the man you run to, the man you confide in, the man you love". He looked up at her. "The man you betrayed your husband for".

He considered her for a moment, listening to her sobbing as she stared at him, eyes wide with fear.

"Shall we send him a love letter?" he asked coldly. "Shall we ask him to join us? Or perhaps I mean *you* should send him a love letter, because he will never believe the message is from anyone other than you. Tell me, what name does he have you under in his own phone? Do you flash up as K. Graham? All cold, bland and innocent? Or, given that he doesn't have a spouse to hide things from, do you think he has you filed under something more intimate? Katie, perhaps? Or maybe just Kate? Perhaps, before I cut out his eyes, I might let him have one last look at the screen. Would that be a good thing? To see your name before he dies? Would it be a nice thing if your name was the very last thing he saw?"

She tried to scream at him but she was stifled by the heavy tape across her mouth and her own need to breath against her sobbing.

"Well, I guess we'll just have to come to that when we come to it" he said. He looked down at the phone, speaking the words as he typed them. "Are you free? Can you come to the house asap? I need to see you v urgently ". He smiled as he looked up at her. "Kiss, kiss, kiss" he said. Then he held the phone out in front of her. "Do you see that? Do you see what you are sending him? You are sending him a scarlet tessera – a deadly invitation. Do you know what a tessera is?"

She closed her eyes and tried to block him out as he drew nearer.

"A tessera is an invitation. A ticket, if you like. A ticket to a show, an *event*. Let's send David his invitation shall we?"

She opened her eyes.

He pressed *'send'*.

*   *   *

David Sachs strode down Farringdon Road towards the Guardian Newsroom Archive Centre. He drew repeatedly on a cigarette, perpetually annoyed by the fact that smoking was becoming next to impossible these days for anyone who worked anywhere other than in a field, and even then it was still probably illegal.

He showed his pass at the entrance, resting his bulging leather attaché case on the clerk's desk. "Good Morning John" he said, self assuredly. "I trust all is well in the world of archives".

The clerk smiled. Most people who knew David Sachs would smile at his comfortable and confident manner. He could put you at ease from the moment he caught your eye. He was a large, avuncular man, but intellectually and politically astute. Journalism had taught him much.

He strode on through the building to the lecture halls at the rear, pausing as his phone beeped. He took it out from his jacket pocket and looked at the source, smiling immediately he saw her name. He opened it up.

"Are you free? Can you come to the house asap? I need to see you v urgently xxx"

He checked his watch. 5pm. There was nothing here that couldn't wait

He put his briefcase down momentarily so that he could text her back.

        *   *   *

Kate Graham jerked in her chair as the phone rang out from the table.

Her attacker picked it up, reading the message out loud. "Will do. I love urgency! See you in a minute. Kiss". He looked down at her. "How sweet" he said sarcastically, before tossing the phone on to the table. "Time to make my preparations".

He sat down on the sofa and took out a small pouch from his inside pocket. On the table he laid out two glass vials and a syringe. He pushed the plunger all the way into the receptacle and took the safety cap from the end of the needle. He held up the first glass vial. "This is Rohypnol. Do you know what Rohypnol does to the human body? It is classed as an hypnotic, and also as a muscle-relaxant. It reduces anxiety, pacifies a person, robs them of their usual defences and causes them to forget exactly what happened to them". He inserted the needle into the end of the vial and drew back the plunger, filling almost half the syringe. He resealed the vial and placed it back into the pouch. He picked up the second vial. "And this is heroin". He glanced over at her. "I think we both know what heroin does to the human body and mind". He inserted the needle into the end of the glass vial and filled the remaining space in the syringe.

When he had finished he resealed the vial and placed it back into the pouch. He held the syringe up vertically, gently pushing the plunger in until a small jet of liquid squirted out at the top. He placed the syringe down on the table and then sat back down on the sofa.

"The combination of Rohypnol and Heroin is used by drug addicts to take the pain out of withdrawal. It allows the addict to enter a semi-hypnotic state where they are still conscious, but so far as their physical body is concerned they feel nothing". He folded his arms. "Aside from regular intake of alcohol, and perhaps recreational cocaine use, I would guess neither you nor your lover are great crack-heads. This little injection should be the best escape you've ever had".

She was sobbing loudly now, muffled and muted by the seal over her mouth but with tears flowing freely. He watched her in her misery, neither seeing nor hearing her distress; just waiting.

*   *   *

When the doorbell rang her attacker got up calmly from the sofa. He picked up the syringe and walked out into the hallway. He could see the shape of the caller through the frosted glass. He opened the door and let it swing slightly ajar, keeping behind it as he did so. He heard David Sachs laugh nervously. "Kate? Are you naked or something?"

The attacker, eyes alive with the focus of a predator, watched and listened for David's first step into the house. When he could see the blurred shape of his outline fully inside he kicked the door, hard, smashing it into David's face. As David fell back against the wall the man drove forward, left hand catching under David's chin, gripping his throat and driving upwards against the wall choking him. Both of David's hands grabbed the man's left wrist to twist it away so he could breathe, but the action left him defenceless against the attacker's right hand which immediately plunged the syringe into the side of David's neck.

He screamed out in pain as he felt the pressured bulging of his neck filling with liquid. And then the syringe was out as quickly as it had entered and he felt a hard blow to the right side of his head. He tried to fight back as he slid against the wall away from his assailant but the man kept coming at him, blow after blow raining down on him. He wanted to scream, to shout for help, but somehow in the melee the door had been kicked shut. The pain in his neck was unbearable. "What the fuck do you want!" he shouted. "Who are you?"

"SHUT THE FUCK UP!" shouted the man back at him. He kicked David's legs from under him and as he fell the man pushed him face down into the wooden floor of the hallway. He drove his knee into David's back and took hold of David's head in his hands driving it repeatedly into the floor.

"PLEASE!" he screamed. "Please!" but the attacker was relentless. Then he felt his arms being pulled back and suddenly he couldn't raise his hands to protect himself. The assailant wound the tape round and round and round until he was satisfied and he rolled David onto his back, standing over him and staring down at him.

"Hello David" he said. "It's been a long time. You won't recognise me, but you do know me. How you came up with the name I don't know, but you know me as The Horologist".

*   *   *

David was starting to lose his normal thought processes. He was slurring his words when he spoke, and his vision was blurred, falling in and out of focus. He felt detached from his body, as if his body didn't matter to him anymore.

"Your girlfriend hasn't had her injection yet, David" said the attacker. "She is experiencing this in all its glory. But I thought I would spare you that, David, because, you see, I have a soft spot for you. I owe much of my reputation to you".

He sat down on the sofa, facing the two of them. David was bound to the chair sitting opposite Kate, like chess players with no board or table between them.

"I have a package for you, David", continued the man. "I shall leave it on the table here. When you eventually come round it will be the only thing you have to hold on to that might make any sense of what you wake up to. I wonder what it will be like for you, David, waking up from a drug-induced haze, confused and paranoid, in the house of your lover's husband, with your lover missing and nothing but an envelope on the table with your name on it, an envelope containing, well, let's not spoil the surprise now, David. We still have a long way to go".

He placed the envelope on the table. "I liked your analysis, David, all those years ago. It was poetic. You were right about the cycles. Yes, I kill according to the moon cycle, and Yes, I leave the bodies at a different Circle Line station each time, but not for the reasons you suggested. And anyway, the Circle Line is no longer continuous these days, although I concede it was back then when you came up with your theory.

"No, David. I kill according to the moon cycle because my killing is about purification. I am purifying these women, bleeding them to death to rid them of their impurities and to release their spirits into a better world, where they don't have to suffer the result of their beauty. In fact, I strip them of their beauty at the very outset by taking away their lips and their hair. The waning moon is the best time for getting rid of things. That energy helps the process. That is why they die in line with the moon cycle. And as for the Circle Line locations, that is simply because it is convenient for me, David. And yet you, with your journalistic must-have-a-story brain turned that into a cycle. A cycle of time itself, no less. And so here I am. The Horologist. Master of Time itself". He laughed. "I like it, David. I have always liked it".

He got up from the sofa. "But you missed the real connection, David. You missed the meaning of the roman numerals. Why is each victim numbered? What does that numbering mean? You will come to know, in time, David, what that means".

David's head was rolling from side to side as he tried to keep himself conscious. He tried to speak but it was a heavy effort to formulate words. He just wanted to slip away, into anaesthetised nothingness.

The assailant took hold of David's hair and twisted his head toward him so he could see his eyes. "Stay with me, David" he said, "because I have one last story to tell before we are all on our way to our various destinations".

He let David's head fall back, and turned his attention to Kate. "Do you know the story of Bathsheba, Kate?". He carried on without waiting for a response. "It is a Bible story, and revolves around King David". He glanced over at David. "Bathsheba was a married woman, living in King David's kingdom. The story says that the King saw her bathing on her rooftop, naked, and he was so taken with her that he had to have her. He committed adultery with her, and she fell pregnant. In order to cover up his misdemeanour he sent for her husband, who was away at war, insisting that he return and sleep with his wife. It was hoped this would hide the true identity of the child's father. But Bathsheba's husband was a man of honour, and he would not indulge himself with his wife whilst his men were dying on the battlefield. King David sent the man back to his unit, and sent with him a sealed message for the man's commanding officer. That message contained the King's orders for the man to be abandoned on the battlefield. Those orders were followed, and the man met a bloody death at the hands of his enemies. Bathsheba then became one of the King's many wives, and legend has it that she was his favourite, for when he died it was her son from her former marriage that took King David's throne, and not King David's own son".

He moved closer to her. "But there is another interpretation of that story, Kate. You see, at that time, buildings were built very close together. Everyone bathed on their rooftops, and because of this, everyone was discreet. It would not have been possible for the King to look down on a blatantly naked exhibition by Bathsheba unless *she* had wanted it that way. Some people think she engineered the whole thing in order to seduce the King and be rid of her husband. Does this sound familiar, Kate? Have you seduced my King David? Have you displayed yourself before him despite your marriage, leading him on so there is only one tragic conclusion?"

He wrapped a tourniquet around her upper arm and pulled it tight, watching the veins in her lower arm swell with blood and offer themselves up. "Well you should read your history, Kate. God was so displeased by King David and his adultery that he struck down Bathsheba's child when it was born and it died within days from sickness".

He filled the syringe again from the glass vials as he spoke. Kate shook her head, trying in vain to plead for her life. "That was the punishment, you see? They lived but the child died. That is even worse than death, don't you think? To be the one who lives on with the loss, day in day out, knowing they needed you but that you could do nothing to help them...."

He put the syringe down, now full with the liquid drugs, and picked up the phone. He held it at an angle so they could both see him scrolling down the names. "Yes, that is even worse than death, don't you think?", he stopped on her daughter's name, "to be the one who lives on with the loss, day in day out, knowing they needed you but that you could do nothing to help them..."

She felt as if her stifled screaming would burn a hole in her throat. She fought for air against the sobs, eyes wide with fear as he took up the syringe and eased it into her swollen vein, saying all the while "Shhhushhh......"

"Shhhhushhh......"

05

6.32pm

Webber knocked and entered without waiting for acknowledgement. "We've found Maria Blakemore".

He handed McMullen a thin file of papers. She turned away to the desk and started to spread them out.

She picked up the most recent photograph on file. "She still goes by the same name then. Jane Lister".

"So it seems" said Webber. "She's worked at the same address for the past nine years.
The only reason she wasn't there today was due to some hearing where she is giving evidence".

McMullen raised her eyebrows. "Anything interesting?" she asked.

"From what Uniform could get out of the receptionist it was down to some teenager who topped himself. The family want answers and the NHS PCT are hoping to pin the blame on someone else. Usual stuff. No doubt someone will get sued shortly regardless of the outcome".

She rifled through the file. "No wonder they took her off witness protection. Look at this - her picture is on the company's website. Hardly keeping a low profile, was she?"

"You know the system", said Webber. "It's all about money. She was reviewed under that legislation because we can't afford to watch everyone forever". He turned to face the glass frontage that partitioned McMullen's office.

"That's what makes it all so difficult to understand. If this guy wanted to find her he could have done easily enough. There was no need to do what he's done. All this public display stuff, and the DVD…." He trailed off.

"Was all unnecessary", she said, finishing his sentence for him.

She picked up the photograph again. "She seems to have become quite a well respected counsellor".

"Hmm.. ironic isn't it? If I were a wannabe psychologist I would say she finds therapy in giving therapy. I suppose we should count our blessings, though. If she had bummed out and disappeared over the last couple of years then she wouldn't have been so easy to find. The fact that she has continued living her life has done us a favour".

McMullen closed up the file. "Where is the hearing? Presumably we can bring her in from there?"

"Uniform already tried that. They knocked off at four. We missed them. The clerk said they resume at ten tomorrow morning so we will get there in advance. The Judge won't be impressed".

McMullen closed the file. "The Judge isn't under threat of being abducted, mutilated and killed. Home address?"

"Still waiting on that".

McMullen handed the file back to him. "Ok, then. Best scenario is that a home address comes through in time for us to pick her up from there. Worst scenario is that tonight is her last night out in the jungle, and we'll pick her up tomorrow".

06

8.37pm

The entrance to the bar and restaurant was wide and spacious, like a hotel lobby. Works of art adorned the walls and tropical style plants stood tall in various places. There was a mottled glass brick wall creating a partition half way down, and he sat in one of the large leather chairs clustered together around several coffee tables. It was a perfect vantage point from which to see the bar.

There were some obvious candidates for Sarah Graham, but there was only one way to find out for sure.

He opened the phone he carried and checked the sent messages.

"I need to talk to you about Dad. Where are you? Can we meet?"

Sarah Graham's response had been immediate and willing. All he had needed to do was to text back a time and a location and she hadn't even questioned the request. Perhaps there was already an issue there and he had just gotten lucky. He smiled. If there was one thing you could rely on in life it was that families had dramas. Human dynamics were just too predictable.

He got up from his seat and walked through to the bar. A waitress offered to find him a table.

"I'm only here for a drink, thanks" he said, moving past her.

With his hands casually in his pockets he walked the length of the bar, listening intently. One hand controlled the glass vial. The other hand controlled the phone. He pressed the *dial* button.

From somewhere to his right he heard a mobile ring. The woman was blonde, slim, dressed in T-shirt and jeans, sitting on a tall chrome bar-stool. He approached her quickly, eyes scanning her position urgently; the body language, any make-up, any jewellery, tattoos, the colour and style of her clothes, her shoes, trinkets, symbols, things that might give her away, things that might teach him something immediately about her, and he saw the drink on the bar.

The drink on the bar.

He stood on her blind side as she rummaged in her bag. She could never have seen the colourless liquid poured deftly into her glass. She looked at the name displayed, immediately accepting the call. "Mum"? she said. There was no voice at the other end.

He felt for the button that turned the phone off completely.

He heard her curse quietly. He saw her re-dialling.

He caught the barman's eye and ordered a drink. A drink he had no intention of touching with either hand or lips.

The woman began talking into her phone. "Mum, it's me. Are you here yet? Your phone cut-out". She ended the message, and was suddenly aware of him.

"Modern technology" he said, smiling.

She simply smiled back.

He paid the waiter for the drink, before saying to her "would you mind just watching my pint whilst I nip to the loo? Sorry to ask, but you can't be too careful these days".

"Sure" she said, distractedly.

He walked away, but not far. He watched her, waiting for the signs. *It won't be long.*

After a few minutes he saw her rub the back of her neck. He sent the text message immediately.

"Sorry! Can't work the phone! Am just coming in. xx"

He returned to the bar. She was frowning at her phone.

"Thanks" he said, smiling again. Then he feigned a look of concern. "Are you OK?"

She nodded. "I just came over dizzy for some reason. It's no big deal. My mum will be here in a minute".

"That's good" he said, scanning her intently for the signs of disorientation. Picking the moment would be crucial.

He turned away from her, typing quickly into the phone. He set up the text to go, then placed his hand, phone intact, into his pocket, and turned back to her. She was looking pale. She was starting to breathe more quickly, complaining of being hot.

He pressed send.

Her phone beeped and she struggled to operate it, finally retrieving the message amid her growing confusion.

"I am here, in the foyer. Where are you?"

"Thank God", said the woman. She tried to move from her stool but stumbled as she did so.

He caught her with both hands now, the phone having been turned off in his pocket. *We won't be needing that anymore.*

"Hey! Steady!" he said, jokingly.

She looked up at him, her pupils dilating. "I think.... I... my drink.... Someone....my drink..."

"What?" he said

"Um.... I need.... the foyer.... the foyer"

"You want to go to the foyer?" he said, close to her ear. She nodded.

"Let me help you".

She walked forward, leaning heavily on him. "My….. mum…" she said.

"Yes, don't worry. We'll get you to your mum".

To the rest of the world they looked like a normal couple as they left the restaurant and hailed a taxi, the woman draped around the man like a drunk woman in love.

07

9.07pm

Maria Blakemore moved quickly through her apartment, turning on the lights as she went.

"I need a shower" she thought, wanting the soporific effect to wash away the day.

She paused briefly to look outside as she drew the curtains and blinds on her way. She checked the locks on each window, the only barrier between her and the outside world. *If only there was a barrier for the soul*, she thought. *How much easier would her life be?*

Her bathroom was a small en-suite connection. She undressed slowly, putting the clothes away in an unhurried reverie, letting her mind slowly switch off. It was only when she turned on the shower, and the sound of the water masked everything else that she thought she heard someone in the bedroom.

She froze for a moment, listening. Then she turned the shower off, and listened again. Nothing.

She put her dressing gown on and went into the bedroom, then to the short circular stairway that lead down to the lounge and kitchen, and then finally down to the front door.

Nothing.

It had controlled her for too long, she thought; the paranoia that had haunted her since the attack. She had never had a lover she could grow close to or trust. She had never had children. She had never been able to form a relationship with anyone that wasn't ultimately polluted by the spectre of what had happened to her, and yet she wanted all those things so badly it sliced the core of her in half, creating a wound that never seemed like it would heal.

She made her way back to the bathroom, turning on the shower to its most powerful and loudest setting. She let it pound onto her skin, closing her eyes as the steam enveloped the bathroom in a fog.

She washed slowly, waiting for the heat and the steam to transport her to a different place. A place where she was cleansed of the effect of other people. A place where she could be herself.

When she stepped out she looked away from her left side, as she had done for the last nineteen years every time she dried her body, or dressed, or was naked anywhere for any reason. She looked away because that was where the tattoo was. She did not recall exactly when he tattooed her, but she knew it was near the end of her captivity. That was why she was sure back then that her death was close. She closed her eyes to try and shut out the image, try and resist the pull of the memory. She didn't want to see herself there again. She didn't want to hear herself screaming when she woke up and saw that tattoo. She didn't want to recall crying for hours at the sight of it, staring at it all the while. It was the imposition, the depersonalisation, the unknown meaning of it that broke her. It turned her into a chunk of meat, like cattle, branded as to ownership. She didn't want to remember any of these things but so many times, every day, without warning, the visions still crashed through her defences, snatching her away from her life and throwing her into the pit of her past.

When she was done, she stood naked before the mirror. If she ever looked at it, this was how she did it. It seemed less awful seeing it in the mirror than it did looking directly on her skin.

She ran her fingers over it, tracing the shapes and being unable to avoid thinking of the sickening meaning.

Three symbols. One number.

☤

✠

⚓

VII

She knew she should have it removed, gouged out, purged from her body. But she hadn't done so far, and she knew deep down she never would. Having it removed would not remove the truth of her existence: That until he was caught she remained his prisoner.

Until he was caught.

And what were the chances of that? Nineteen years of post-traumatic hell, seventeen of those spent under police protection. And even after so long she was still, at thirty-eight years of age, looking at a lifetime of dealing with the fact that she awoke every morning believing she should have died, and that he was somewhere, out there, coming for her still. That was not life. That was existence without point.

She wrapped herself in her towel. Days like today were rarer than they used to be. Despite the triggers each day that made her remember she could, most days, muddle through, consoling herself with her work. Counselling others through their trauma was the best therapy. At least that way she put something back; made something good out of something bad.

Everyone has their cross to bear, she accepted that. It was just that there were some days where she wished hers was not indelibly marked on her soul, or her skin.

When she heard the knocking at the door it didn't immediately register. When it came again, loudly, she leapt from the bed and put on her dressing gown. She turned off the light and drew the curtain back slightly to see if she recognised a car, or a face.

There was nothing familiar.

The knocking came again. It sounded as if someone were thumping the door. She heard her name called. Jane Lister.

She hurried down the stairs, through to the hallway, and stared at the outline of the people standing on the other side of the door. She walked slowly toward it, placing the chain on the door.

"Who is it?" she called out.

"The Police" came the reply.

She opened the door against her better judgement as far as the chain-lock would allow.

Webber held up his warrant card. "My name is Detective Inspector Joseph Webber. I am looking for Miss Jane Lister. Are you Jane Lister?" he asked.

She didn't reply. She just stared at him.

"It's OK" he said, trying to reassure her. "I don't wish to alarm you, but you do need to let me in".

She glanced at his colleague. A tall blonde woman, with sharp features, ice-blue eyes, but a familiarity that threw her immediately, even in the half-light of dusk. Her fingers pressed hard into her palms as she held DCI McMullen's gaze.

"Hello, Maria. I am Detective Chief Inspector Claire McMullen".

Maria fought back the immediate urge to slam the door shut and run. She took in the face, the demeanour, the sound of the woman's voice. At first she said nothing, feeling only a weakness seeping into her limbs.

"Claire" she said, finally.

"Yes" replied McMullen, without apology.

08

11.17pm

He turned the key in the outer lock and entered the inner storage area. Here he kept the items he needed for his work. He walked slowly from one locked door to the other.
Two rooms.
The work required time, like all worthwhile work. Time did not come easily. To start time running at one end of a candle meant that time must be started on the mirrored candle. Everything had two parts. For the dark, there must be the light. For the end, there must be the beginning. Cycles. Circles. These were the things of life. These were the inevitabilities that no-one could escape.
He lit the candle outside the first room, pausing to stare at the locked door. She was a clever one this one, which was why he was sad to see her here, but perhaps that made it all the more important that she was here. He glanced down at the water. She was not drinking enough. She never had. She refused. There would be some punishment for that. She had to learn that it was not good.
He walked slowly to the second room. The light was not so good in this latter end of the tunnel. He had to be careful with such things. The spotlights used up excessive amounts of electricity. The generator would need replacing. That was difficult – exceptionally difficult – given the location. But he had to remain mindful of

everything. Maria, the salvatory Maria, his scarlet tessera, would have told them everything. It was only a short hop from there to deduce that he needed power without power. Down here, there were no sockets. He could picture them sitting round their investigation table. Discussing what she would have given them. Seeking to find those remote places where electricity was being consumed in large amounts, disproportionate, perhaps to its functionality. He smiled. That would throw them miles off. Yes, all these things, all these tiny nuances, were what made the process difficult. But when something is difficult, it is worth doing. Nothing good ever came from anything that was easy.

He paused outside the second door and lit the candle. He filled his lungs, as if to ease his anxiety. Now they were alight he could speak with them. Their spirit beacon was there, in the dark, where it had always been. He had simply bought it to the fore on their behalf. Is that not love? To know what someone needs even when they do not know that they need it?

Love.

Yes. Love.

Love is so many things, but in the end, it is only what it means to the receiver that gives it meaning. So these physical beings here would not say that he loved them. He didn't expect them to. But perhaps their spirits, their deeper intuitive spirits, might. Yes, perhaps. But their physical cages would spit and fight and say that he doesn't understand love.

He smiled. "But I do understand love" he said to himself. "It was not love that scarred me in this way. It was evil that scarred me in this way. And so I seek to ensure others do not suffer the same fate". He touched the shaft of the candle, stared at the flame.

"It is time" he said quietly. "It is time to talk".

He walked to the other end of the crescent. He turned the key in the inner lock. He heard movement as he entered. She was awake. She was always awake. He frowned. And then he heard her voice.

"I know you're there you bastard!"

He locked the door behind him. And turned toward the darkness. The switch for the spotlights was down to his left. He stood, motionless, trying to read the feeling in the air. He closed his eyes, turned his head to one side.

He heard her spit. "You sick piece of shit! For God's sake! You are going to go down for fucking years for this and you know it! And if I have to be the one that sends you down I fucking well will! Down to Hell!"

"SILENCE!" *he shouted into the darkness. He could not think when they shouted so much filth into the air. He closed his eyes again and tried to read what he felt. He shook his head and slammed on the lights.*

The bank of spotlights lit up like a thousand burning suns. There was a scream as he stormed into the room, walking up to her without hesitation. She scrambled backwards, slamming herself against the wall, shielding her eyes from the searing light. He stood before her. Inches between them. "Screech like that again and you will be dead within minutes. Do you understand?"

She spat at him. He stepped forward, ignoring her nakedness, grabbing her throat.

"Do you understand!" *he bellowed. She refused to acknowledge him. He turned his head away in disgust. He had touched her. He could not afford any mistakes.*

He walked back to the door, shaking his head again.

"That's it!" *she screamed.* "Run away you little piece of shit!"

He turned the key in the lock and pulled the hose from its housing. He reached around to the tap on the pressure tank and turned it on, moving swiftly back through the inner door. He could not afford this. Resources down here were scarce and he couldn't ever guarantee undisturbed time to bring extra resources down from the surface, especially given the difficulties. This is why they had to obey him. He pushed the bucket toward her. The one she used for excrement.

"Scrub yourself! All over!" he barked.

She held her head high. "Fuck you!" she screamed.

He turned on the hose and she screamed as the water hit her. She was thrown back against the wall. He soaked her as she continued screaming. He moved forward as she fell to her knees under the power of the water.

"PLEASE!" she screamed as he walked toward her.

He focused the hose on her neck where he had touched her. She tried to raise her hands to protect herself against the jet but the chains held her and he pushed the hose harder in to the area of his touch. The force of the water almost choked her. Satisfied he backed away, saying nothing. He watched her, crying and choking.

"It need not be this way" he said as he walked away.

She said nothing and he turned off the lights, plunging her into darkness.

He locked the door, ignoring the sound of her sobbing, and kicked it hard in anger.

He turned to look at the candle that flickered and danced in the disturbed air, filling his lungs repeatedly, trying to regain control.

He rested against the door, staring at the wall, counting the tiles.. one, two, three...

Eventually he pushed himself up, walking slowly to the other end of the small section of tunnel.

He turned the key to the lock and moved inside.

He heard the shuffle of the steel chains on the floor.

"Is someone there?" *came the woman's voice.*
"Yes. I am here".
She started to cry. "Please", *she said,* "Please…. Why am I here?"
He switched on the spotlights and she screamed.
"You are here because you are unhappy" he said, staying behind the light.
She wiped her eyes. She was crouching down, huddled with her knees drawn to her chest, head bowed to shield her eyes from the light. "But I wasn't unhappy" *she said.* "I have friends. I have family. I liked my life". *She began to sob heavily, her voice turning to a whine.* "I was happy", *she said.* "I was happy…"
He stared at her. Her long dark hair falling over her shoulders. Her nakedness hidden by her defensive crouch. "That would have been taken from you eventually" he said.
"By what?" *she said, hardly able to speak.* "By you?"
He stared at her, in her meekness.
"By life itself" he said, and he turned off the lights.
He locked the door and slumped against it. The process of understanding them was so draining. He could not help them if he did not understand them, and it was so hard to understand them, so hard to hear them in amongst the noise they created.
He sat for several minutes, gathering himself, turning over what they had said to him.
"Time and chance happen to us all" he said, resignedly. "I can no more predict who I take than they can predict who will take them".
He pushed himself away from the door and pictured her, on the other side, in her nakedness, shielding herself against the bright lights and yet having no need to shield herself. He began to cry. He thought of her, moving

through life, beginning to live and to love, so beautiful in her acceptance of everything. He saw her making things work with the father to her children, innocent in her naivety, taking the misery of life without really knowing why she had ended up with so little when life had promised so much.

He reached down on the ground, took up a small piece of smashed tile and ripped it, hard, along the flesh on his inner forearm. Blood flowed freely and he squeezed his hand, pumping it out onto his skin. He ran his hand over it, collecting it, and smearing it onto his face.

"God has given you one face" *he said, shaking,* "and you paint yourself another".

He took deep breaths, trying to control the heaving in his chest, and hauled himself to his feet.

Stumbling along the corridor to the other door, he turned the key in the lock. He slammed on the lights and the blonde woman scrambled to her feet. "Back again you piece of shit!" *she screamed.* "You see how I was ready for you? Do you! Do you see how you cannot break me?"

She was holding her chained arms up to her eyes against the light.

When he stepped out she screamed at the sight of his blood-smeared face.

He walked slowly up to her. "I have a guest here" *he said quietly.* "She is like you. Held here for the work I must do".

The woman scrambled backwards, straining at her chains as she pushed herself as far away from him as her restraints allowed.

"And she deserves to be released first, for she is not so far down the line of sick debauchery as you, you fucking little whore. You... you must stay here and suffer. You must stay here and learn".

"WHY!" *she screamed*, "Why does she get to go free when I have to stay! What am I to you!". *She scrambled to her feet.*

He stood before her, his face smeared with his own blood. "You must stay and she must die" *he said calmly.* "You are sick, but you do not know it".

"ME! I'M SICK!?" *she spat at him.* "There is only one sick piece of shit round here you twisted freak!"

'You are shrieking at me now' *he said silently to himself,* ' but it matters not. Your companion's fate is sealed'.

He closed her box. Shut her away and moved down the tunnel.

When he turned the lock in the other door he didn't hear her move.

He picked up the tattoo gun, and its battery pack, and placed them inside the door. He closed the door and turned the key in the lock, listening all the while for her movement. Nothing came.

He stood against the locked door, in the darkness. All he could hear was the quiet sound of her sleeping.

He waited for a moment, wanting to hear her react, but all he heard was the low, breathy, in and out of her slumber.

He held up the syringe against the half- light, and drew down one half from a glass vial he held in his left pocket. Then he took out a glass vial from his right pocket, inserted the syringe, and filled the remaining space from the pale liquid.

He pressed the plunger, lightly, and the toxins squirted out from the end of the needle.

He moved toward the border between the spotlights and her space.

He stood there, waiting. She did not move.

He reached behind him and turned on a small torch, running the beam over the wall. She was lying on her side, the chains pulled across her.

He placed the torch on the ground. The beam directed at her face and neck.

He moved slowly toward her, kneeling down beside her, away from the beam that lit her upper body.

Briefly, he watched her sleeping, then placed his gloved hand over her mouth and plunged the needle into her neck pushing hard on the plunger. She emitted a startled sound and jumped awake but he pushed hard on her mouth and straddled her so that he could finish administering the dosage.

She fought for a while, in her clouded confusion, and then she was gone.

He climbed off and unlocked the wrist clamps, pulling her into the centre of the floor. He slapped her face to ensure she was out. Satisfied, he walked back to the access door and turned on the spotlights. She lay, prostate, ignorant of what was happening.

Solemnly, driven by a deep belief, he picked up the tattoo gun and its battery pack.

09

11.36pm

At the door to the custody suite Maria paused. Webber hardly noticed as he punched in the code to the security door.

"It's been a long time since I've been inside one of these", she said.

"Don't worry", said Webber, smiling. McMullen, who followed behind them, said nothing.

As they entered the building a young man who was emptying the pockets of his tracksuit into a plastic tray wolf-whistled as Maria walked past.

"Do you mind keeping your dogs on a lead?" Webber said loudly in the general direction of the custody sergeant.

He punched in another security code to a dividing door and led them into the heart of the station.

Maria's eyes darted around the corridor, taking in the surroundings with an urgency she hadn't expected. It was if she was suddenly a prisoner, forced into a hasty reconnaissance of the route to her captivity, searching for her means of escape.

Webber knocked on the first door that was ajar. When no answer came he pushed the sign on the door to "engaged" and held it open for them. "We can use this room", he said.

Maria walked in slowly, still scanning the inner sanctum of the station. Memories gatecrashed their way back into the core of her, sucking her back through the years of resistance and denial. She saw herself, younger, thinner, clutching a plastic cup, hand shaking as she read letters, heard place names, and listened to the warm words of assurance and encouragement that come from the officers in front of her. Officers who would achieve nothing and, ultimately, let her down.

She looked up at Webber who drew back the chair, offering her a place to sit. He was smiling. She held his eye contact momentarily. Another officer whose heart was in the right place, she thought. He would be eaten alive in the frustration and the fear, of that she felt sure. It was something in his tone that gave him away. The matter-of-fact *we-can-deal-with-it* approach. The assumption that the Met was a mighty machine, with resources, talent, skill, knowledge; that all she had to do was surrender herself to it and good would prevail. She sat down slowly and rested her elbows on the table.

"I cannot believe I am here again", she said, almost to herself.

She clasped her hands together in front of her in a prayer-like position, sliding back in time to when she once sat opposite McMullen, her dark hair tied back from her stick-thin shoulders, her face gaunt and drawn, McMullen reaching out, re-assuring her... doing her job. And then it struck her: The difference between who she was then, and who she was now. "I wouldn't worry about me this time, Clare" she said. "I'm faithless now". And then, more clearly, as if her voice and strength had suddenly returned to her, "I'm faithless. So come on. Tell me why the life I tried so hard to rebuild is suddenly being torn apart in seconds. Tell me what is so bad that I have Met officers sent for my protection, and why normal life has suddenly evaporated right in front of me. Tell me why I am back here. Again".

McMullen considered her for a moment. She wanted to say that neither she, nor the Met, had anything to apologise for. She wanted to say that sometimes things just don't go to plan. She wanted to go through every single murder investigation she had ever been a part of since that first, barren experience, and tell her that everyone is human, that people make mistakes, and that yes, sometimes the best just isn't good enough, but do you know what? It is the caring that makes the difference; it is the understanding and the empathy that keeps you coming back time and time again. It is the damned human element that keeps you addicted to the buzz of finally catching some evil bastard and putting them away and going home at night and saying *in this endless stream of twisted fuckers there is at least one less of them now....*

She glanced briefly at Webber, suddenly grateful for his presence there. "Three days ago we found the body of a young woman. Her head had been shaved. Her lips had been cut from her face, and she appeared to have bled to death somewhere other than where her body was found. We have now identified her as a 19 year old model who was living and working in London. She had been reported missing a month before she was found".

Maria clasped her hands together again to try and hide the shaking.

Webber spoke up in an effort to support his colleague. "We have good reason to believe that the person who carried out this attack was the same person who attacked you. That is why we felt we had no option but to bring you back into some form of protection. We haven't given any thought yet as to how that might be done. That is something we need to discuss with you".

Maria didn't appear to be listening. Her eyes, welling with tears, were fixed on McMullen. "All this reason-to-believe bullshit", she said quietly. "It's more than that, isn't it…. That's why *you're* here. That's why it's *you* and not someone else sitting there".

No Cotton Wool thought McMullen. *Not this time.* "The girl was tattooed", she said. "Number Eight in Roman numerals, and also the same three symbols".

"Oh God!" cried Maria. She thrust her hands into her lap, rocking back and forth.

"Jesus", said Webber, unable to control himself, "do you have to be so fucking brutal about it?"

McMullen remembered, fleetingly, Webber's own recent loss, but said nothing. *No cotton wool. Not this time.*

*   *   *

They talked around the edges of the horror for a while. Somewhere in the recesses of Maria's mind reality started to take hold. McMullen spoke about the implications of the Serious Organised Crime Act under which Maria's protection had ultimately been removed, and how such protection might best be restored. Maria felt the fabric of things being unpicked as they organised the ensuing days and what her employers would be told. It hurt when McMullen asked about family.

"There is no family" said Maria, solemnly, and then the conversation moved on to the logistics of her safety and the constant reference to liberty, rights of privacy…. Rights to Life.

She got up. She couldn't help herself. The conversation stopped. "Rights to Life?" she said incredulously, almost laughing to herself. "What life do I have now? What life did I ever have?"

She turned to face McMullen. "Nineteen years ago you promised me that you would catch him. I gave you everything I had. All my trust, all my faith. You made me believe in the system, and all that happened was that he taunted and taunted and he kept on doing it until he had stripped me of everything I had left. He walked away a free man and I was the one who got the jail sentence. I was the one who got Life. That is what my life has been like Claire, since you held me in some sick suspended reality. Every single day, every *single* day under that police protection, that new life, I used to wake up and think 'maybe it's today…. Maybe today is the day that they phone me up and say I am finally giving evidence' because you had charged someone, because you had found someone, because you had tracked them down and brought them in… because you had done your fucking job".

She could feel her chest pounding. Tears were forming in her eyes. "And yet everything just went on and on with everybody who had promised so much gradually losing interest. Do you know what? Cutting me loose from the protection programme was the best thing you ever did for me. I knew it wasn't because I had become low-risk. It was because I was an expensive luxury. But that was fine because all of a sudden I was out there alone, fending for myself, taking my chances". She laughed to herself, wiping the tears from her eyes. "But I was alive. I was living. I was normal".

She sat down, wringing her hands. There was a sense of urgency in her voice. "Put me back out there" she said. "Put me back out there and let me live. He let me go, remember? I was number seven. It's over for me. I have been passed by. I cannot be number nine, don't you see? I cannot be nine, ten, eleven. I am tattooed, Claire. I am branded with the number seven".

McMullen glanced furtively at Webber. "I cannot see a way that you could return to a life without protection, not in the short term".

"But why? Surely this is my decision now? I have no family left. Both my parents are dead. I have lived looking over my shoulder for as long as I can remember. There is nothing that this man hasn't already taken from me".

"Apart from your life" said Webber.

Maria switched her attention to him. "Yes. Apart from my life. You are right. And do you know what? I don't value that and haven't done since all of this first happened to me. I know I was supposed to walk off into the sunset, blessed with my freedom and grateful to be alive to taste the air, to watch the rain and feel the sun on my skin, but it was all bullshit. All of it. I went into a prison cell with no bars. I went into a chamber with endless space within and no way out. Trust me – I may as well have been dead for all the good being alive brought me".

She turned back to McMullen. "So why don't you just let me get back to what little life I had. Yes, he is clearly out there, like he always was. I am sorry for what has happened because I, more than anyone else, know what that poor woman would have been through, but I am in no more danger than I ever was, am I?"

McMullen got up and walked slowly over to the two-way mirror set behind them. She watched her reflection as she approached, looking into her own eyes as she did so. "I will not let you go back out there without protection, not now". She turned to face Maria. "I know how let down you feel. I am not stupid. I can see why you wouldn't trust me, or the Force, again. But understand this: You are in danger. Not in the way you were when you were first released, and not in the way you were in subsequent years. This is different. This is the same man, suddenly out again from whatever stone it was he has hidden under for the last nineteen years, and his reason for being back in the sunlight is you".

"You cannot know that for sure", Maria protested.

"But I do know it" said McMullen flatly. "I would not have dragged you in here for a second time, knowing what that would do to you, unless I had good reason. I would not have pulled every string available to get myself transferred down here, unless I had good reason". She went back to the table and sat down opposite Maria. "And I would not promise myself that I would not let you down a second time, unless I had good reason".

She paused for a moment, scanning Maria's face, looking at her eyes for something, anything, that would show the message was getting through. *No cotton wool. Not this time.* "With the body of the girl we also received a DVD. It contains a recording of the girl when she was still alive. Despite her injuries and terrible distress, she is being forced to say your name. It is quite distinctive, and it is very obvious. She is saying 'Maria'".

Maria stared back at her. "I want to see it" she said, her voice suddenly devoid of animosity.

McMullen shook her head. "I understand why you might want to, but I don't think there is any real need to see it. What can it offer you, apart from upset?".

Maria started picking at the skin around her thumbnail. "I need to see it".

"It won't change things" said Webber.

Maria looked up at him. "I know it won't change things, but I need to see it. It was, after all, meant for me. Isn't that what you are saying?"

"Maria", said McMullen, "there is a man out there who is killing. Whether or not he intends to kill you is something no-one knows. Only he knows that. But what I will say is that leaving us visual evidence of his mutilations may actually have little to do with you and everything to do with his own vanity".

"Let's face it", retorted Maria, "whether I see it or I don't see it, it makes no difference. If I am a target then I will always be one. I just need to know what he's capable of". She stopped picking at herself. "I need to know what he did, what he has done, what I was spared from. He never took me that last step, did he? I never got to that stage. He let me go and no-one knows why, and I know I shouldn't care, but I lay awake at night, going over it and over it, trying to see what it was that was different about me – why he let me go. Sometimes I think I will go mad trying to work it out, and perhaps that is what he wants, but part of me thinks it is something simple. That it is something no-one will have expected, hidden in a place that no-one would ever look, and we don't know – I don't know – where that might be, which is why I have to look at everything. I have to see and hear everything about it so I can work it out for myself".

"Isn't that our job" said Webber, half-smiling.

Maria looked at McMullen and they held each other's stare for a moment.

"Maybe" said Maria, looking away, "but I don't trust anyone anymore to do that job".

"I cannot give you free rein to get involved with a Police investigation" said McMullen. "I will give you all the transparency I can, and I will make sure you are not kept in the dark over significant developments, but I am throwing the weight of all the resources I have against this man and I will succeed here where we failed before. Whether you trust me or not we are all different people now. You, me, the Force itself. It may not be as simple as a matter of trust anymore. There are more things to consider".

Maria got to her feet. "By *transparency* I guess you mean I can see it".

McMullen was silent for a moment, before she nodded slowly. "Yes", she said. "But on one condition".

"Which is?"

"From this point on you do as you are told. Your safety is now the responsibility of the Met. If we are to keep you safe, you have to do what we tell you".

She looked from one face to another. *Voices* she thought to herself. *Such tiny voices lost in the dark.*

*   *   *

The three of them walked through to the main investigation room. McMullen turned the remote over and over in her hands. "I want the FME here before we start" she said solemnly. "Just in case".

Webber picked up the nearest phone to make the call.

"You are liability free, Claire" said Maria. "You needn't worry about protocol. I know this is my own doing".

"Nevertheless…" she trailed off and paced the room.

They listened in silence to Webber explaining matters. There was a brief conversation which sounded like nothing more than questions and answers. "Yes" Webber said to some, "No" to others. Then, eventually, "He's on his way up".

Maria pulled a chair from behind one of the desks. Webber sat down next to her. She watched McMullen as she turned on the television and opened the DVD tray. She took a slim case from an evidence bag. The DVD looked like any other. A small round disc, with nothing written on it. Plain. Uninteresting. Normal.

The door clicked behind them and a stressed looking man entered the room, carrying a black medical bag. He was slightly out of breath. "You were lucky you caught me", he said, dropping the bag heavily on the table in front of him and removing his jacket. "I was on my way out".

"I appreciate this Philip" said McMullen.

He moved swiftly to Maria and extended his hand. "I am Dr Philip Gill" he said, almost as breathless as when he had entered.

Maria shook his hand but said nothing. He smiled. "You don't need to look so concerned" he said. "As I am sure DCI McMullen explained, this is just a precaution. I have some mild sedatives in my bag, that's all, and I will stay for a while afterwards in case you want to talk, or…" he shrugged his shoulders, "I think you know what I mean".

"Or throw up" said Maria, coldly "Or have some kind of breakdown or delayed shock reaction, or feint". There was a hint of mockery in her voice.

Webber frowned. "Officers who have served for years and who think they've seen everything can be affected by little things totally out of the blue. No-one knows how people react to upsetting images. Suppressing it and being a tough guy isn't always the best way".

She fixed her eyes on him. "Whatever I see now, Joe, it is at least one step removed. I doubt anything on that TV screen is going to feel worse than how it felt when I was physically there. Fearing for your life tends to have a strange sobering effect on you. It puts pretty much everything else into perspective".

"Perhaps", said Dr Gill, "but it's a precaution. That's all".

"Well", said Maria, "now all the precautions are in place let's just get on with it".

McMullen looked disapprovingly at Webber, but he averted her eyes. Politics would not serve them well now.

McMullen pressed play and the screen came to life with the dark, out of focus image of a wall. She had purposefully kept the sound low and when the woman's face appeared, mutilated and screaming, she held her finger over the red button that would kill the sound and screen dead. She glanced at Maria who had her hands to her mouth.

"Jesus Christ" said Maria, staring, transfixed, at the screen.

The DVD played through its' sickening motions. The screaming. The suffocation. The violence.

And then the name.

"SAY IT!" shouted the male voice over the screaming. "SAY IT!"

"Ah – eee – ah" came the desperate cry. "Ah – eee – ah… Ah –eee- ah"

"SAY IT! SAY IT!"

"AH – EEE – AH!" came the scream, frantic and pleading. "AH – EEE – AH! AH – EEE – AH!"

"Say it properly you unclean bitch before I rip your fucking tongue out!.......... Now you say what I fucking tell you to say you filthy whore!"

Maria wiped the tears from her eyes, her hands shaking. "Turn it off!" she pleaded, her voice almost failing her, and then again, before her composure left her, "Please! Please turn it off!"

McMullen killed the systems, and bowed her head.

Webber put his arm around Maria, whilst the FME watched them. It was several minutes before she stopped crying and regained herself. She eased away from Webber, wiping her eyes.

McMullen said nothing. *'No Cotton Wool'* she kept thinking to herself, over and over. *'No Cotton Wool'*.

It was Dr Gill who spoke first. "Do you…" he paused.

Maria heard him but didn't turn around. "Do I need anything" she said finishing his words for him. "No, thank you Doctor. Other than to get out of here".

McMullen got to her feet and nodded to the FME who gathered up his things.

She took a breath thinking she might have her *'I-told-you-so'* moment, but she caught the look on Webber's face and let it go.

"Are you alright, Maria?" she said mechanically, hardly sounding like a question.

Maria pushed herself up and wiped her eyes again. "I'll live" she said. "For now, at least".

July 3rd

10

8.03am

Webber was at the scene within minutes of getting the call, but despite his early arrival he couldn't get his car more than a few feet at a time, even with the siren going. Traffic was queuing on all roads away from Farringdon tube station as uniformed officers directed people along other routes. Police cars were positioned on Vine Street and Clerkenwell bridges. He parked up on the kerb at the side gate on Farringdon Road opposite the Post Office. There was no way he was going to get anywhere near the front of the station.

He climbed out and ran up to the police cordon, showing his badge and ducking under the tape.

Officers were ushering people away from the brick walls and vantage points that overlooked the station. He ran across Clerkenwell Bridge, pausing briefly to haul himself up a few inches and peer over the wall. The wall was head height. He put his hands on the top and jumped up a little way, coming to rest on his forearms, his legs hanging free.

He could see a tube train in position but empty, and SOCO officers getting gowned up with their protective clothing. There were other officers milling around, but the normally packed station was now drained of its' public. He could see McMullen, talking on her mobile phone, looking up in his direction.

As he dropped to his feet a uniformed officer said "When we first got here this bridge was lined with people all doing exactly what you've just done".

He hurried over the bridge into Turnmill Street, then ran the rest of the way to the front of the station. Several police officers stood at the entrance and motorcycle traffic officers blocked the approach roads from each direction, their sirens silent but the intermittent bright blue flash of the lights unmistakeable.

The station echoed in its' hollow emptiness. A few uniformed officers busied themselves with some witnesses, but the desertion was tangible. He passed through the turnstiles, all of them locked open, and then down the steps to the Southbound platform.

McMullen was talking to a uniformed officer with her back to Webber as he approached. In front of her, in the direction she was facing, he saw the SOCO's, in their white suits and blue shoe coverings, entering and leaving the forensic tent which had been set up over the area where the body was found. They moved slowly and meticulously, bringing out small containers and vials, cataloguing everything.

"Jesus, it's a fucking nightmare out there" he said, standing next to McMullen.

"You should try being in here" she said. "I saw you poking your head over the bridge up there. My best guess is that the body was thrown from that very point. The fucking media are going to put two and two together in the next few hours and come up with five. Too many people saw the body. This time there was no warning, no tinkering with the signals to draw attention, no quiet placement of the body to the side of the track. This was just thrown down for all to see. It was hit by a tube train at 6am this morning. The train was pulling-in to the station and the driver saw it early, thank god, so it's all still in one piece. All the early birds were peering over the walls at Vine Street and Clerkenwell bridges to see what the fuss was about. By the time uniform got the roads sorted out I couldn't tell you how many people had seen the body".

They started walking down the platform. "For all we know" she said, still looking up at the vantage points that overlooked the station, "he might still be out there somewhere, watching the chaos he has created".

They stopped at the far end of the platform where an engineer's wooden step-down had been placed. McMullen climbed down first and they picked their way over the rail track, stopping a few yards from the tent to put on the protective clothing.

"Ready?" she asked, as she pulled her hood on.

Webber nodded. SOCO's made them both turn round several times to check their suits.

"Let's go" she said.

Inside the tent there were two forensic officers. When they saw McMullen approaching they nodded and moved to give her access.

The woman's body was laying on her side, her head twisted to the left, facing away from where they had entered. She was covered in scratches and one of her arms, the one on which she lay, was outstretched, above her head. The other arm was twisted backwards, laying behind her, her hand almost in the small of her back. Webber looked at her wrist. There were heavy blood stains around it.

He walked slowly up to the cadaver. The tent created an unreal space; A quiet place. A place set apart from the outside world. He could hear the noise of the people outside, but it was if they were from a different time, a different era. This small enclosure, with this poor woman's body central to it; These silent men photographing her, collecting samples from her, treating her like the riddle she was – something to be solved… it was all so surreal.

He stared at the woman's face. Her lips had been cut off. Her teeth and gums exposed. It was like some garish smile. With all of her hair removed she looked freakish. Like something evil.

And then McMullen saw what she had been looking for. The tattoo. It was in the same place as all the others. On the top of the victim's left leg, on the outside of her thigh. She had to crouch down to see it, but there it was.

Three symbols. One number.

☓

※

⚓

IX

She was number nine.

McMullen stood there for several more minutes, looking at the cuts, looking at the way the girl had landed

"Enough?" she said to Webber, eventually.

He nodded, following her solemnly out of the tent. They removed their protective clothing in silence.

As they walked back over the track toward the sanity of the platform McMullen said, "We think we know who this girl is. I have had DS Shah trawling missing person reports. Usually these girls are held for some time before we find a body. Well, in this instance it seems we have gotten lucky, if you can call it that".

They stopped by the side of the platform, standing on the track itself.

"Last night, uniformed officers were called to Hammersmith tube station. A woman was found on the tube train, completely out of it. Stoned, apparently. Talking absolute gibberish. The paramedics took her into St Hugh's where she eventually came round. Because the casualty department didn't have a clue what she'd taken they ran blood tests". She fixed her eyes on Webber. "She tested positive for both Rohypnol *and* Heroin".

Webber raised his eyebrows. "What has a user got to do with our investigation?"

"She wasn't a user", continued McMullen. "Her medical records didn't suggest any history of drug abuse, and neither did her physical appearance. The only conclusion was that she had been drugged, and then left on the tube train. If it wasn't for the fact that the Circle Line has an extension, so a train actually terminates, she would have gone round and round for hours".

Webber folded his arms, listening intently. "What does she have to do with this girl?" he asked.

"The woman was identified by the drivers licence in her purse. Katherine Graham, forty-nine years old, works for the Guardian newspaper. Even though she was barely coherent she was still telling the same story over and over about someone who was going to hurt her daughter. CID there had the good sense to get on to the newspaper, and despite the late hour they got a lead on the daughter. The only trouble was, when they got to the girl's flat, her flatmate said she had received a text message from her mum and gone to meet her at a bar somewhere but she didn't know where".

Webber frowned. "Would be nice to know what the message said."

McMullen nodded. "Agreed. But I'm not sure it would actually make much difference. The woman didn't have her mobile with her. She said her attacker took it".

Webber drew breath. "Shit. The message was from him".

"Exactly. And she responded in good faith without knowing. The flatmate gave a scar on the girl's leg as an indentifying mark. Motorbike accident apparently. Did you see the scar?"

Webber shook his head.

"It's definitely there. This girl is therefore most probably Sarah Graham, and whoever attacked her also drugged her mother last night for some reason. It could mean some serious leads, or even a suspect. He hasn't taken such a risk before so far as I can tell. This is a new thing. To take someone so quickly, and for this to be done so quickly. This is why there is more blood at the scene than the last one, and the others from before. There wasn't time for him to do what he normally does".

Webber climbed up the steps to the platform, and then put out his hand to help McMullen.

As they walked she continued talking. "I think this is significant because it is such a departure from the norm. He does not strike me as someone who takes risks. But this opportunistic killing seems deliberate in its opportunism. What do you think?"

Webber shrugged. "I guess it depends on whether we really do think this is the same guy as before, and not just a well researched copycat. The M.O of the first six was all the same. Why deviate? I agree with you. The deviation is important, but I wouldn't like to say whether that was simply because it's not the same man doing it now. Nineteen years is a long time".

McMullen stopped on the platform and looked up at the vantage points again. "It's the same man, Joe. I would stake my life on it. I can smell his shit in the air everywhere I go in this city".

Webber was about to interject when McMullen's mobile rang. She retrieved it quickly, glancing briefly at the number. "It's the station" she said to him, taking the call.

"DCI McMullen" she said, self-assuredly.

For a few moments she stood motionless, listening. Webber looked expectantly at her. She was staring back at him, but her stare was vacant, unfocused. She was engrossed in whatever she was being told over the phone.

Finally she said, "tell me the ward again". She looked at Webber. "Remember the Middleton Ward, in the new building".

McMullen exchanged a few more instructions before slipping the mobile back into her pocket. "We need to go back to St Hugh's. David Sachs walked into A&E this morning claiming he'd been drugged and demanding someone test him to find out whatever poison he'd been given"

"Who the hell is David Sachs?"

McMullen glanced fleetingly at him before glossing over the question. "Get this. He tested positive for Rohypnol and Heroin. Uniform attended and called it straight in".

"You talk of him as if you know him" said Webber flatly.

She focused on him, as if suddenly becoming aware of his presence. The tone in her voice changed. "I used to" she said solemnly. "He was the one who came up with the sound-bite *The Horologist*". She almost spat the word out, frowning as she said it. "He's a very colourful character. Well respected".

"So why does that make a difference?"

"It makes a difference because he is familiar with the background. He said he was given an envelope. An envelope with his name on it, but that he wants a senior officer to see him before he will hand it over. He says he was given it by the man we are hunting".

"Then we need to get down there" said Webber, urgency creeping into his voice. "What are we waiting for?"

McMullen took out her rosary.

Click-clack. Click-clack.

"If what he says is true", stated McMullen, "then why isn't he dead? You have to ask yourself, Joe, why is he walking out into the sunset with nothing but a drug come-down to deal with? If what he says is true, then this guy wanted him to come to us, and, worse, it means someone wants him back in the frame, back in the forefront with his pen in hand, ready to chronicle the next fucking horror story". She began to walk toward the exit. "We are being hit from all sides" she said, quickening her pace, "and I don't fucking like it".

She rolled the rosary beads between her fingers as she thrust it back into her pocket.

Pray for us sinners.
Now, and at the hour of our Death.

11

11.31am

McMullen left Webber to find out what he could from the admission desk. Sachs' room was at the end of the corridor. She listened to Webber's conversation with the admissions nurse fading into the background as she made her way past the open wards and more private rooms. At the end of the corridor she stopped and peered through the small glass rectangle in the door to Sachs' room. He was sitting on the bed with his back to the door, staring towards the window. She noticed his white hair, still long and thick despite his age, and his broad shoulders, hunched over. She remembered him to be more than six-feet tall. *So it would have taken some strength to bring him down* she thought.

She entered the room and he turned slightly, but painfully, toward the door. They held eye contact for a moment before DCI McMullen identified herself.

At first he said nothing, his eyes narrowing slightly. Finally he said, "Once a young, inexperienced WPC. Now a DCI".

"You remember me then" she said, although it wasn't a question, more of an acknowledgement.

"I have thought of nothing else since I came round. It seems the past is rushing back in all its forms, and none of it in a good way". He pushed himself to his feet, trying to straighten his hospital gown. The pain made him catch his breath. "Broken ribs" he said, almost apologetically.

When he stood to his full height he was every bit the hulking frame she remembered him to be. A deep, resonant, gravelly voice. A voice for radio she had always thought. A large, dominant physical presence, his flowing white hair giving him a god-like appearance. An investigative reporter for the whole of his working life he had gravitas and respect.

He limped over to the small table beside his bed, taking small, tentative steps. McMullen noticed that his hands were shaking as he reached for an A4 sized manilla envelope. She had to remind herself that this man was still under the influence of the drug concoction that had been forced into his system.

"The man who attacked me left this behind. It was obviously meant for me". He handed it to her.

It looked innocent enough. The name *David Sachs* was printed in black text on a small white label. The label was stuck in the middle of the brown envelope. There were no other markings. "No-one has touched it but me" he added, trying to be helpful.

McMullen opened it up and took out the few sheets of A4 paper inside. They were photocopies of handwritten letters. She read over them for several minutes, her own memories seeping back through the cracks of the defences she had built against this case over the years.

David coughed, and then winced in pain. He took a sip of water with a shaking hand before saying, "do you see how certain words and sentences are highlighted?"

McMullen nodded slowly. "I recognise the letters", she said. "These are the letters that were written to Maria Blakemore by her abductor after she had been released".

David sat back down on the bed. "And I take it this is no co-incidence, you being here, I mean. One minute I am being attacked by someone I once wrote about and who was never caught, a man who leaves me in no doubt about who he is, and the next minute, when I ask to see someone senior, you turn up. You, the woman who sat with Maria Blakemore day after day when she was released. You will forgive me for being cynical, but despite the fact that I am lucky to be alive and I really therefore shouldn't question anything, I can't help but feel I just walked into something major".

McMullen put the letters down on the bed and considered him. "Whoever this man is, he is active again. It is not a copycat. It is him. We know it's not a copycat because of what happened to you, because of these letters, and because of a number of other factors which are not yet public knowledge".

"Am I in danger?" asked David.

"It's doubtful. If he wanted you dead Mr Sachs you would already be dead. You were a messenger". She picked up the letters again, before adding, "and you have delivered".

She looked over the letters again. "These phrases that have been highlighted, do they mean anything to you?"

He shook his head. "I wrote a lot about him back in those days, but that didn't mean I understood him. Circle Line killings, time cycles, circles. It was all a long time ago".

The first letter was two pages long. McMullen scanned the highlighted passages, reading them aloud.

"You will remember what I said to you when we were together, Maria: That God had given you one face and yet you painted yourself another".

And then, at the end of the letter:

"You cannot see me now, but I am smiling. Remember me, Maria. Remember me when I am gone".

She turned to the second letter. This was shorter than the first, but the highlighted sections were bigger. She continued reading.

"Do you know what duality is? It is the concept that two things are interlinked. Inseparable. One needs the other and without the other the two things, whatever they may be, do not exist".

Do you exist without me, Maria? Are you able to uncouple yourself from me? Or have recent events forged us into one, and never again will we exist without stopping briefly to remember the other?"

And further down the page:

"Duality is also wrapped up with the concept of deception. Duplicity. Perhaps shown in the fact that God has given you one face and you have painted yourself another".

She scanned down to the end of the letter.

Do you remember the mirror, Maria? Do you remember looking at yourself? How did you find that face, Maria? Remember the mirror, Maria. Remember the Mirror for in it you will see the truth.

She turned to the final letter. The first highlighted passage was halfway down the page.

"Do not let yourself down, Maria. You are an intelligent woman. Do not let them taint you toward me. I have tried to set you on a path toward a clear understanding as to how you may become immortal. This is no small thing, Maria. Do not close your mind".

She found the final highlighted section on the last page:

"The wind blows to the south, and goes round to the north; round and round goes the wind, and on its circuits the wind returns

'So there it is. I have given you the Book, the Chapter and the Verse".

McMullen replaced the letters in the envelope. They sat in silence as she checked through her notebook. David was motionless, hardly even looking up as Webber entered the room.

As Webber introduced himself, he discreetly passed McMullen a folded note torn from his notebook. It read *"Have spoken to uniform. Sachs knows about Katherine Graham but <u>doesn't</u> know about Sarah Graham"*

He took up position at the end of the bed.

"Mr Sachs", began McMullen, "What was the nature of your relationship with Katherine Graham?"

Sachs continued staring at the floor. "We had been having an affair for a long time, but I do not want that on record". He snorted in disgust at himself. "Who am I kidding? The truth has a habit of coming out, right?"

He eased himself back onto the bed.

"And the wider family, her daughter and husband, do you know them, too"?

"Not really. We didn't broadcast our relationship and we were always careful. Sarah has her own life, and as for Kate's husband, well….. I know who he is but that's as far as it goes".

McMullen folded Webber's note in half and placed it slowly into her trouser pocket. "Nevertheless, I am going to have to ask you some questions about the extent of your relationship with Sarah Graham, what she knew about you, what you knew about her, and what sort of relationship she had with her mother".

He looked up at her, trying to read her cold demeanor. "Why" he said slowly. "What's happened?"

July 4th

12

1.08pm

Webber sat at his desk, one hand cradling his coffee cup, the fingers of the other drumming incessantly on the table-top. The room had taken on a life of its own. The desks were covered in papers and notepads, the paraphernalia of the teams' thought processes and leads spread everywhere. Yellow sticky notes adorned computer screens. In-trays overflowed with files. Statements, taken by hand, waited to be typed. Phones rang, people answered self-assuredly but mechanically. He pulled one of the buff coloured files toward him. Numerous A4 size standard issue stationery, all full of their own little horror stories within.

Following the body at Farringdon, the violence of the killings had reached the public domain. Now there was no choice but to open things up. A Press Conference. A Public Statement. That meant increased pressure and increased scrutiny. The world of policing no longer allowed quiet analysis and the pursuit of leads with space to get it wrong. This would now become a world of retrospective-perfection. Every decision would be up for discussion by the wider press. Every lead would be subject to its own external analysis. Every member of the Press and public would be sitting in judgement, expecting results, because it is, after all, so easy to catch a murderer.

McMullen came in, closely followed by several other members of the team. They were greeted with a hush as conversations were ended mid-sentence. She nodded at those in the room, was greeted with some discreet "Ma'am" responses, and made her way to Webber's desk.

He pushed himself up in his seat. She looked at his desk, at the doodles on the pad and the coffee cup. "Busy?" she said.

"Thinking" he replied curtly.

"Yes, well, we won't have time for that shortly, that's for sure. You can save your thinking time for reading the press analysis of our inadequacies once this briefing is over."

"I'll be sure to read them on the crapper so I can flush them away with the rest of the shit".

She half-smiled. "Along with our careers no doubt".

She moved to the boards that now lined the far wall. The two victims, their locations, other possible connections, formed a maze before them. She walked slowly from one end to the other, her finger tracing a line through the pictures and notes. The faces of the mutilated bodies, garish in their skull-like appearance, stared back at her.

"Staring at it won't solve it", said Webber, as he got up from behind the desk.

"Oh I don't know, Joe. Call it thinking time".

He snorted. "I thought we'd dealt with that".

She touched the pictures of the victims. "Have you noticed that in each of them, their eyes are open?"

Webber looked from one to the other and back again. "Odd that both are found with their eyes open, I suppose, but hardly significant. They died under serious trauma".

"Yes, but did they? We already know the method of death in each case is probably blood loss. If we are right on that then consciousness would have been lost and that would have meant eyes closing as strength and mental capacity is lost".

Webber looked over the photos again. "So what are you saying?" he said. "That their eyes were opened after death".

She looked back at the photos, repeating his words. "Their eyes were opened after death. Yes. I am sure of it. Perhaps in more ways than one so far as the killer is concerned".

They both stood in silence, staring at the boards. Then Webber finally said, "we should get on with it. The Press Conference is at two".

"I know. Can you make a note to get the photos of the previous victims, the first six. I need to see whether their eyes are also open".

"Of course" said Webber.

She turned to face the team. "Right people" she said loudly, "can I have your attention whilst we go through what we've got. We have this press conference at two and I want to run through everything with you beforehand so we all know where we are. Joe will take this one".

They stopped what they were doing. Several people moved seats. Webber stood at the centre of the boards, hands in his pockets.

"We now have two murders in three days" he said solemnly. "We need to make a public appeal for witnesses and give some greater background to the Press than the piecemeal information they have already had. It is no longer of any benefit to us to keep the gravity of the situation under wraps. Any hopes of finding a lead and a suspect in the early days have now gone".

"Very little has been extracted from the original files. It is much the same now as it was then. The bodies are mutilated in the same way. The victims all died the same way. They have all been tattooed with these odd symbols and numerals, and they were all deposited either at or in the vicinity of a Circle Line tube station".

He pointed to the picture of the first victim. "The autopsy report on this woman will be here tomorrow. It's taken longer than expected due to certain materials found in the victim's stomach that needed to go for analysis. We don't have any more information on than that until the report arrives. The DVD is also currently undergoing sound analysis in the hope we can get some idea of what was going on in the background, something that might give us an idea of location. So far as the victim is concerned, we have identified her as Hannah Farrell. She was reported missing three months before her body was found on the tube line between Gloucester Road and South Kensington. DC Collins is heading up the investigation into her life and contacts before the abduction. She was an East London girl, born and bred. Usual methodology, mobiles, computers and all known places of recreation, work and questions asked of anyone who knew her from the boyfriend she was sleeping with down to the shopkeeper who sold her a newspaper. There is obviously a link into the missing persons investigation but from what I have seen from the records that had not produced a great deal. Neither did it appear to have been progressed either, probably due to resources, so we can expect a kicking over that when the Press get hold of it".

He turned back to face the team. "We can also expect a kicking over how this is being done right under our noses. We are assuming the last victim was thrown from the bridge above Farringdon tube station. We are checking traffic cameras in the area for the last forty-eight hours. We are not sure we will get a shot of the actual place she was thrown. Tube stations themselves are covered with cameras as are major traffic junctions but this bastard is clever. It seems there are certain areas around all of these last two locations where there is no coverage. When CCTV was first introduced to stations everyone was so wrapped up in covering the entrances, exits and platforms for security that the blind spots around the outside of these places were never given a second thought. We are paying the price for that now and it does of course have wider implications for terrorist activity, so you can expect the press to rip the Met apart over the next few weeks on that issue, apart from anything else".

The Press conference this afternoon is simply to appeal for witnesses and confirm victims details to widen the investigation. We don't want to go into chapter and verse and we are certainly not saying that each victim was found with a DVD of their own murder. We have to retain something that will allow us to weed out the cranks, and this DVD is absolutely vital in doing that because not only is it an important part of the killings that only the killer himself would know about, it is also the one thing that is different this time round from the original murders. Nothing in the old files shows any sort of recording of the killings. So this is an important difference and one that, as we already know, appears to be specific to the only surviving victim".

He walked over to the picture of Maria that was attached to the far end of the board. He looked at the sadness in her face. The picture had been taken shortly after she had been found on the waste ground in Newcastle.

"On that subject, Maria Blakemore will continue to be held under police protection for the foreseeable. She remains here at the station until the Press conference is over. We are doing our best to find a safehouse, but most of what we have at present in that department is tied up on terrorism issues. The most likely scenario is that she will be kept within the station".

He looked back at the team. "Any questions?"

No-one responded. "Ok. Be ready for the onslaught. When this goes to press we are going to be crucified".

*   *   *

He sat motionless in the chair, his hand hovering over the remote control. He didn't need to hear what they were saying any more. He had listened and re-wound, listened and re-wound, and played them over and over until they were etched on his memory, ready to be analysed to find the meaning. Now he wanted to memorise their faces. Every nuance of their faces. Every tell-tale giveaway sign in their body language, their glances at each other, their mannerisms, their gestures, their transparency. Everyone gave themselves away in some small way, eventually. He muted the sound and watched them over and over. Talking, gesticulating. He watched them when they were not talking. He watched them when they were questioned. He watched them when they wrote things down.

Then he froze the screen at the individual points where he could see both their name plates, placed helpfully in front of them, and the information name tag displayed at the bottom of the screen.

DCI Claire McMullen.

DI Joseph Webber.

"Finally", he said quietly to himself. "Finally I get to see the eyes of those who would seek to stop me. Finally I get to know their names and see their faces".

He stared at the freeze-frame of the officers for several minutes, before eventually killing the screen from the remote.

In the darkness, he closed his eyes and pictured them again.

DCI Claire McMullen.

DI Joseph Weller.

"So Ezra the priest brought the Law before the assembly, both men and women and all who could understand what they heard, on the first day of the seventh month".

He filled his lungs and exhaled, slowly.

"I am the priest. You are the Law".

July 5th

13

6.47pm

McMullen and Webber sat opposite each other at McMullen's desk. Webber held a thin black DVD case in his hands, sealed within a plastic evidence bag. The outer cover of the case bore their names and job titles in full.
Detective Chief Inspector Claire McMullen
Detective Inspector Joseph Webber
"This time it's specific" said McMullen. "The last one was just blank".
Webber nodded, but didn't answer.
She looked up at him. He looked tired and drawn, like he hadn't slept. He was distanced, almost disinterested. "Are you okay?" she asked, expecting a stoical response that gave nothing away. She had worked with a lot of officers who put on a brave face. Although she had Webber down as perhaps being smarter than that, she had learned never to expect it. Regardless of its politically-correct approach to policing, the force was still a testosterone driven entity.
Webber put down the DVD case and sat with his elbows on the table, hands clasped together as if in prayer. "Today would have been Chloe's birthday" he said, staring blankly into nothingness.
"Shit. Sorry. I didn't know. I…..", she trailed off.
"Perhaps you shouldn't be here. Perhaps it was wrong to

come back to work with something like that on the horizon".

He didn't raise his eyes. "It had been seven months, Claire. I couldn't keep putting it off".

She nodded. "But even so. You've only been back a few weeks, and you've chosen to come back right at such a difficult time. You should have said. We could have made arrangements for you to be elsewhere or something".

He continued staring at nothing. He looked resigned to it as he said "What does it matter? There will be no more birthdays. Not for her, and not for Sarah". He paused, frowning slightly as if he couldn't remember what it was he wanted to say. When the words finally came they came flatly and without emotion. "And not for me. I am dead too, Claire, which is why I am back at work, and why I shall always be at work now for as long as the Force will have me. This is my life now".

She picked up the DVD case from the table, the plastic evidence bag rustling as she did so. "The job isn't everything, Joe. I've heard a lot of people say it is, but eventually they all admit they were wrong. The job is just….." she searched for the right words, "…. Somewhere to hide".

He didn't look up at her. He just continued staring into the vacant space in front of him on the desk. "When I go home, to my flat, they are all I see, Claire. At first, I couldn't bring myself to put their things away, and then, after a while, I ended up exactly the opposite, unable to stomach the sight of it all. I did it gradually though, with love and respect, and now everything that was theirs has been put away, packed up in boxes like they might need it again, like they're coming back or something. But it doesn't matter whether the stuff is there or whether it's buried in boxes in the loft, the two of them are all I see.

When I wake up, I hear them, even though they are not there. When I sit alone, I see them, even though they are not there". His eyes hardly flickered as he spoke. It was as if he were reeling off facts. Undeniable truths that were not worth emotion because they could not be changed. *It is what it is.* "So perhaps you're right" he continued. "Perhaps this is my place to hide, because here, twisted as it is to say it, the horror of what we do blocks out my thoughts. The demands of the job, the way it gets inside your head and fucks you up….. I need that. I am a better copper now I am alone. And sometimes, God forgive me for saying it, but sometimes I think they are better off without me because I saw things in my job that I couldn't speak to them about. I saw things I didn't want to *have* to speak to them about. But you have to carry it around, don't you, in your head, and try and pretend that home-life is real life when you know, deep down in your guts, that home-life isn't real life. The real life is what is going on out there on the streets. The filth, the shit, the dark shadows that are always just a fucking whisper away from the life you call real". He shook his head, still staring into nothing.

"I can't pretend to know what to say, Joe", said McMullen. "I don't mean this unkindly, but you should think about using the counsellors, every day if need be".

He filled his lungs, breathing in slowly and deeply, pursing his lips as he exhaled. He looked over to her, and smiled slightly. He reached forward and took the DVD case from her. "The best thing I can do, Claire, is get on with my job". He walked over to the television and turned it on. "So let's do exactly that" he said, taking the DVD from its' case as the machine's disc-tray slid silently toward him.

*   *   *

There were several seconds of blank, soundless display before the woman's face appeared on screen. She was scared. Confused. She jerked visibly as the man's voice was heard. From the way she moved they could tell she was restrained in some way, but they could only see her face. Her make up had run under her tears. McMullen guessed this must be early on in the woman's abduction. Perhaps even the very beginning.

"Women" came the man's voice. "God has given you one face and you paint yourselves another".

The woman began to cry as she stared ahead of her, toward the camera but not at it. Then a hand came into view, covered with a surgical glove, and the fingers swiped hard over the woman's lips, smearing the lipstick over her mouth and chin.

"He must be holding her head" said Webber pointing at the screen. "I can just see what looks like his other hand at the top of the screen".

The woman sobbed loudly as the gloved hand rubbed her make up hard into her skin, smearing it round in circles until she appeared as a mottled, bloodied mess.

The hand fell out of shot, and the camera held her in view for several more seconds, crying but seemingly too scared to protest.

Then the screen went blank.

Several more seconds passed before the screen burst into life again. This time the woman was screaming, her hair had been cut back to nothing but clumps and her face had been cleaned of make up. Mucus ran from her nose as she stared, wide eyed with fear, at somewhere above the camera. She was pleading, over and over for him to stop, for him to let her go. She offered him money. She promised she would never say anything. She promised him whatever he wanted but please, please, please……

Then the picture went blank but the sound continued. The woman began screaming uncontrollably. There was a sickening cutting sound in amongst the screaming and McMullen felt her body tense.

Then the sound died, and they were left staring at a blank screen in silence.

Several more seconds passed, and suddenly there it was on screen. No sound. Just that garish, repeated mutilation. The woman's head had been completely shaved. Her lips had been cut from her face leaving the skull like smile of horror. McMullen retched. Webber stared motionless, transfixed by what they were watching.

Then the sound returned and it was exactly as before.

"SAY IT!" shouted the man, his shouts barely audible over her screaming. "SAY IT!"

"Ah – eee – ah" came the sound, breathless and desperate. "Ah – eee – ah… Ah –eee- ah"

They could not see what he was doing to her off screen but McMullen thought she heard repeated thuds. As if the woman were banging her feet against the floor, possibly the only movement her trussed up body could make to express her suffering. "SAY IT!" he shouted. "SAY IT!"

"AH – EEE – AH!" she screamed. "AH – EEE – AH! AH – EEE – AH!"

Then his body came in and out of shot as he struck her across the face.

"AGAIN!"

"AH – EEE – AH!" she screamed.

He struck her again.

"LOUDER!"

"AH – EEE – AH! AH-EEE-AH!"

He struck her again, and again.

"LOUDER! LOUDER FOR THEY DO NOT HEAR!"

The woman couldn't raise any more energy and he struck her repeatedly until she obeyed him, the sobbing uncontrollable now as she struggled to form words without the lips to do so.

"O LORD I CRY BY DAY AND BY NIGHT BUT YOU DO NOT ANSWER!" and then he stood out of the way and the woman, bloodied, mutilated and now falling in and out of consciousness, filled the screen whilst they looked on, helpless.

And then the screen went dead, and the silence prevailed.

At first neither of them moved. Webber was about to get up when the screen jumped back into life. There was no screaming this time. No victim. The screen showed only a bank of spotlights. Then came the man's voice again.

"You may think this is a game of some sort. You may think that these victims are here for my own sick amusement. Well, let me assure you that there is nothing amusing about this for me. I take this work extremely seriously because these women need the spiritual release and cleansing that I give them".

McMullen glanced over at Webber. He turned the sound up.

"You know the symbols mean that I, a cyclical God, bring purification to women. But I wonder whether you *accept* that as the truth. You see, *knowing* something is not the same as *accepting* it. Humans *know* they are going to die, somehow, sometime, somewhere, but even when the time comes they do not *accept* it. You *know* from what you have just seen that this woman will die. In fact, by the time you are watching this she will already be dead. In seeing me do this once again you must surely *know* that until you catch me, if indeed you ever do, then there will be another cleansing, and another, and another. Yes, you *know* this is an inevitability, but you do not *accept* it. The same way you *know* that any given day could be the die on which you die, but you do not *accept* that. Why would you? To accept such a truth would take away your ability to live.

"So I am going to give you the evidence you need to *accept* and understand that what I am doing is the work of a God. Consider the tattoos that you have seen on the women. The numbers. Do you know what they mean? They rise incrementally according to the order of death. How many cleansings have there been now? Eight overall, and the woman you have just seen will be number nine.

"So when you find her, and don't worry, I shall make it very easy for you to find her, she will carry my usual markings, and she will carry the number nine, in roman numerals, just like her predecessor carried the number eight, and the one before her, my beloved Maria, carried the number seven. Three symbols, and one number. Always three symbols and one number. But what do the numbers mean, other than the order of death?"

McMullen reached into her jacket pocket and took out her notebook. Webber stared, transfixed, at the screen. "He wasn't joking when he said he's make it easy for us to find her" he muttered. "She couldn't have been dumped in a more public place".

"To understand what the numbers mean" continued the voice "I want you to think back to the letters I wrote to Maria after she left me. I am sure you have not forgotten them, because by the time you are listening to this recording, over and over scouring for clues and something you may have missed, the Guardian reporter... let's call him my Scribe... will have delivered to you, in some mild state of shock no doubt, the reminder I gave him to pass on.

"The wind blows to the south and goes round to the north; round and round goes the wind, and on its circuits the wind returns".

McMullen glanced quickly at Webber. "That was in one of the letters" she said.

"I like this quote because it perfectly sums up the Circle Line. When you stand on that platform, and the train approaches, and the wind rips through you. That wind has been dragged and pushed all the way round that line. It is stale air, trapped underground, pushed and pulled by the backdraft of the tunnels. But the real point is this: Higher powers chose my location for me. You should find yourself a Bible and brush up on your scripture knowledge. Ecclesiastes chapter one, verse six reads 'the wind blows to the south and goes round to the north; round and round goes the wind and on its circuits the wind returns'. Do you see now how my location was chosen for me? I did not choose it. It was chosen for me".

McMullen wrote down the bible reference.

"And it is not only the location that was chosen for me. The victims themselves are dead before I have even taken them, their fate sealed by their number. I wonder, did you find Maria? Did you do as I instructed? When you found her, did you ask her? Did you ask her about her tattoo? Did you ask her how she sees it? 'Do you remember the mirror, Maria? Do you remember looking at yourself? How did you find that face, Maria? Remember the mirror, Maria. Remember the Mirror for in it you will see the truth'."

"The letters again" said McMullen in hushed tones.

"You should ask her. You should ask her how she sees it, because I know how she sees it. I have watched her, before this current cycle. I have watched her on occasion over the years. She looks at it in a mirror. She thinks this somehow protects her from it, or defeats it. But she does not yet know the final horror that awaits her, for in looking at her number in the mirror she looks at it in all its' ultimate potency and meaning.

"What does the roman numeral seven read when it is viewed in the mirror? V, i, i, when seen in the mirror is i, i, V. Two away from five, which is three. In the flesh it is seven. In the reflection it is three. If you multiply these two numbers together you get twenty-one. What is Book twenty-one of the Bible? It is Ecclesiastes.
Book twenty-one, chapter seven, verse three reads 'sorrow is better than laughter, for by sadness of face the heart is made glad'. Do you see the irony? Do you see why I let her go? I have made her happy in her misery. Sorrow is better for Maria than laughter, for in her sorrow she keeps herself pure. Her sorrow prevents her from whoring herself. She hides her beauty because she is sad. She refuses to enjoy life because she is sad. She stays in the shadows because she is sad. Yes, sorrow is better than laughter for her, because it is all she knows. In her sadness of face, my heart is made glad".

"This is bullshit" said Webber. "This is just a smokescreen. In fact, why are we listening to this bollocks anyway? This is ego. It is a fucking indulgence. He's got us as a captive audience and he fucking knows it".

The voice continued. "Revisit the letters. Revisit the clues. You will see that the last thing I said before you lost me and I disappeared was *'So there it is. I have given you the Book, the Chapter and the Verse'*. And I have. Think back. Think Back to the last cleansing. Number eight. What is the roman numeral eight in the mirror? It is two. i, i, i, V. Three before five, which is two. Eight on the flesh, two in the reflection. Eight multiplied by two is sixteen. Book sixteen of the Bible is Nehemiah. Book sixteen, chapter eight, verse two reads 'So Ezra the priest brought the Law before the assembly, both men and women and all who could understand what they heard, on the first day of the seventh month'. I am the priest. You are the Law. I brought you before my assembly, and the Guardian reporter, and all who could understand what they heard – all those who were part of the cleansings nineteen years ago – and tell me what day did you find her? Yes, the first day of the seventh month. The first of July".

   His voice quickened. "Are you beginning to understand now? Are you beginning to see that this work is predicted? Are you beginning to *accept?*"

   He was talking louder now. His voice more agitated. "Take this girl as an example. When you find her she will be number nine. Nine on the flesh is *i, x*. In the mirror this is *x, i*. Eleven. Nine on the flesh, eleven in the reflection. Nine multiplied by eleven is ninety-nine. There is no Book ninety-nine. Oh, but there is! Count them through. Count through the Old Testament Books and when you get to the end keep going from the start again and count through, and through, and through!" He was almost shouting now. "Book ninety-nine is Ecclesiastes again. Book ninety-nine, chapter nine, verse eleven reads 'Again I saw that under the sun the race is not to the swift, nor the battle to the strong, nor bread to the wise, nor riches to the intelligent, nor favour to those with knowledge, but time and chance happen to them all'. Did you not think it odd? Did you not question my methods? All these other women have been held for a long time before they die, but this woman? She is only a day old! She has only just joined me! She was in the wrong place at the wrong time because it does not matter what you do in life to protect yourself, Time and Chance will happen to us all! Do you see now? Do you see how it is all predicted. This is the work of a higher power.

I do not get to chose! Do you understand! I do not get to chose! It is all chosen for me, for them, for you, already!"

He was ranting now. Shouting the words. "You go away! You go away and work it out! Play with your numbers and play with your calculations but understand this – it ends with number fifteen. That is all the time you have. You have until number fifteen. Why? You work it out! You go away and play with your numbers! Fifteen on the flesh is five in the reflection. Fifteen times five is seventy-five. Count it through, top to bottom and back to top again. Book seventy-five is Zephaniah. Book seventy-five, chapter fifteen, verse five reads 'A day of wrath is that day, a day of distress and anguish, a day of ruin and disaster, a day of darkness and gloom, a day of clouds and thick darkness'! Do you understand me now? Do you! A day of ruin and disaster! A day of distress and anguish and of clouds and thick darkness! Do you understand me! Do you!"

Suddenly the camera was smashed from its' tripod and McMullen jumped in her seat. The sound ended and the screen went blank.

Webber stood up and stormed over to the TV tower. He slammed the DVD machine until the disc ejected and he threw it across the floor.

"Joe, what the fuck are you doing?" said McMullen.

"This is ego, Claire. Pure and simple. He knows we are going to sit here like lame ducks writing down every little snippet and he is fucking loving it".

McMullen picked up the DVD from the floor.

"Whatever you feel about it, Joe, it's evidence. You know as well as I do that whether it's egotistical indulgence or not it all counts toward what will hang him and get us our conviction. Go and get yourself a tea or something and calm the fuck down, for all our sakes".

He picked up his jacket and made for the door. "Fuck tea", he said coldly. "I'm going to get a fucking drink".

McMullen sat back down and stared at the blank screen. She opened her notepad and drew the roman numeral *VII* on a blank page. She took out a mirror from a small make up bag in her desk drawer and held it up to the number. Studying it closely it read *IIV*.

"Two numbers" she said to herself quietly. "The one on the body is always the Chapter. The mirror image is always the verse. The two multiplied together give the Book number".

She put the mirror away slowly and went back to the DVD. She skipped the violent images and started the recording from the point where his voice began.

She picked up her notepad, and turned up the sound.

14

9.07pm

Webber pulled into a side road, taking the risk that he could conduct his business before a traffic warden tried to book him. He already had two unpaid fines in his glove compartment and he wished one day that he could trade places with someone at the council. Perhaps they would see how impossible they had made life. Then again, perhaps, they wouldn't. The truth was, since the loss of his family, he wasn't sure he cared anymore. What was the worst they could do to him? Fine him double?

He walked with head down toward the off-licence. It wasn't that drink was an escape for him, it was just that, in light of everything, it helped him retract into himself. It helped him block out the world and let him think in a way that he couldn't when the noise and the filth and the pain was live in technicolour around him.

He turned the corner and headed towards the shop door. A group of girls came out, laughing and joking, each of them clutching a bottle of vodka. They couldn't have been more than sixteen. He tried to smile, but all he saw was the life his daughter would never have now, and how these girls seemed not to value theirs at all.

"Cheer up Mister!" said one, as she brushed past him, purposefully bumping her backside, adorned in short skirt, into him.

He stumbled slightly, and carried on, ignoring them.

Inside the shop he took down a bottle of gin from the shelf. He looked at it for a few moments before taking down another one. It wasn't so much the fact that he would run out, but more the fact that having it in the flat comforted him. The irony was that he had never been much of a drinker, and even now, in the face of his trauma, he preferred sleep to anything else as a soporific. If he was going to escape he would rather pull the duvet over his head and pretend the world wasn't there.

But that was the problem these days. The old escapes were not working. When he pulled the duvet over his head he couldn't sleep. When he pulled the duvet over his head he felt the presence of his dead wife, and he heard the delighted squeals of his dead daughter as he tickled her first thing in the morning and last thing at night. Things he would never have again. He heard them sleeping. He felt them next to him as if they all slept together. And yet he could not erase from his mind the pictures of them dying. He should have been there. He should have *been* there. And that was why, when he pulled the duvet over his head, he could not sleep. It was because he was sleeping in blood.

Sleeping In Blood.

He paid for the bottles and made his way back to the car. Ticket-free he put the carrier bag on the passenger seat and drove home.

There was no reason now for him to be embarrassed. At first, after the accident, he had found it difficult to face people, not only because of his own issues, but because he saw on their faces how they struggled themselves to relate to him. It was almost as if, in the shrouds of death, he had become unreachable. Something to be avoided because he carried the ultimate trump card. *There is always someone worse off than you* was how the saying went. All of a sudden, in the eyes of his immediate world, he was that person.

But even serious trauma fades over time. It was that simple fact that he clung to.

He pulled into a resident's parking space and made his way up the small flight of stairs to the front of the building. He could have punched in the code but he felt the need to touch base with someone, to ground himself in a world that wasn't polluted by the case. He found he often did this over recent weeks, especially since returning to work, and his neighbours, knowing his circumstances, were more than happy to oblige. Another example of embarrassment.

He pushed a familiar button.

"Hello?" came the voice on the intercom.

"Hi Dan. It's Joe. How you doing?"

"Oh, Hi Joe. Yep all fine. You want me to buzz you in".

"Please"

"Twice in one day huh? I guess you needed some air. Pop in when you can Joe".

He tried to hit the button again to ask what twice in one day meant, but the door buzzer was ringing out and he kicked the bottom plate with his foot to open it.

Once inside he made his way up to his front door, bottle bag clutched to his chest to stop the chinking of the bottles.

When he reached the front door he froze. He put the bottles down slowly. He took out his mobile phone. He dialled McMullen.

Her voice came almost instantly. "You calmed down yet?", she said sternly.

"Claire" he said in hushed tones into the mobile. "I have just got to my flat and the door has been forced. Can you arrange for some uniform back-up and maybe put forensics on notice? I am going to go in".

"Joe, don't go – "

He ended the call. What did he have to lose.
Sleeping In Blood.

He put the phone back in his jacket and pushed the door open slowly. It had been smashed from its lock. Something heavy had been rammed against it. Not a clean cut. Whoever had forced access had not been shy about advertising the fact.

He reached down into the bag by the door and picked up a bottle of gin by the neck, raising it like a weapon.

Walking into the flat he flicked the light switch. No sound or reaction from within.

He moved through the hallway, pushing open the doors to the kitchen diner and the sitting room as he went.

Nothing.

He pushed open the last door that lead to the small bathroom.

Nothing.

With all the lights on downstairs he edged up the small seven-step staircase to the two bedrooms set off the main floor. The builder had squeezed extra space per flat by using an interlocking design and it made the small flats seem like they had an upstairs even when they didn't.

He flicked the switch in what used to be Chloe's bedroom.

Nothing.

He flicked the switch in what used to be his marital bedroom.

He stared at the mirror on the side wall of the room above the dresser. He gripped the neck of the bottle as he entered the room.

The picture of his wife and daughter that he normally kept by his bed had been ripped from its frame and was stuck on the mirror. Underneath it, in what looked like lipstick, which he could only guess was lipstick of his dead wife and which had been taken from the small bathroom downstairs, were written the words:

Do you think they called out your name?

He could hear sirens in the distance, and he lowered the bottle.

Then he sat down on the end of the bed and surrendered to the wave of grief that engulfed him.

July 6th

15

9.03am

"The sound analysis is back from the lab" said McMullen, striding through the desks to reach the front of the room, "along with the first post-mortem report".

She reached the photo-boards displaying the pictures of the victims so far. "Copies are being distributed but the result is clear. Admittedly it's a best guess only, but they are placing their money on the fact that the low rumble picked up in several places on the tape is a train. I know that's probably no surprise, given where the bodies are found, but that's my point: the tape suggests that the victims are almost certainly held near to a train station, which no doubt facilitates the killer's goal of leaving the bodies in or around a tube station".

"That could mean they are held anywhere" said one of the officers. "I was on an investigation two years ago where I interviewed some guy running a porn shop in a basement near Farringdon. We went into the back office and I could hear trains in there. You are not suggesting house to house around every tube station , Guv, are you?"

"Better than that" said McMullen. "This bastard thinks he's clever, but the reports show otherwise".

She held up the forensic report. "Again, copies are being made and will be distributed, but there are two important points from this report. Firstly, the girl had a substance in her stomach that was granular and hadn't been digested. It matched the traces of substance found ground into the end of her fingers. The nails on each finger of each hand were broken and splintered. The skin at the ends was torn and cut – but they were tiny cuts. In some places she had scratched away the skin almost down to the bone"

"She was trying to dig her way out of something" said Webber.

"Exactly" replied McMullen. "And the substance itself, the one in her stomach, and ground into the tips of her fingers, was similar to grout. The stuff they stick between tiles".

There were murmurs among the team. "Are we saying she was held somewhere were the walls were tiled?"

"That's what the reports are saying" said McMullen. "Toilets. Bathrooms. Not to mention public stuff. Disused toilets"

"Disused tube stations" offered someone else. "All those walls are tiled".

"Why the hell would she be eating it?" came another voice. "How come it was in her stomach as well?"

"No idea" said McMullen.

"She had her fingers in her mouth" said a woman in the corner. "She was trying to comfort herself, and also ease the pain in her fingers".

People turned to see who had spoken. McMullen dropped the reports onto the desk in front of her, incredulous at what she saw. "Maria, you shouldn't be in here" she said. She glanced back at Webber as she made her way to the corner of the room, her face suggesting a *what-the-fuck-are-you-doing* judgement.

"Joe said it would be OK" protested Maria, not making any attempt to move.

They stared at each other, McMullen conscious that this was a test of authority amid staff who were not ordinarily her own. "You need to leave, Maria" said McMullen. "Whatever DI Webber said to you, it is not fair on you to listen to what we discuss here, and we have no clearance for a civilian to be in here". She glanced back at Webber for support but he sat, impassively, saying nothing.

"It seems I am more of a prisoner than I thought" said Maria. She got up, pushed past McMullen and made her way to the picture boards. "This is me" she said, pointing to the picture of herself in the bottom corner of the display. She turned to face the team. "But I am not a picture. I am real". She studied the faces of the officers who sat silently, but she ignored McMullen. She turned back to the board. "This woman here" she said, pointing to the first victim. "I have seen the recording of her. I have seen her trying to say my name. And this woman", she pointed to the second victim, "She would have been made to say my name, too". She turned back to the team. "But none of you will say it, will you? None of you will speak to me as if I am here".

She stared at the team. No-one spoke. She walked over to Joe. "Detective Inspector Joseph Webber" she said. "Please tell me who I am".

Joe looked up at her. "You are Maria Blakemore, the sole surviving victim of the serial killer known by some as The Circle Line Killer, and by others as The Horologist".

"Thank you", she said. "And why am I here?"

"You are here because your life is in danger. We don't know why you were released by your attacker, we don't know why he spared you, but we do know that he is active again, and your name is being given to the victims as if it may save them. It is the use of your name that has given us cause to bring you into police protection. That, and the fact that he has made direct reference to you himself in recorded messages sent to us".

"Wrong" she said coldly. "That is not why I am here".

She turned to face the team. "I am here because I am the key" she said, this time engaging the stare of DCI McMullen. "I am the key, and yet you put my picture in the corner here, as if that is enough". She looked from one face to another. "Well, it isn't enough. Nineteen years ago everyone made promises to me. 'Trust me, Maria, we will catch him'. He made a mockery of the Met then and he will do it again now, I know it. The only way I can have any faith in this system is if I am part of it. I want to hear everything, see everything, and put my ideas forward. At the end of the day, if he isn't caught, it is me who is likely to die, not you. You owe me that, at least".

She engaged McMullen's stare again. "My life being in danger is not the reason I am here. The reason I am here is because I have information and experience that will contribute to this investigation. I am going to catch my own killer, and I am going to do it with your help".

Still no-one spoke. McMullen glared at Webber but he didn't respond. She took a few steps forward. "This is lunacy. You are a civilian, Maria. We are not the people we were nineteen years ago. Techniques are different. Technology is different. We will catch him, and we can do it whilst keeping you safe at the same time".

Maria was already shaking her head. "You can't hold me against my will, that much I do know. Police protection or not there is nothing you can do if I walk out of here. And I *will* walk out of here if I do not become part of this investigation".

Some of the officers shifted position, no-one wishing to comment. Webber felt the glare of McMullen, but he remained expressionless. After last night, and the invasion into his home, nothing was off limits.

There was silence as McMullen looked from one member of the team to another, eventually settling on Maria. Slowly, McMullen walked up to the picture board and took Maria's picture down. "You will have to sign the Official Secrets Act, and you will do as you are told. You will have no powers of arrest and you will remain in the station at all times unless otherwise authorised by me. If I do authorise leaving the building you will be accompanied by at least one officer, and possibly several, at all times. You have stated your terms, and now I have stated mine. Are we agreed?"

Maria bowed her head. "Thank you" she said.

There was an uncomfortable silence as Maria made her way back to her seat, but as she sat down, the officer next to her put a hand on her shoulder and smiled.

"This is the line we are going to take" said McMullen, addressing the whole team and regaining her composure. "Regardless of where we think the victims are being held, the killer clearly has some intimate knowledge of the railway network. I want British Transport Police included in the loop now and a check on all the personnel records of every underground and overground employee. I want you to look for patterns, for anything out of the ordinary. Look for specialisms – engineers who have access to disused parts of the railway or who have access to areas or equipment without supervision. Look at managers, and people in senior positions but most of all look at sickness records and absenteeism. This man needed time to do all these things, and he needed knowledge and equipment to get his bodies onto the tracks. Look for anomalies, like long term sick or regular sickness, or someone with definite shift patterns over the last three weeks. Look at contractors as well. Anyone who knows the underground but who does not work for them currently".

"It will take days" said one officer.

"No, it won't take days. Get on to the Transport Police now and get them to do it. They have better contacts within the employer itself. They will get it done a damn sight quicker than we could. Also keep in mind the fact that the sound report also suggests the rumble could be aeroplane engines from a distance. Apparently, the deep resonance falls within the same acoustic waveband. Look at likely remote locations that fall within a mile of London Airport. Any questions?".

People were already busying themselves with the task. Maria sat silently watching the activity as it began. The wheels of the Met, turning laboriously into action.

Webber stood up, preparing for the bollocking that would inevitably follow. He needn't have worried. One of the officers shouted for him first. "Joe, I've got a guy on the phone says he will only speak to you, no-one else".

"Who is he?"

"He wouldn't say. Just says he has information".

Webber nodded and made his way to the desk. "This is Detective Inspector Joseph Webber. Who am I talking to please?"

The voice was deep. Restrained. Considered. "Do you have a pen, Detective Inspector?"

"Who is this?"

"I am known by many names, but you will know me as The Horologist".

Holy Fuck

He gestured manically at his colleague to patch the call through to loud speaker so the team could hear.

"How do I know you are not another time-wasting crank?" said Webber.

"Because I know about you, Detective Inspector. I know a lot about you".

"Anyone can do their research" replied Webber.

The call was now on the speakers, and their conversation filled the room.

"I know that next to your bed you keep a picture of your dead wife and daughter. I know that because last night I took that picture out and placed it on the mirror with my question to you that is: Do you think they called out your name?"

"You sick mother-fucker!"

"Do you think they called out your name when they were burning in their car Joe? Did your wife call out for Joe? Did your little girl call out for her Daddy?"

"Fuck off you sick shit!"

McMullen stepped forward and took the phone away from him. "This is Detective Chief Inspector Claire McMullen".

There was a brief silence at the other end, before he said "Blessed are those who have not seen and yet still believe. Do you still believe you can catch me Claire?"

"There is no need for belief or faith. We will catch you. That is a matter of fact".

He laughed. "I much prefer Joseph. He is more…. Real. He feels pain and deals with it. You just shut it out, as if it is not there. Well understand this, Claire, it *is* there, and I will show you that in a way that will change you forever".

"I do not believe you".

"I thought you said there was no need for belief".

She didn't respond. She glanced at Maria who was chewing her fingernails and staring at the floor.

"Well" came the voice "if our conversation is over I believe I still have enough of my three minute window to go before you trace me, so give me Joseph Webber's mobile telephone number. I will call him in fifteen minutes, and trust me, you will want the call".

"You can use this number"

"DO NOT MAKE ME ANGRY!" The voice dominated the room and some officers jerked at the volume. "Give me the mobile number. If you are afraid, simply change your mobile afterwards. It makes no difference".

McMullen gestured at Webber. He shrugged. McMullen relayed the number. The phone went dead.

She replaced the handset slowly. Webber said to his colleague "Is there any way we can rig up the mobile to the speakers? I don't want to be the only person who listens to this sick fucker when he calls back. There's no telling what it will be".

His colleague nodded and took the phone from him.

When the phone rang again it wasn't who they expected. Through the speakers, in answer to DI Webber stating his name, came the voice of a woman. Frightened. Sobbing.

"Is…. Is that the Police? Oh God, please let it be the Police"

"Yes" said Webber. "This is the incident room of Kensington & Chelsea CID. I am a senior officer. Who am I talking to?"

There was a brief pause, before she gave her name. "My name is Cathy Norris. I am being held in the back of a van but I don't know where I am. I live at Flat 2a, Corrington Road in Fulham and I must have been reported missing by now. It has been weeks, I think… I…." she trailed off.

"Alright, Cathy" said Webber. "Stay calm. You are going to be fine. Can you tell me where you were when you were abducted?"

There was a scream and the phone went dead.

Webber looked up, frantic. "What the fuck happened? That had better not be us who cut her off?"

His colleague shook his head. "No. It was her end".

The phone rang again. Webber answered immediately. "Joseph Webber"

"You now have a victim, with a name, and an address, and she is still alive. You have a chance to save her. You already know she is in a van. Let me help you some more. It is a white van. A transit van. It looks like all the other white transit vans. It will be on the move in a moment, just in case I overstepped my time limits and you happened to trace me. I will call one more time when I reach my destination. You will not need to speak at that point. You will simply need to listen".

The line went dead.

Webber put the mobile down.

"Jackie" said McMullen, "get on to missing persons. Get uniform down to the address given. Get everything you can on this girl".

"Yes Guv".

The officer left the room and no-one spoke. A desk phone rang and it was answered immediately. Anxious faces were waved away as it was clear it was only a usual information call. Gradually, people began to return to their work. Maria still stared at the floor, biting the skin around her nails.

Webber got up from the desk on which he had been sitting. "It's a lead, at least" he said.

"You could say that" said McMullen. "But all it says to us is that someone whom we already know is missing is actually still alive".

It was forty-five minutes before the mobile rang again. Webber let it ring for a while so they were sure the call was heard by everyone. Silence fell on the room as he answered.

"DI Webber"

"OH GOD, PLEASE HELP ME! HE'S GOING TO KILL ME!"

"Alright Cathy, calm down. Try and calm – "

Her screaming filled the room and Maria put her head in her hands.

"He's coming for me! He says he is going to make me pure again! What does he mean? Why is he doing this? Please, please help me! Please help me! Oh God!"

The screaming took over again. There were muted thuds from the line. Then his voice came over the speakers. "I will tell you how you can save this woman. I want Maria".

Maria's head jerked up. Eyes wide with fear.

"I want her in place of this woman. I know you have her. You give me Maria. I give you this innocent lamb. If you do not give me Maria, then this woman dies".

There were muffled voices at the other end of the line, before the woman came back on.

"Maria? Is that your name? Maria? He said you can help me. He said you can save me? Can you? Who are you? Oh God, please Maria! Please help me! Maria!"

His voice came on the line again.

"You have twenty-four hours. I will call again to tell you how the swap will happen".

The line went dead.

16

11.33am

"No" said McMullen. "I will not even ask you the question".

McMullen sat opposite Maria at her desk. Webber stood at the window with his back to them.

"There is no question to answer, Claire" said Maria. "I will do it. If it means we have a chance of catching him then I will do it".

McMullen flicked the rosary back and forth over her hand.

Click-clack. Click-clack.

"We don't know what the current investigation will turn up first" she said, flatly.

"Forty-eight hours is a long time. There are a lot of resources working on this".

"Don't fool yourself", said Maria, "I will do it. I have nothing to lose after all".

"What about family" said Webber, "or friends and boyfriends".

"We've been through this. There is no-one"

"Maria", began McMullen. "I need to ask you about the letters he sent to you after
you were first released".

"Why?".

McMullen took out a small bundle of papers from the drawer next to her. "These copies were given to David Sachs, the reporter who published theories about the killings when they first occurred. He was attacked recently, along with his lover, and told to deliver these to the Police. His lover's daughter was one of the recent victims".

McMullen read out part of the letter: *"Do you remember the mirror, Maria? Do you remember looking at yourself? How did you find that face, Maria? How did you find it when you looked at it, all sad and unhappy? Did it suit you?*

Sorrow is better than laughter, Maria. For by sadness of face the heart is made glad.

Remember the mirror, Maria. Remember the Mirror for in it you will see the truth'.

She looked up at Maria. "Does that mean anything to you?" she asked.

"I remember the mirror" she said defensively. "I remember it because its' sick fairground image is burned into my memory".

She got up from her seat and walked to the window where Joe was standing. "During the years following the attack I withdrew into myself, and I didn't care what people thought of me, or how I looked". She folded her arms, staring out of the window. "Part of his mental torture was to expose me to bright lights and make me look at myself. He always gave me a mirror. Not a handheld vanity mirror or a dress mirror, but the kind of mirror a showgirl would use or a performer. One with bright, piercing bulbs around the outside. It always reminded me of the mirror a clown would use to do his make-up, or the kind of thing you would see on backstage shots of big TV shows, where everyone is smiling and looking like the world awaits them. But all I ever saw in my mind's eye when that mirror came out was the clown. Every time he wheeled the monstrosity in front of me I could almost see it – the clown, weeping in misery painting himself a false smile".

'God has given you one face and you paint yourselves another', said McMullen from behind her.

"Perhaps" said Maria, not really hearing what was being said. She was back now. Back in the walls of the prison that once held her. "For a long time after I came out I couldn't deal with my appearance. Do you know how insane that is? To keep the curtains drawn all the time, to get up only at night and avoid the day? As my hair grew back I found myself shaving it off again. I would walk around like a freak almost on purpose until I finally accepted that my behaviour was hurting me".

She turned away from the window, making her way back to her seat. "But I wanted to hurt me. He had hated the way I had looked, which is why he cut off all my hair. And for a while I hated myself for being attractive. It took me a long time to remove that self-blame from my head. And then the flip side came several years later. I began to see myself with a detached pair of eyes. I could see I was beautiful, but whereas I had once been proud of that beauty, now I resented it because I realised that people did not see "me", they saw instead a brooding, dark-eyed woman with red lips and long black hair. They saw a slim waist, good legs. They saw breasts and they wondered what it would be like to taste me, to touch me."

She glanced up at Joe, but he was still staring out of the window, his back half-turned away from them. "I am not proud of those years. I abused myself, and ended up back at square one, talking endlessly to my counsellor as to the reasons for my behaviour. That in itself wasn't easy. No-one knew the truth about me. I just healed, so far as I could, over the years and found some twisted balance where I gained enough benefit from helping others so that I stopped hating myself".

"Hence you are now a counsellor" said McMullen, nodding.

"Yes" said Maria. "Do you judge me for that?"

McMullen shook her head slowly. "Why would I judge you?" she asked, frowning. "I do not claim to be perfect. You do not claim to be perfect. If either of us thought we were beyond criticism or failure or weakness, what use would we be to others?" She looked down at the papers. "He never mentions the tattoo in the letter, does he?"

"Should he?" said Maria. "Maybe he thinks the permanence of such a thing speaks for itself. Whatever he was trying to say in that tattoo has already been said. I never look at it. It was hard at first, but after a while I trained myself to never look at it".

"Never? Not even by accident?"

"Never".

"What about other people? Has anyone else ever seen it?"

Maria sighed. "The hurtful behaviour I mentioned….. Some men would ask what the tattoo meant. I would just say it meant that I wanted them to love me. That seemed to be enough for them. I guess that says a lot about the type of men I slept with. They weren't exactly there to see my tattoo. The tattoo was the last thing on their minds".

"But they all saw it" continued McMullen, "and you didn't have any hesitation in explaining it away".

"Meaning?"

"Meaning that it didn't stop you hurting yourself with these meaningless encounters. You could say it showed you were able to live your life even with it there all the time".

"I wasn't living it though", protested Maria, "that's the point. I was dying. If one of them had stopped to go into a conversation about it, I mean, if someone had really banged on about it, that would have been it. I liked the fact that they didn't give a shit about it. I liked the fact that they saw it and dismissed it. The fact that they saw it, and then saw me, and chose having sex with me over having a conversation about the weird markings in a weird place on my leg, meant that somehow its power was taken away. The same way as when I look at it in the mirror. Whenever I look at it, I only ever look at it in the mirror, because it's not the tattoo he gave me when it's in the mirror. It's something else".

"Like what?"

"Like a different number. Not the one he intended. When I was lying there, drugged into unconsciousness and he took such pains to mark me as number seven, well, I'm not number seven thank you very much. In the mirror I'm number three and I'm quite happy with that because it's not what he intended. It's a small victory. Does that make sense?"

Webber turned to face them. "On the last DVD we received he told us to ask you how you looked at your tattoo. He said he knew that you looked at it in the mirror"

"What?"

McMullen interjected. "He was implying that he had seen you over the years since he let you go".

Maria was shaking her head. "That's not possible. I was under police protection, and later, when I wasn't…. no, that cannot have happened".

Webber pulled a chair up beside Maria and sat down. "He said that the mirror was important for the exact reason you have just given. In the mirror, the tattoo shows a different number".

"What's the point of that?" asked Maria. "Even if it were true, what's the point of it?"

"He said that if you multiply them together you get a third number. That third number represents a book of the Bible. The tattoo number itself is the Chapter number of that book, and the mirror image is the verse number".

McMullen read one of the highlighted passages from the letters: *"So there it is. I have given you the Book, the Chapter and the Verse"*.

"I looked it up, Maria" continued McMullen. "If you are number seven on your tattoo, then you are number three in the mirror. Seven times three is twenty-one. Book twenty-one of the Bible, Chapter seven, verse three, was the message he claims set your destiny".

Maria stared back at her. "What does it say?"

Webber took out his notebook. "Ecclesiastes, chapter seven, verse three says *Sorrow is better than laughter, for by sadness of face the heart is made glad"*.

"He claims he is purifying women" said McMullen. "I believe he let you go because he thought he had ruined you, and that you would be so traumatised that you would live like a Nun. You were to be his living proof that a beautiful woman could stay pure, and that her beauty would not corrupt herself or others. Yes, you were sad, but as the quote says, by staying sad you would have stayed pure, hence the heart being made glad".

"But I didn't stay pure" said Maria. "I…." she didn't finish her statement. "That's why he wants me back, doesn't he? This time, I must die. There will be no mercy. He granted me life and I abused it".

Webber put his hand on her shoulder. "He held you for so long Maria that he conditioned you. I don't believe that he has been anywhere near you since he let you go. He conditioned you, subconsciously, by his actions and by his words and by his letters, to link your pain with mirrors. He knew that was how you would see it when he let you go because he planted that seed when he held you and made sure that it grew".

"This is why I would think very carefully, Maria, before agreeing to do anything" said McMullen. "You will always be the weaker party against this man. Even now, sitting here with us, he has reached you via the message he gave to us and the seed he planted in your head all those years ago. He is dangerous and manipulative, and you should leave things to us".

There was a knock at the door and one of the team poked his head round. "Sorry, Guv, but we have an address worth checking out. A forty-five year old white male by the name of Andrew Garner, works as an electrical engineer on the underground, hasn't been at work since twenty-eighth of June, and lives in a basement flat near Farringdon station".

McMullen put the papers into the drawer and the rosary into her pocket. "Maria, you stay here. Joe, you come with me".

17

1.07pm

They parked several hundred yards away from the address. "Let's just take a casual walk past first, see what the general impression is".

As they walked McMullen went over the information they had obtained. "Andrew Garner. Forty-five year old IC-one male. Self-employed electrician up until two years ago when he became a London Underground Limited employee"

"Convenient" said Webber. "Two years to gather information and learn what he thinks he needs to learn".

"According to the records he has been an electrician all his working life, with sub-contracted London Underground work being a part of that from the beginning".

"But other than that we have nothing on him" added Webber.

"Not yet, no" said McMullen, "which is why talking to him, and finding out why he hasn't been at work since two days before the first body was found, will be interesting".

They slowed as they walked past the address. A basement flat, accessed by a small flight of concrete steps from the pavement above. There were no obvious signs of life. The curtains were pulled but the outside looked well maintained.

They carried on past the target. "What do you think?" asked Webber.

"Odd that the curtains are pulled in the middle of the day" said McMullen. "Did you see any other possible access points?"

Webber shook his head. "Looks like it's just the front door or bust".

"OK. Lets have a word".

As they made their way down the steps Webber glanced up at the building itself. "Looks like three other flats I reckon".

McMullen banged on the door. There was no answer. She thumped on the door again and dropped to her knees to try and look through the letterbox. Webber knocked on the window to their left but there was no answer.

"We should put the place under observation" said Webber. "If he's not in then he must be coming back at some point".

"And if he is in, then he must go out at some point" added McMullen.

From somewhere above them came a woman's voice. "If you're after Andy then you've missed him. He's working".

Webber looked up at the face of the elderly woman who was leaning out of her window. He shielded his eyes from the glare of the sun. "What time is he due back?"

"He comes and goes all funny hours. He does lots of overtime, you see. For the money. I only know because he always buys me a half bottle of whiskey on pay day".

Webber smiled. "We all need friends like that. Have you noticed anything different about his patterns recently?"

The woman frowned. "Who are you? The Police?"

"Yes" said Webber.

"Well I can't help you I'm afraid. Like I said. A half-bottle of whiskey on pay day and I give him a frozen home made shepherd's pie in return. That's all I know". She closed the window.

"I'll nip up there" said Webber.

"Don't bother. I want this place under surveillance. If we haven't seen anything worthwhile by this time tomorrow we can go in under a search warrant. I am not pissing around with whiskey-drinking old ladies".

They made their way up the steps. "We'll put a car down there", said McMullen, "and get some bodies down here to see what the chances are of getting a flat over the road".

Webber's mobile rang. He froze, momentarily, staring at McMullen, before reaching into his jacket to retrieve it. "It's the station" he said, his relief obvious.

"DI Webber" he said as they walked back to the car.

Suddenly McMullen became aware that he wasn't alongside her anymore, that he had stopped walking. She turned back to see where he was.

He put the mobile back into his pocket slowly. "We need to get back" he said. "There is another DVD".

"Addressed to us?" asked McMullen.

"No", said Webber, quickening his pace toward the car, "addressed to Maria".

18

2.42pm

The team assembled in the incident room. Maria sat at the front next to Webber.

McMullen held the package in her hands. "This is the third DVD we have received" she said to the team. "The first was unmarked. The second was addressed to myself and DI Webber. This one is addressed specifically to Maria. He has no way of knowing that she is here. He is taking a punt. Equally, he has no way of knowing what we have discussed with Maria or what we are planning regarding his request that we give her up in return for Cathy Norris. We have the upper hand at the moment. He said he would call again with instructions. Well, we will have a few instructions of our own. SO19 are working on Operation Blackarrow which will dovetail with our own plans. We have the address of a potential suspect under observation in Farringdon, and a search warrant application for the premises being processed as we speak. This is not the one sided war he thinks it is".

She walked over to the TV tower and loaded the disc. "Whatever is on here changes nothing. Keep that in mind".

The screen came to life and they saw the face of a woman. She was crying but she did not appear to have been harmed. She looked confused initially, but then seemed to settle enough to begin speaking.

"My name is Cathy Norris. I am 23 years old and I am being held prisoner". She fought to control her breathing. Her eyes darted around her, as if she were expecting someone to appear in the room with her. It distracted her to the point where her speech was hesitant and stunted. "I have been here for weeks. I don't know how many. I have been told that I am ill, but that I will be purified and that things will be better after that". She began to cry. "But I don't want this to happen. I don't know what he is planning to do to me but I know he will kill me. I just wish it would happen quickly". She hung her head, composed herself.

"I just want to go home. I just want to see my mum and my dad and my brother. God, I hope they haven't given up on me. If you are listening, if you get to see this, I love you all so much. I love you....". She began to cry again, taking several minutes before she could carry on.

"So much has been taken away from me that now there is just fear. Fear of what pain I might suffer. Fear of Death being prolonged. I know there is no way out now. He is going to kill me and I know that from his change in routine. He comes more frequently now than before. He is more agitated. He is insisting that I eat and there is punishment when I refuse to do so. Most of the time he keeps me in the dark". She paused, her face becoming contorted, like she was trying to remember something but couldn't.... "And I hear something in the dark. It is a sound I always hear. It troubled me in the early days, but now I am resigned to it in the way I have become resigned to my own death. I think I hear the sound of someone else. I think I hear someone else here, in this Hell, screaming for help. I think I hear her, but even if I do, there is nothing I can do for her. We are ghosts now.... Lives taken..."

The picture jumped back and repeated itself. "We are ghosts now….. Lives taken" and it jumped back again, repeating the same phrase. "We are ghosts now….. Lives taken. We are ghosts now….. Lives taken".

It took McMullen a few moments to recognise that the recording had been deliberately spliced so that the final words would repeat endlessly. She walked over to the DVD and turned off the screen.

"Where is the necklace?" asked Webber.

"There wasn't one" said McMullen.

Webber turned to Maria. "With the first two DVD's of the victims there was a necklace"

"A Tessera" said Maria. "He used to call it a Tessera. It's like a ticket. An invitation. If you are given it, you are invited to the show, that's what he used to say. I wore one when I was held. In fact, Claire, put that screen back on. That woman is wearing one too".

McMullen turned the DVD back on and fast-forwarded a little way before freezing the frame. Cathy Norris stared back at them, a small piece of stone hanging around her neck on a black cord.

McMullen went into her room and retrieved a file. "Material Analysis Report" she said, placing the papers on the desk in front of her. "The necklace was held by forensics for several days before we got it off to the labs for material analysis". She thumbed through the papers saying quietly to herself , "I know I have seen it somewhere", and then, almost triumphantly, "Yes, here it is".

She pulled an A4 sheet from the file and read aloud from it. "The object of the necklace is almost certainly London Clay. Testing revealed high levels of Pyrite and also of Selenite both of which are characteristic of London Clay. There was also noted a high degree of fossilisation debris within the body of the object lending further weight to the conclusion given. London Clay is only found within the London Basin, but that area itself is wide, encompassing parts of Essex, Kent, and stretching down through the South as far as the Isle of Wight. However, it is quite possible that the objects might theoretically be linked in some way to the areas where the bodies are found as the underground system itself is cut into the clay basin. The presence of a malleable but stable clay basin was instrumental to the early construction of the London Underground". She put the paper down.

"He's in the tunnels, isn't he?" said Maria. "He's right underneath our feet. He has to be".

"Which is why Cathy Norris was in a van when the mobile calls were made. He had to be overground for that", said Webber.

McMullen gathered up her papers. "Joe, get that warrant chased up. I am not waiting any more. I want whatever is in that suspect's house".

"And if he's nothing to do with it?" asked Webber

"Then at least we can rule him out, and put our resources into another line of enquiry before we are forced into Operation Blackarrow". She glanced at Maria, ignoring the clear animosity in the look that Maria returned to her.

July 7th

19

6.38am

McMullen climbed into the back of the dark blue Audi A4 parked a few hundred yards down from the target address.

"Morning Guv" said the officer in the driving seat as she closed the door. "Thank God it's summer. It's been a while since I've done an all-nighter. It's not so bad when the sun comes up at four-thirty and you're having coffee and donuts at six. My last obbo was in the pissing rain outside a betting shop for a no-show in November"

"With luck like that you should think about the lottery" said McMullen. "Anything to report?"

"Sweet F.A" said the driver. "Nothing here, and nothing from the boys opposite".

"OK. I take it you have the Big Red Key in the boot?"

"Always"

"Good. Meet me up there".

She climbed out of the car and walked up the road a few metres to meet with Webber. He was focused on a building further up the road. "Here they come" he said, spotting the other officers leaving the building. "You got the warrant?" he asked.

"At last, yes".

"Ready Guv" came a voice from behind them. A short, stocky officer held the red metal bar used to break door locks.

"OK" said McMullen into her radio. "All units have visual. Please confirm".

Confirmation came back rapidly.

She visually checked her own team. Assessed the distance the two units had to cover, and then made the call.

20

6.50am

The stairs to the front door only allowed single file. McMullen took the lead followed by two other officers. She thumped on the door, then the window. She shouted their identity repeatedly. Satisfied, she stepped aside.

The stocky officer took one swing with the red metal Enforcer and the officers piled in as the door swung violently open.

The stench hit them hard.

"Jesus Christ" said Webber, putting his hand over his mouth and nose.

They pushed open doors, checking the rooms, some officers still remembering to identify themselves, others simply doing their best to fight the smell.

They didn't have to wait long for the raid to be over. The officer who entered the bathroom began to retch as he collapsed on to colleagues behind him. It was McMullen who managed to stumble across the threshold of people first.

The bathroom was a small, badly ventilated room. There was no window, only a tiny extractor fan which had long blown its fuse, hence the smell. But the smell wasn't only damp. In the bath lay a naked, male body. To his right wrist was tied a red cord, and on the other end of the cord was a bird. McMullen couldn't tell what type of bird, probably a crow, but it was almost dead itself, flapping pathetically against its restraint. The bath was filled to the brim with water and the dead man's face was turned to face them, his mouth stuffed full of something that looked like twigs but McMullen couldn't say for sure. She guessed that either his throat or his wrists had been cut because the bathwater was full of blood and the bloodied water that had spilled over the side had long since dried into congealed, globulous red patches.

Webber appeared behind her. "Jesus" he said, wincing at the sight. "Are you going to call for forensics or shall I". It was sarcasm, not a question.

"We may not have found the right man, Joe", said McMullen, "but at least the right man has been here. We can't be that far off".

Webber's mobile rang. He pulled it quickly from his pocket, glancing at the number.

Unknown number

He turned it quickly to show McMullen.

"Take it", she said.

21

7.12am

Webber identified himself as he answered, eyes locked with McMullen's.

"Hello, Joseph", came the voice.

Webber indicated to the officer's behind him to keep quiet. "Who am I speaking to?", he said, looking back at McMullen.

"Please don't insult me, Joseph. I shall tell you who you are speaking to. Let me tell you by perhaps describing what you see".

"Go on", said Webber.

There was a sigh, followed by several seconds of silence. "Pass me to McMullen", said the voice. "I think this is more her domain than yours, Joseph. No disrespect, but I am not sure you should be back at work so soon after your loss". He began to laugh. "Do you think they called out your name, Joseph?" The laughter grew louder. "Did your baby call for her Daddy? And was Daddy unable to get to her? Tell me, where were you, Joseph? Where were you when they died? Where were you when they burned alive calling out your name?"

"Shut the fuck up! Understand this you sick fuck, we will catch you and I will make sure that when we put you away you spend the rest of your fucking life facing a wall with nothing. You understand me? Nothing! Just your own fucking madness staring back at you day after day until you put yourself out of your fucking misery".

McMullen took the phone from him. "This is Detective Chief Inspector Claire McMullen. Who am I talking to please?"

"At last...", came the voice. "Someone who knows what they are doing. Tell me, Claire, how is life from your position of detachment? How much easier is the job for you these days, given that you are so good at keeping that professional distance? Is this why Maria does not trust you? Is this why Joseph never opens up to you?"

"What do you want?"

"I want to tell you what you are looking at".

"Meaning?"

"Meaning that someone is going to have to fix that gentleman's front door. Anyone could walk in if it's left wide open like that".

She hurried through the flat to the front door and stepped out of the flat, looking up to the pavement. "Where are you?" she said, scanning the buildings above her.

"It does not matter where I am. What matters is where you are. Tell me, is the bird still alive? Like most living things it can go without food for some considerable time, but it cannot go without water. Given the state of the water in that place I wondered if it would end up drinking the bathwater because it had no choice, or whether it would let itself die rather than drink blood. How is it doing? Is it dead yet?"

She walked back through the flat. "Why would you care. You are beyond reason and you are beyond feeling".

He laughed. "And there was me thinking that it was Maria who was the counsellor these days".

"I am not playing this game" she said flatly. "I am ending this call now".

His words came urgently and his tone changed. "You are looking at a man laying in a bath of blood. The bath was originally filled with water, but now it has the contents of the man's veins in it too. To his left wrist is tied a red cord, and to the end of that cord is a crow, probably half-dead but still in two minds as to whether the water it could drink to keep it alive is actually water or something else. The man's head is turned to the left, to face the door. His eyes are open, watching for his saviour, but that saviour did not come. You were his saviour, Claire. He waited and waited for you but you did not come. In his mouth are twigs. These are twigs of cedarwood".

McMullen looked over the body as he spoke, verifying everything he said. The wooden shards that had been forced into the man's mouth had pierced his cheeks, some jagged pieces protruding right through the palid skin to the outside. Blood had clearly flowed heavily from the internal throat and mouth wounds. McMullen wondered if he had choked on his own blood even before the blood loss from his other wounds killed him.

The voice continued. "The man's wrists were cut, to purify him. To drain him of his filth. Above him, if you pull the shower curtain all the way back, you will find another crow. A headless crow. Some of the blood in the bath water is the blood of the crow, just to help your forensics along".

McMullen took a tentative step forward and pushed the shower curtain to one side. It wouldn't move all the way. Some of the dried blood had stuck it to the rim of the bath.

Behind the curtain hung the headless corpse of the bird. Tied by its feet to the shower rail above.

"Around the sides of the bath, probably near your feet, you will see some other twigs. These would once have had blue flowers on them but I expect they are withered now. They are hyssop. A simple plant to grow".

McMullen backed away from the bath, conscious of the fact that she was standing in some of the blood, and that she was contaminating the scene. "Why are you telling me this?"

"Because he carries a tattoo, Claire. I doubt whether you will see it immersed in the bath of blood, but he carries a tattoo. He carries the three symbols of my work – purification by death via the moon cycle – and he carries the number fourteen. Your forensics team will confirm all this to you, but I wanted to be there with you, Claire. I wanted to be there at the scene to stand by your side and explain to you what you see, because what you see will confuse you, and it mustn't confuse you, Claire. It is important that you understand it because only by understanding it can you ever hope to save yourself"

"I don't understand anything that you do" she said flatly, "and neither do I want to. I will just simply catch you, based on modern policing techniques that none of your smoke screen mumbo-jumbo bullshit can hide behind".

There was a short silence. Then he continued as if he hadn't listened to anything she had said. "The man is tattoo-ed with the number fourteen, which makes him fourteen on the flesh and six in the mirror".

"Fourteen and Six" said McMullen

"Yes".

"Fourteen times six is eighty-four. Based on your madness you will tell me that I should look up Book eighty-four, Chapter fourteen, Verse six of the Bible"

"Very good, Claire. I thought you said you didn't understand me".

"Are you going to tell me what it says?"

"I would, but there is a problem. You see, when your people finally extract this body they will tell you that the tattoo does not show the number fourteen in the usual way. Instead it is written as two sevens".

"Two sevens are still fourteen" said McMullen. "In the mirror it would show two threes, which are still six. It is still fourteen times six, which is eighty-four".

"But why would fourteen be written as two sevens, Claire? Why not write it simply as fourteen?"

"You're the fucking expert" she snapped. "You tell me"

"Because seven is half of fourteen"

"Meaning what?"

"Meaning that you were right about fourteen times six being eighty-four, but that you are looking for half that".

"Forty-two then" she said, frustrated

"Yes, Claire. Forty-two"

"Book Forty-two, Chapter fourteen, Verse six"

"Yes"

She heard the rustling of papers in the background, then his voice came again. "Book Forty-two is Leviticus. Leviticus Chapter fourteen, Verse six reads *"He shall take the live bird with the cedarwood and the scarlet yarn and the hyssop, and dip them and the live bird in the blood of the bird that was killed over the fresh water""*

McMullen looked over the scene before her. "Listen to me" she said slowly. "You are a very ill man and if you give yourself up we can help you. Whatever it is that you believe you are doing I can tell you now is nothing but the expression of your illness. You are mentally ill. For your own sake, please give - "

"You seem to forget that I gave you forty-eight hours to prepare Maria for her salvation. A life for a life. Maria Blakemore for Cathy Norris. This is her good deed. This is your good deed. Prepare her now. When you get back to the Station, you tell her that I am coming for her, and that, even worse, you are delivering her to me. You have angered me, Claire, but I forgive you. The reason I forgive you is because you do not know what you are saying. You must be wondering why you have stumbled on a victim marked with the number fourteen. Do you not wish to know where the others are? Perhaps not. Perhaps this is an irrelevance for you, but we are running out of time now. I want Maria, and I will have her, and please understand this, Claire: It ends with number fifteen. I will not labour the process. I will make it easy for you. When body fifteen is rolled on to the railway tracks you will do your analysis and you will count through your bible books and you will find yourself reading Zephaniah, fifteen, and you will see that such a day is the end of the world for you, Claire. It reads *'A day of wrath is that day. A day of disaster and anguish. A day of ruin and devastation. A day of darkness and gloom. A day of clouds and thick darkness'*, but trust me Claire, by the time you read those words, you will already know what those words mean. I will call you in two hours. Have Maria ready".

The line went dead.

She paused for a few moments, the phone still held to her ear, her eyes still scanning the body, before slowly handing the phone back to Webber.

"We need to get forensics in here" she said, regaining her composure.

22

9.41am

"We will be able to hear you but you won't be able to hear us".

McMullen was sitting on the edge of her desk, watching the surveillance engineer rigging up Maria's wire.

"Are you ok with that?"

Maria nodded. "I don't care what it takes, Claire. I have waited a long time for this, to have a chance of making a difference against him".

"You don't need to get carried away", said Webber. "Just keep hold of the phone to listen to the instructions we give you. It may be that he talks directly to you. Do you think you can handle that?"

"If it means we catch him, I will handle it"

"Eventually, it is likely that he will ask you to leave the phone behind" continued Webber. "When he does, just drop it. He will be expecting the phone to have GPS and at some point he is going to have to take a risk that you will be able to follow the last set of instructions without guidance, otherwise he knows your ultimate destination will be pin-pointed if you are still holding the phone".

"Don't be afraid when you throw the phone away" added McMullen. "You just follow whatever directions were given, and keep talking as to where you are going, what you can see. It doesn't matter what it is. Road names, shop names, anything so long as it's a permanent structure. Just keep giving us as much description as you can. That's all we will need".

Maria nodded as the engineer finished his concealment. He asked her to walk up and down, then out of the room, then down the corridor, and finally to the front desk, outside, and back to the starting point, testing reception and clarity all the while.

When he was satisfied he left to get the mobile unit ready. An unmarked white transit van, with two duplicate units, one in an unmarked car and the other, a smaller emergency duplicate reception device that could be used on a motorbike, fed through the rider's helmet. As McMullen cast her eye over the specification and hardware documents she couldn't help thinking how much this operation was costing.

Maria twisted her body left to right, feeling the pull of the tape and the wire against her skin.

"Is there anything you want to ask?" said McMullen.

Maria shook her head.

"S-O-nineteen have been briefed and are on standby. There is some reluctance to have them involved because we anticipate any arrest is likely to be in a crowded area. The idea that he may be armed seems remote, and if we go in guns blazing in the middle of London we will never see our badges again. However," she glanced at Webber, "your safety is paramount, which is why we have that option available to us if we need it".

Maria didn't answer her, she just stood by the window, staring out.

"And Joe's right about heroics. I know how much you want to see this man dead, but this is a police operation and you will be protected at all times. There is no need for you to feel that you must take matters into your own hands. Are we clear?"

Maria nodded, but still didn't break her gaze down onto the London streets.

McMullen checked her watch. "Well, we are expecting the call in the next few minutes, so I will go and have a quick word with the troops".

She gestured toward Joe as she left, expecting him to make Maria open up. He nodded almost imperceptibly, but had no intention of doing so. In his own mind, this was madness, played out by two people who were clouded by past issues. The sooner this operation came to a close the better.

The minutes that passed before the call came passed in silence. Eventually, looking more solemn than even Maria thought she ever would, McMullen opened the door reluctantly and said, "It's time"

*   *   *

As they filed into the incident room Maria could hear screaming. The call was on loudspeaker. The faces of the officers said all she needed to know.

"I'm waiting" came the voice.

McMullen picked up the mobile phone. "She is here", she said calmly.

Maria thought she heard his breathing grow heavier. "Good" he said slowly. "Maria, I do not want you to be afraid. This is your destiny, to return to me. This is a good thing that you do here today. Cathy will owe you everything". He paused to allow the screaming in the background to seep through.

"What the fuck is he doing to her?" said Webber, shaking his head.

"If this is to happen" said McMullen, trying to hold on to some credibility, "then it needs to happen now. We are not here for your indulgence".

"What is the matter Detective Chief Inspector? Are you worried how your career might be affected by having thrown my only surviving victim back into my hands?"

"We are close to finding you" she lied. "Perhaps we should leave it at that and you just lay awake at night listening for the sound of officers at your door".

He laughed. "Please, Claire. If you were anywhere near locating me you wouldn't be sitting there now operating such a high risk strategy to draw me out. You are down to your last chips already and the wheel has hardly been spinning. It's not even warm yet, Claire, and yet you are almost broke".

She cleared her throat. "Instructions from now on are to be given by the designated mobile for this operation. Are you ready?"

There was a pause, before he said "Of course".

She gave him the mobile number, and then the line went dead.

"What now?" said Webber.

He didn't have to wait for someone to answer. The mobile rang and McMullen answered.

"Head for Chelsea Bridge" said the voice.

23

10.16am

The van left the building first, turning onto the main street. Maria, Webber and McMullen travelled in the car behind driven by one of the area car drivers. A motorcycle outrider weaved through the traffic ahead of them.

McMullen, sat in the back with Maria, cradled the mobile in her hands. Webber, in the front seat, passed instructions to the units on the ground.

"Get as many bodies to either end of Chelsea Bridge as you can. Get ready to seal it off. Get on to River Police and ask them for an ETA for the nearest vessel and to get as many down there on standby as they can. Let the eye in the sky know the location and get him in the air asap. No blues and twos unless it's absolutely necessary. If he's on that fucking bridge then he's coming home with us today".

The mobile rang. McMullen snapped it up.

"When you get to the city side of the bridge, I want you to park up. I don't want any surprises and if I see an attempt to close the bridge at any point, she will die".

They could still hear screaming in the background. McMullen's mind was racing. If he was with Cathy, and yet had to get to the bridge, then Cathy Norris must be being held somewhere nearby. "How far away are you?" she asked.

"Far away enough to mean you will have a short wait. So I am sure all your scrambling of units will ultimately end up in the whole place looking like the Secret Policeman's Ball by the time I get there. No matter. All you have to do is make sure you don't close the bridge. If the bridge closes, then the swap doesn't happen".

The line went dead and the car slowed as it hit traffic.

"Are you ok?" asked McMullen, glancing over at Maria.

"Yes" she said coldly. "I just want it over with".

The car edged forward as the traffic moved. Webber was being fed updates as things moved forward. River Police had a vessel there already. A back up vessel was on its way. The helicopter was five minutes away. All plain clothes units were in place at both ends of the bridge. Initial reports suggested that pedestrian use was heavy.

After several minutes they arrived at the city side of Chelsea Bridge. They parked up on the kerb so as to make themselves obvious. The main tracking vehicle parked up further down the road. The motorcycle outrider, still being fed tracking information, carried on over the bridge to the other side.

No-one reported anything out of the ordinary.

They got out of the car. "Let's make ourselves visible" said McMullen.

Maria could see the River Police vessel trawling the waters beneath the bridge. She looked out over the Thames, at the smaller boats, the working boats. She looked at the pedestrians using the bridge, eventually hearing the sound of the helicopter as it approached.

Webber was shaking his head. "He won't show. Look at this place. Cathy Norris will be in a right state. He will stick out like a sore thumb if he shows his hand here"

"Maybe this isn't the place" said McMullen. "Maybe we get further instructions".

The phone rang in her hand.

"McMullen"

"Well, it's always nice to see more Police on the streets" came the voice. "I am sure the people of the Borough of Kensington and Chelsea are feeling exceptionally reassured by the Metropolitan presence today".

"Can you see us?" said McMullen. "We are on the city side, as you asked".

Webber was some distance away, alerting units to the fact that the phone was being used.

He didn't answer the question. "I want you to walk to the start of the bridge" he said. "I shall stay on the line".

Maria and McMullen started to walk toward the start of the bridge. Webber walked with them, eyes scanning the pedestrian usage on the bridge.

When they arrived McMullen said, "OK we're here. What now?"

"I want you to give your personal phone to Maria"

"We are using this phone" said McMullen.

"Not any more".

She reached into her pocket and handed Maria her mobile phone. "She has it"

"Good" said the voice. "Get her to phone me. The number is in the phone box behind you". He rang off.

McMullen threw the phone down in disgust. "He can fucking see us!" she shouted at Joe. "He's on that fucking bridge somewhere!"

Joe was shaking his head. "We don't know that for sure. Even if we close the bridge now and arrest every fucker on it there's no guarantee he'll be on there. We need to get closer, to narrow it down".

"Well he's right under our fucking noses somewhere!" she screamed. She wrenched open the door to the phone box. "Get this box sealed off for forensics now!"

She scanned the inside of the phone box, picking up a small piece of paper she found with a number written on it.

"Phone it" she said, thrusting it in to Maria's hand.

Maria looked down at the phone and the number.

"Now!" said McMullen. "I don't want this mother-fucker on our streets a moment longer!"

Maria dialled the number, carefully, methodically.

"Hello Maria" came the voice

She couldn't bring herself to answer. Her head was starting to spin with the noise and the urgency and the presence of so many officers unable to stop her walking again into oblivion.

"Maria, all I want you to do is walk, alone, to the middle of the bridge. I will stay on the line. When you reach the middle of the bridge I will give you more instructions. Do you understand?"

She nodded, but didn't speak. She turned to McMullen. "He wants me to walk to the middle of the bridge, alone".

McMullen nodded. "We have officers at both ends of the bridge. We have boats underneath, a helicopter in the air. Nothing can happen to you, Maria, I promise you".

Maria nodded, but hesitated. Eventually she said into the phone. "OK. I'm coming now" and started walking.

She walked slowly, watching the faces of those who came toward her. They could never know what this walk meant to her. They could never know how many years were being sucked away between who she was now and who she used to be, young and naïve and happy, nineteen years old and in London for the first time. They could never know what happened to her after that and they could never know what was to happen to her now. But someone did. Someone on this bridge knew. She was sure of that.

She reached the middle of the bridge. "Is this far enough?" she asked.

"Yes, Maria. That is far enough. I want you put the phone down on the ground, but don't hang up. Do you understand? I want you to put the phone down on the ground and then take off all of your clothes. I need to know that you are not wearing a wire, or a GPS device, or anything that will betray me. Do you understand?"

A tear rolled down her cheek. She bent down slowly and put the phone on the ground.

"He wants me to take all my clothes off" she said, her voice breaking. "He wants me to strip so that he can see I am not wearing a wire or anything that might track me".

McMullen was listening in, flicking her rosary back and forth over her hand.

Click-Clack. Click-Clack.

"It's OK" said Webber, almost to himself. "All the while we have visual it doesn't make a fucking difference. She's going nowhere and he knows it".

Maria started to remove her clothing. Passers by smiled at her. Some, who saw her tears, stopped to ask her if she was OK, but she waved them on. As each item of clothing came off she dropped them on the floor. The tears came more freely now, and as she stood there in her underwear, thin black wire encircling her body, she felt she had been exposed to the depths of her soul. She bent down and picked up the phone.

A crowd was now gathering around her. Some were amused, some were concerned. Some hurried by.

"Hello?" she said, tentatively, into the phone.

"I do not blame you, Maria. I blame DCI McMullen for your humiliation. Please remove the wire, and your underwear. I will not take this process further until you are naked and pure. Put the phone down, don't hang up, just do it, and then we will talk properly".

McMullen swore. "We have to go now, Joe!"

"And arrest who? The crowd? We don't even now if he's on the bridge. Christ, we don't even know who we are looking for or what he looks like! This was always a fucking fishing expedition and you know it! We have to see it through. She isn't going anywhere. We have full visual for fuck's sake".

Maria peeled the wire away from her body and dropped it to the ground. Slowly, she took off the rest of her underwear. The crowd around her was substantial now. People were taking pictures, calling out to her.

She bent down and picked up the phone. "It is done" she said, wiping her eyes.

"Good, Maria. That's good. Now I want you to count to twenty. Nice and slowly, as you walk back towards DCI McMullen, but you will know, Maria that it is not the numbers that matter. It is the destination".

Her tears choked her. She could not answer.

"Seven on the flesh, three in the mirror". He paused to let his words take effect. "Remember this, Maria. Remember that ultimately it began exactly where it ended"

There was silence on the line before he finally said, "I want you to go straight to Unit F on the Paragon Industrial Estate in East London. Can you remember that? Tell McMullen that you must be delivered there naked as you are now. And remember, Maria, when it comes to the switch, ultimately, it can only end exactly the way it began".

He rang off.

The crowd around her were discussing her openly now, asking each other the questions she wouldn't answer.

She put the phone down on the ground and began to count.

One.... Two... Three...

McMullen and Webber stared at her.

Four…. Five…. Six…

"What the fuck is she doing?" said Webber

McMullen shook her head, saying nothing, just staring at throng that had gathered around Maria.

Twelve…. Thirteen…. Fourteen…

"We should do something" said McMullen

"Like what?" replied Webber. "She's not in immediate danger and we don't have a suspect".

Then she turned and started walking toward them. The crowd of people followed her, walking with her.

"Jesus Christ" said Webber, "it might as well be in the Evening fucking Standard". He ran to the car and took out a blanket from the boot. By the time he was back Maria was trying to get the words out to McMullen.

"Unit… F… Paragon Industrial Estate. East London. That's where we have to go. That's where the….. the switch will happen".

Webber threw the blanket around her and left McMullen to take her to the car. He called in the latest development, arranging back up support to switch location.

"Your clothes, Maria!" he called out as they made their way to the car.

She put her hand on McMullen's arm. "He said I have… to be delivered naked".

"Alright, Maria, stay calm. You are not being delivered anywhere". She turned to Webber. "Get uniform to collect everything and take it back to the station. We need to get to this industrial estate before he does"

"If he was ever here" said Webber.

"He had to be" said McMullen, glancing out over the bridge as Maria climbed into the car. "He couldn't have seen such detail if he wasn't at least close".

24

12.21pm

The car pulled out, sirens wailing now. McMullen figured that if they were to race to a location half way across London against whoever was doing this then they were sure as hell going win that fight, even if they won nothing else today. Whatever, or whoever, was in that warehouse was going to be under the control of the Met before they were put on the backfoot again.

Maria sat in the back, blanket pulled around her, tears still seeping down her face.

Webber's mobile rang. He glanced down, relieved to see the station number staring back at him.

"Webber" he said, placing a hand on the dashboard for support as the area driver swung them the wrong side of a zebra crossing, narrowly missing an oncoming taxi.

"You need to hear this, Joe". It was DS Shah, the man who had thought he had drawn the short straw being left at the station. "It's come through on the mainline number, the one he always used before. Put your phone on speaker, I can use the MPLS network to patch it through to you. You should hear the whole lot then".

"Hold on" said Webber.

He took out a connector from the glove compartment and rigged up the phone to the car speakers. "Ok" he said. "Put it through".

Screaming filled the car. McMullen winced.

"Fucking bastard" said Webber.

Maria put her head in her hands.

The driver ploughed on. London flashed by. The sat-nav, programmed by Webber with the post code phoned in from the station, was the only sound that broke the call they were subjected to.

"This is your destiny" came the voice.

"How the fuck are you in two places at once?" shouted Webber…

… but his words were met only with the incessant screaming and pleading of Cathy Norris.

Maria, sobbing heavily now, put her hands over her ears. "Please…" she whimpered, but her voice was drowned out amid the sirens, the screaming, Webber's raised voice…

McMullen leaned forward. "I want S-O-nineteen there, Joe. Tell them Operation Blackarrow is inevitable".

Webber nodded and pulled the plug on the car-speakers. He barked into the phone. "Raz! Can you hear me?"

"Yes mate" said DS Shah.

"We're minutes away. Do S-O-nineteen know the location?"

"Yes. Do you want me to speak to them about deploying?"

"We don't have an option anymore. The DCI says codeword Blackarrow is live. Do you understand me?".

"Understood".

Webber put his phone back into his pocket and turned to face Maria. "This is just part of the mind games, Maria. Nothing has happened to you so far, and nothing will".

She still had her head bowed and her hands over her ears.

He glanced at McMullen, but didn't think it the time for in-fighting, so turned to face the front as they sped out of the congested central London roads.

25

12.59pm

As they approached the industrial estate the driver killed the sirens, slowing to a speed where they had reaction time. The motorcycle outrider dropped back.

The two other unmarked cars which had followed from the bridge fell in behind.

Webber spoke to the control room at the station over the car radio.

"Commander Allinson advises that SO19 have taken strategic positions. Over"

"Received" said Webber. "Who's the commanding officer on scene? Over".

"They are happy to defer to DCI McMullen. Over"

"Received".

He turned to face them both. "Looks like you get the bullet call" he said.

McMullen looked over at Maria, who was now watching the warehouses pass by. "There is no call to make, Joe. I am going to have this mother-fucker shot and that's that". She turned back to him. "In the leg, I mean, I obviously".

The cars slowed to a standstill with the warehouse in sight.

McMullen got out of the car and made her way up to the small group of people shielded from the warehouse by some stationary skip lorries.

"Guv" said one of the officers in acknowledgement. "This is Sergeant Rickson, S-O-nineteen".

The man shook her hand. "Happy for you to make the call on this one" he said. "Let me show you what we have".

Through various sight points in the trucks, the officer showed her where the live points were situated. "Basically, because we don't know what we are dealing with we have set up basic cover of the courtyard entrance area. Initial reconnaissance suggests exit points at both front and rear, which are both covered, but there is no other way in unless we go through the windows. Window units on the other buildings look like standard stuff and there is no reason why this is different, but we haven't been able to get hold of any detail yet – like plans from the landlord – so we have no idea what's on the other side. There is no guarantee every warehouse is identical, even though they all look the same".

McMullen nodded. "Any sign of life?"

"None" said the officer. "Although we decided against an initial look-see until we knew what we were up against".

"Ok" said McMullen. "Hold position until I say otherwise. To be honest, we don't know exactly where this guy is, or even if this place is a red-herring. You know the brief. This is about a switch. I can't see how a switch can happen here. He's holed up in a building with no obvious exit route. It doesn't add up. He had more chance of switching on the bridge".

She made her way back to the car.

As she got in, Webber turned the sound slightly on the car-speakers. "Raz still has the same call as before" he said to her. "Nothing but screaming and every now and then he says *This is your destiny*. We've tried getting him to talk but it's like he's transfixed. Whatever the fuck he is doing to her I don't know how she is taking it. It's been going on since we left the bridge"

McMullen sat impassively, staring out of the car at the warehouse. She scanned over the live points where the S-O-nineteen officer had told her they were located. She glanced over at Maria, hands clasped in her lap, body hidden under a blanket in the July heat because she had no choice.

"I don't understand this, Joe" she said. "This doesn't bare any relation to what he was after".

"What do you mean?"

"Think it through" she said. "If Cathy Norris is in that warehouse, and he is torturing her right now, like that phone call suggests he is, and we have Maria sitting here with us….. who was stripped of anything that could give away her location….. " she trailed off.

"Guv, there isn't time for this. Are we going in or what?" urged Webber.

"Joe, she may as well be wearing a wire and a GPS unit and God knows what else so far as this place is concerned because this place is a gold fish bowl. There is no way in, and no way out. It makes no sense to go to all that trouble on the bridge to make Maria untraceable, and then send us here – to a dead end".

"What are you saying?"

"I am worried, Joe. Something doesn't stack up. What if he has wired the place. You know, explosive device or something"

"What?"

"Look at it, Joe. If you were going to give up Cathy Norris, and take Maria away you would have no choice but to make sure you were in a public place, where S-O-nineteen couldn't get a shot, where you had multiple exit routes and opportunities to double back. This…." She gestured toward the warehouse. "This is bullshit. The bridge made sense, in a strange sort of way, but this…..". She was shaking her head.

She got out of the car.

Webber got out quickly to follow her. "What are you doing?"

"I am going to send S-O-nineteen in after a full external reckie. If they sweep the place and think there is a live target inside I am sending them in".

*   *   *

He sat quietly in the corner of the bar, reviewing the text message he had sent. He hoped it was said in the right tone, but then, texts were texts. How do any of us know they come from the person themselves? This is the beauty of the electronic age.

We are all faceless….

…Which facilitates all manner of horrors.

*   *   *

The black-clad officers moved swiftly in single file. The front door secure. The rear door secure. One on the shoulders of the other. A view through the window. Nothing. Lead officer places weapon on safety and leaves it on the ground, covered by two colleagues. He places a probe just under the door clearance.

There are sounds. Definite sounds of a woman screaming, but nothing else. It is hard to tell the distance they might need to travel with no visual information to back it up. With no lay-out plan they are going in blind and no-one is comfortable with that.

The lead officer relays the signal to the sergeant. McMullen has heard enough. She is bringing an end to the madness now. Webber protests for the life of Cathy Norris, but Maria, huddled in the back of the car is evidence enough for McMullen that sometimes we cannot save everyone.

*   *   *

He is pleased at the message.
"OK Mum. See you in a few minutes. Hope all is OK. You can buy lunch!".
A few minutes.
That is all.
He reads it again.
"OK Mum. See you in a few minutes. Hope all is OK. You can buy lunch!".
He smiles.

26

2.17pm

"You don't have to stay in here" said Maria. "I am not about to top myself, or do a runner".

Maria emptied her clothes from the evidence bag onto the closed toilet lid in the cubicle.

"I didn't say you were", said McMullen. "I am just here for support".

She was standing outside the cubicle in the woman's toilets of the CID floor.

"I don't need your support, Claire. I had it once, and I appreciated it, but you know as well I do that promises were made, and those promises were never kept". She put on her underwear and wriggled back into her skirt. "And I don't expect the promises made now to be any different".

McMullen stared at herself in the mirror. So much older than before. "Nineteen years is a long time" she said, matter-of-factly. "People change".

"But the promises don't" came the voice from the cubicle. "It's always *we'll catch him*. Only you didn't then, you didn't today, and there is no guarantee that you will in the future. Face it, Claire, he's always been one step ahead of you".

She didn't answer.

Maria buttoned up her blouse. "I mean, how did you feel, with armed police breaking into a disused warehouse only to find a CD recording going over and over? How does that say that the big Met machine has its finger on the pulse?"

"It was a timed electronic device that dialled the mainline number at a specific time and played the recording down the phone. The same principle that plays your favourite CD when your alarm goes off in the morning".

Maria snorted. "Favourite CD. Yeah right. It sure sounded like it. Along with a bank of sirens and misplaced police officers to back it up". She tucked her blouse into her skirt, reaching for her jacket.

"We did the best we could, Maria. We can only ever react to the hand we are dealt".

Maria slipped on her shoes and straightened her clothes. "That's my point. You cannot predict what comes next. We are continually at his mercy, reacting but never being able to predict".

She flicked the lock and exited the cubicle. "I just want to be able to get one step ahead of him, that's all. It's possible. You just have to think like he does".

McMullen stepped aside for her. "And can you?" she asked. "Can you think like he does?"

Maria shrugged. "In some ways, yes, in some ways no".

"That isn't exactly the insight I was hoping for" said McMullen.

Maria didn't reply. She checked herself in the mirror, making her final adjustments. "I look like a corporate suit" she said.

"It was a necessary evil to cover the wire" said McMullen, instantly regretting it.

"Perhaps they should call this the freedom range. Run an advert where the woman throws the suit off on Chelsea Bridge and liberates herself". She looked at McMullen in the reflection of the mirror. "Only she doesn't liberate herself does she?"

McMullen looked away, no longer having the energy to rise to the bait. "We can talk about this later. Can I have my mobile, please".

Maria shook her head. "I don't have it".

"It was with the clothes you left on the bridge".

Maria became agitated. "I didn't *leave* any clothes on the bridge. I was *forced* to strip on the bridge in full view of the Great British fucking Public. Speak to whoever picked the clothes up".

McMullen made her way quickly back to the main incident room.

"Who picked up the clothes and other stuff from the bridge today?"

No-one answered.

DS Shah said "The guys left that box there on the table. That was everything".

McMullen tipped it toward her, scanning inside. "Where is DI Webber?" she said.

DS Shah pointed to the small office partitioned off from the main area, the place McMullen considered to be her own office.

"Joe", she said as she walked in and closed the door. "Where the fuck is my mobile phone from earlier".

He looked up from the file he was reading. "Everything is in the box" he said. "They recovered everyth – "

She banged the table in front of him. "No, Joe! They didn't recover everything! My fucking mobile is missing and you know what this man is capable of! Do I have to mention David Sachs, his girlfriend and his girlfriends daughter?"

And then it dawned on her. "Oh Dear God"

She stormed out of the small office. Grabbed the nearest phone. She punched the numbers in frantically. The phone connected. It went to voice mail.

"No! No! Shit no!"

She did it again, and again. It was the same every time.

Joe came out of the office. "Claire?"

She turned to him with tears in her eyes. "He's got my daughter, Joe, I know it. That's why today didn't make any sense. He was buying time. It was only ever about my mobile". She began to cry. "It was only ever about...."

Joe stepped forward to catch her.

He hauled her to her feet. "Concentrate Claire, don't lose it now.. where will we find her…? where will she be..?"

She fought through the tears to give him what he needed.

"University campus" he said to Raz. "South Kensington Pathology lab, she is in the halls of residence".

When Maria emerged from the women's toilet she found McMullen in a crumpled heap, Webber cradling her as she sobbed.

"Jesus", she said. "What's happened?".

27

10.58pm

She woke up in darkness. The cold stone pressed against her skin, hard and unfeeling. She raised her hand to her face, felt the pull of the chains that held her, and the weight of her sorrow flooded back, crushing her as she remembered where she was. Slowly, she became aware of herself, cradled in the foetal position in which she had been sleeping. It was as if, in death, she was regressing.

She forced herself to move, easing her aching body to its feet. The chains scraped against the stone floor like some ghostly cliché. But that's what she was now, almost. A ghost. A life taken, and never seen again. That's what he had made her say: *We are ghosts now... Lives taken.*

She put her hands behind her to touch the wall. In the darkness she felt for something familiar. Something to ground her. Pushing against it she moved slowly along the wall until she felt the cold metal ring to which the chain was attached. This was her point of reference. When he punished her with darkness this was how she found her way to the water bottle in order to drink, this was how she found the bucket to urinate. Odd, how we learn to survive, even when we do not want to.

Through the silence she heard the click of the outer door. His footsteps, firm and deliberate echoed through the chamber. She froze in position, listening intently, heart thumping in her chest. *The outer door* she thought. *The outer door*..... Usually he would stop and lock the outer door again. But this time he didn't stop. Just the click of the outer door, footsteps, and then he was unlocking the inner door – the door to the hell in which he kept her chained.

He said nothing as he entered the room, but she sensed him in the darkness, watching her. She spread her fingers out against the wall, seeking solace where there was none as she began to weep. And then he threw the switch plunging her into the searing heat of the spotlights. The glare burned onto her skin. The chains scraped as she raised her arms to protect her eyes.

For a while there was silence. She had learned not to say anything when he first entered. In the early days she would spit obscenities at him, insult him, threaten him, but he would simply turn out the lights and leave and she would never know how much time passed before he returned. Sometimes she slept, sometimes she stood, shaking with fear and anger, refusing to be beaten. Perhaps it was hours, even days on those occasions when she stood in defiance, living only for when the lights came back on and she would shout and scream her way back into immediate darkness.

But there was only so much she could give before the tears and the futility took over. So she learned after a while to stay silent when the lights came on. At least that way she would receive food, and perhaps even have the chance to learn something about where she was being held. It was through obedience that the lights stayed on long enough for her to learn the layout of the room, despite the searing light.

She let her hands drop slightly as her eyes started to accommodate. She listened intently, trying to concentrate through the fear. Why didn't she hear the familiar click of the locks to the inner door? Why had he left both doors open? She wiped two small beads of sweat from her face. The lights had started to drain her now. Pulling the life from her as she stood, shielding herself. She listened for his footsteps, like a blind woman, head tilted, heartbeat pounding in her ears. She wanted to be strong, to be defiant, to go fighting against the inevitable. But the doors should not have been open. Something was wrong, because something was different. Her body was shaking now, her legs weakening, and when his voice came through the void she almost cried out.

"Behold! A light in the darkness…."

He stepped past the bank of spotlights and she screamed. He had never let her see his face since he had taken her.

"Please…." She whimpered. "Please, no….."

He came closer to her. It would not have mattered what he looked like. The simple fact of seeing his face after so long was enough to break her. She stared at him, transfixed by the face of the one she knew would end her life. It was devoid of all humanity. It was an alien face, and it bred within her a loneliness the like of which she had never known. A true, cold emptiness born from the shock and horror of realising that there is no mercy and there is no escape.

She was shaking uncontrollably now, arms still raised. He was almost upon her.

"Put your arms out in front of you" he said flatly.

She forced her arms away from her face, squinting hard against the light. "Please… don't hurt me…" she said, weakly and then recoiled as he raised his hand at her.

"Silence!" he barked. And then in a flurry pulled her wrists toward him and unlocked the wristclamps that had held her for so long. Almost in one movement as the chains fell to the floor he gripped her by the throat, squeezing, and pushing upwards forcing her against the wall.

He stared at her for a moment, pushing her hair away from her eyes. He ran his fingers over her lips and then struck her across the face. Screaming, she fell to the floor and covered her head, cowering in fear of the torture starting.

But she felt nothing. Squinting upwards against the light she could not see him. She pushed herself up against the wall into a sitting position, hands, *free* hands, shielding her eyes from the light. Still she could not see him.

And then all at once her adrenalin exploded in her body. She scrambled to her feet and ran toward the light, blind as she did so. She passed by the bank of spotlights and in the mass of power cables and discarded rubbish behind them she found the inner door. She spun round as she exited, checking behind her. There was no sign of him. She was panting heavily now, panicking. Outside was darkness. She smelled oil, and dirt. Her feet felt as if they were walking on sand, a sort of gritty dust. She could hear trains somewhere in the distance, and then, in the darkness, as her eyes adjusted, she could see steps. *The outer door* she thought, heart almost bursting in her chest.

And then she heard him somewhere behind her. She ran up the steps, legs almost buckling beneath her as she stumbled in the darkness, body slamming into the door as she gripped the handle.

"PleaseGodPleaseGodPleaseGod" she said, over and over. It was locked. She screamed and twisted at it, kicking it, rattling it, push, pull, push, pull....

And then her head jerked back. His hand twisted her hair round and round until she was looking up at his face, her body arched backwards. He kicked the back of her knees and forced her to the floor. Hr gripped her throat, squeezing hard. Her arms flailed above her as she fought for breath, taking a deep gasp as his grip released.

And then she screamed as his fist crashed down on her, again and again, until the darkness around her swamped her brain and she lost consciousness.

When she came to, she knew immediately she was moving. She forced herself up, taking in her surroundings. She lunged for the doors, kicking with what strength she had left. She felt for the handle but there was nothing. Just the cold metal of the doors and sides. She was screaming now. Screaming for her life, for her freedom. Kicking the sides of the van and pounding, pounding, pounding until her hands bled.

After a while it became futile. She lay on the floor of the van, rolling with the movement. She gave up trying to think how much time was passing as she listened to the low hum of the road, the changing gears and the increasing miles. Time had long since lost any relevance to her. There was only life or death now it seemed, and nothing else.

When the van finally stopped she lay silent. Of all the things she had done since he had taken her the only things she had come to know as absolutes were that escape was impossible – he was too clever for that – and that death was inevitable.

She heard footsteps outside the van. He was pacing up and down as if he were collecting something or preparing something.

And then one of the doors to the van opened. She heard his voice. He didn't show himself, he didn't reach for her. There was just his voice from somewhere outside.

"I have set before you an open door, which no-one can shut. Remember these words, Cathy".

Her heart was pounding as she crawled to her feet. It was the first time he had ever used her name. She moved toward the door, expecting to see him at any moment and be cut to pieces, but the prospect of freedom drew her inexorably forward. She moved closer and still nothing happened.

And then the voice came again. "Remember these words, Cathy. I have set before you an open door, which no-one can shut".

She edged toward the opening, and freedom. She hesitated at first. And then she leapt from the van, screaming, arms pumping hard as she ran, convinced she was running to her death. She drove herself on, not caring or knowing where she ran to, hardly realising she was running through open fields in total darkness. Her bare feet pounded into the grass and mud as she forced herself forward, expecting at any moment to be cut down and to find him standing over her, dispensing the final act.

She did not know how far she had gone before she fell into exhaustion and collapsed, body alive with the sensations that came from the realisation that she was free…

And the fear and confusion that came from not knowing why, or for how long.

July 8th

28

4.21pm

Webber and McMullen waited impatiently outside the FME's room. Since being brought in Cathy Norris had been under medical examination and psychological assessment. The process had taken longer than McMullen anticipated and she was keen to get started.

Maria sat impassively on one of the small, hardly-fit-for-purpose plastic chairs that were lined against the wall.

When the medical examiner emerged he nodded to McMullen. "She's fit enough to be interviewed" he said. "The hospital have replaced a lot of her fluids but there wasn't a need for anything else. She has cuts and bruises and according to the blood tests results she has low iron levels, but there is nothing else of note. She has lost a lot of weight but nothing that would give immediate cause for alarm. Other than that, mentally, she is how you might expect someone to be who has been through what she has".

McMullen glanced over at Maria, but Maria was still staring at the floor, listening but not contributing.

"Ok" said McMullen. "Thanks. Joe, bring her through to interview room three. Maria, you can come along with me".

As they made their way along the corridors and down to the interview rooms, McMullen said, "I won't pretend to second guess what she is feeling. We all accept that you are probably the only person in the world right now that she will find any affinity with, and I don't under-estimate how hard this is for you. If you want out at any time, just say".

"I won't let her down like that" said Maria flatly. "Whatever she says she won't be saying anything I haven't already heard".

They entered the interview room and sat down. The dark grey faceless room Maria remembered from when they first brought her in. "What's the plan for Cathy" asked Maria, "after you've spoken to her?"

"A re-union with her family. Counselling. A safe-house".

"The same as it was for me, then?"

"She is a witness, Maria, in the same way you were and still are. Her testimony and yours will be crucial when this comes to trial".

"Assuming you catch him" said Maria, holding eye contact with McMullen.

"We *will* catch him"

"That's what you told me last time. Are you going to promise Cathy Norris the same thing?"

Webber knocked and entered, ushering in a frightened, dark-haired woman, dressed in jeans and T-shirt and cradling a cup of tea in her hands. He introduced them all quickly, and when she found out who Maria Blakemore was she stared at her in a way that made Maria immediately uncomfortable. Then she burst into tears and threw her arms around her. "Thank you" she managed through the tears as she cried into Maria's shoulder.

Maria eased her away. "I didn't save you" she said coldly. "That was a trick he played on you". She looked away. "No-one knows why he let you go".

She looked stunned. "But he made me say your name, he told me only you could save me, and here I am. I owe you my life"

"No you don't!" snapped Maria. "Don't fall for it"

Maria sat down heavily. Cathy turned to McMullen. "Is this true?" she said.

"Please" said McMullen. "Please, sit down. We have a lot to talk about".

She sat down, still looking confused, and pulled her plastic tea cup toward her, wrapping her hands around it again.

"Maria was a former victim of the man we believe abducted you. Her ordeal happened nineteen years ago. He let her go in the same way he let you go. Since the suspect became active again, Maria has been helping us with the investigation in any way she can. We believe that Maria was right in what she said to you. The man did make you say her name, but that was to taunt Maria, rather than to give you a means of release. It is nothing more than the sort of manipulation and mental torture we have come to associate with him. The truth is, he has potentially led us into a trap by using Maria, and you, as bait. A trap that may have allowed him to abduct an alternative victim". She held the words together for as long as she could.

Webber stepped in. "So the best way in which you can help us catch this man is to start from the beginning, and tell us as much as you can about how you were abducted, where you were taken, what happened to you whilst you were there, how you escaped. Anything at all that you think might help. Don't worry about having to analyse things as you go. You just tell us as much as you can, and we'll do the rest, OK?"

Cathy nodded. She sipped her tea, then wrapped her hands back around the cup.

"It was a simple thing. I was out shopping, getting stuff for me and my flat mate".

"You're an accountant, is that right?"

"A trainee, yes. Still doing the exams. My flat mate is doing the same. Whilst I was in the supermarket, a guy started talking to me".

"Can you describe him?" asked McMullen.

"Yes. He was one of those people who always look familiar. Dark hair, a little bit of grey at the sides. Brown eyes. Italian looking. Slim, looked like he kept himself fit. Squarish jaw, sort of light tan to his face, not pale or anything. He made some comment about the apples, or something like that, I can't remember, but he asked my opinion on something he said he was cooking for his daughter. He said something about cooking for his daughter always being the easy part but that he never knew what the boyfriends liked and he asked me what I would like to be served if I bought my boyfriend home to my Dad. It was all over so quickly. The conversation was maybe only a few seconds as we passed by each other and you never think about it, do you? It's all so… natural".

"Go on" said Webber.

"I paid for the shopping, made my way out to the car-park. He saw me again in the car park and thanked me for my help. Then he drove off. I don't remember the car. It was silver, that's all I remember". She began to cry, "the only reason I remember him from the supermarket is because I recognised him when he walked toward me outside my flat that night. I was coming home from a meal with work, and I looked at him, and I couldn't place him at first. He was smiling, and I slowed down. And that was all that he needed"

"Ok, Cathy, take your time".

"He linked his arm through mine as he passed by, and I felt something sharp in my neck. I remember looking at his face as I lost consciousness. I remember he was holding me like I was his girlfriend or something, one hand round my waist, the other holding my head. I remember thinking that he was going to kiss me and I didn't want him to, and then…"

Webber kept her momentum. "That's good, Cathy, keep going. What else do you remember?"

"That's it. After that I was in a windowless room, mostly in the dark save for a bank of spotlights that came on when he spoke to me. He always spoke to me from behind the spotlights. I never saw his face again until the night he let me go. Part of me wonders whether it really was him but it couldn't have been anyone else. It just couldn't".

"What about the room you were held in? What can you remember about that?"

"It was dark, always dark, until the spotlights went on. Then I couldn't really see anything anyway, they were so bright, and never on for long enough for me to see anything other than what was right in front of me. The only thing I can compare it to is with being on stage. When the lights are so bright that you see only the stage you are on but cannot see the faces of the people who watch you or anything past the first few feet".

She hung her head down. "I lived like that for what seemed like ages. I managed to see where he kept the water bottle for me, and the bucket I had to… you know. I had my period whilst I was in there and he bought me things for that". She blinked back the tears, her words coming slowly now. "You have no idea how bad that was for me. It was just so.. humiliating… and yet he banged on about it all the time. About how cleansing blood flow is, about how the moon drew blood from the impure".

She fixed McMullen with a desperate stare. "Next time you're having a period, crouch down and sort yourself out in a combination of dust and total darkness with your hands pulling against chains that hold you to a wall".

She broke down completely. Maria put her arm round her, but said nothing.

McMullen didn't respond.

"Tell me about the day you escaped" said Webber. "Tell me how that happened".

She wiped her eyes.

"One thing about living in darkness is that your senses start to compensate. I listened all the time to everything because it was my only connection to things, apart from touch. I knew there were two doors that he came through every time he visited. First I would hear the outer door unlock, and then I would hear footsteps, until the inner door unlocked and he was in the room.

"On the day I made a run for it, I heard the outer door unlock, and he didn't lock it again. I knew that was not normal. Then he unlocked the inner door and didn't relock that either. When the lights came on everything was different. He unchained me, and at first I thought that was it, I was going to die, but then he disappeared. I got to my feet, still blinded by the lights, but I was free. God, I just ran. I didn't know where I was going but I just ran. I remember when I ran out of the room I slipped in a lot of sand, or dust or something. It was cold and loose, like fine snow. And there were amber lights, or what looked like amber lights somewhere in the distance, and a steel hand rail, I remember that. And then I heard a train. I remember looking around thinking maybe I could run for it, but I couldn't see it. There was only this amber glow in the distance, and the sound of a train. I gripped the rail, and pulled myself up because I thought I could see a door at the top of the steps. When I got there, it was locked, and that's when he caught up with me".

She twirled the now empty, cold, plastic tea cup round and round in her hands. "After that I was in the van. God knows how far we went, but when it stopped there was no sound from anywhere. I didn't know where we were. Then the doors opened, and I remember covering myself because I expected him to climb in and do something to me. But nothing happened. He just said something about open doors and him being the only one who could open them, but to be honest I was so desperate that once I realised he wasn't coming in I just ran. And I ran, and I ran, and I ran. And then I woke up on the wasteground where the woman with the dog found me".

"What type of train was it you heard" asked McMullen.

"It sounded like an underground train. I am pretty sure, from the smell and the sound, that I was in the underground system somewhere. I don't know where, but nothing else smells like that, at least, the only smell and sound that was anything like where I was when I ran out of that room that day, to me, is the underground".

McMullen looked over at Webber.

Before he could say anything, DS Shah knocked on the interview room door. "Sorry Guv, I need you both upstairs urgently".

"Can't it wait" said Webber, exasperated.

"No", said DS Shah, opening the door further. "It really can't".

As they got up to leave Cathy looked directly at Maria. "He told me that if I ever saw you I should give you a message".

Maria stiffened slightly. "What was it?" she said slowly.

"He told me to say that you should remember the mirror, because in it you will see the truth, and that you must also remember that it will end exactly as it began".

29

6.39pm

They took the stairs two by two.

"It's definitely him" said DS Shah. "Joe's mobile is on divert. That's how we picked it up".

McMullen entered the room first. People looked away as she entered, not sure what to say or do.

She put the head set on.

"This is Detective Chief Inspector Claire McMullen".

There was a pause, then the voice came through the speakers. "At last…"

"Who is this?"

"Oh, the formalities. I feel for you, Claire, bound by the rules of the game".

"We have a lot of crank callers", she said. "You sound just like one of them".

She jerked her head back at the sound that leapt from the ear piece. The speakers spat the volume into the room.

Screaming.

Screaming followed by pleading. "Oh, God, Mum? Mum are you there? Where am I? He says you can get me out of here? Can you? Mum, please God Mum help me! Help Me!".

The screaming took over again and she ripped the headphones off, running from the room.

Webber picked them up. He put them on slowly. "Hello you son of a bitch" he said, calmly. "Looks like you've got me instead".

"Put McMullen back on the line" came the voice.

"Why? So you can torture her and taunt her and take us round in fucking circles".

"I have her daughter!" bellowed the voice across the room.

"Which is why I am on the line. Surely you didn't expect her to function after that little display".

There was a long pause. Then, "Do you function, Detective Inspector Webber?"

He didn't answer.

"What do you think your colleagues make of you these days, Joe? If they were to be honest? You had a little girl once, and a wife, and because you were trying so hard to live for them in the confines of your Metropolitan straight-jacket, they died. Just like that. Burning and screaming your name. Do you think they called out your name, Joe? Do you think they called out for Daddy, for Joe the saviour?"

He stood still, eyes welling up, taking the pain. If for no other reason than the fact that someone else's daughter was still out there, still alive, he held fast, fighting for control, refusing to look at those around him.

"Nothing you can say can hurt them now" he said slowly. "The only person you can hurt with those words is me".

"Do they hurt Joe" came the voice, almost hissing the words. "Do they hurt like the tiny shards of pain that they are, slicing you to your core? Do they hurt like swallowing broken glass should? Do they course through your veins and cause your heart so much pain that you cannot go on?"

He drew a deep breath, ignoring the tear that fell from his cheek, fighting to keep his voice together. Team members looked at each other, not sure what to do. "Nothing you can say can hurt them now", he said. "They are in a safe place".

"But what about you, Joseph, where are you? How are you supposed to go on with the memory and the misery and the constant daily reminders and the fact that I now have someone else's daughter and you are no better placed to save her than you were to save your own? What about you, Joseph?" came the voice "How are you supposed to live with the pain?"

He let the words and the volume die away before he said "I no longer feel pain".

There was a silence.

"I did, once" he continued into the phone line. "You want a fucking confessional? I'll give you a fucking confessional. I did feel the pain, every day and every night for so long. But after a while it was so bad I blocked it out. I drank it away night after fucking night until I didn't feel it anymore. And after a while the lie became the truth. I didn't feel it. And I don't feel it".

"You will, Joseph", came the voice. "You will".

The phone went dead.

He pulled the headphones off and threw them onto the desk. He slumped heavily into his chair and started to sob.

"I'm sorry, honey" he whimpered. "I'm so sorry".

One of the female officers put her arms around him. He wiped his eyes and looked to the ceiling, unable to stop the tears from rolling down his cheeks. "I do feel it" he said, sobbing into the air above him. "I do fucking feel it".

"I know, Joe" said the female officer. "I know".

July 9th

30

9.01am

McMullen handed each member of the team a small manilla file. Webber watched her as she passed from one to the other. She looked drawn. Pale. She had refused to take any time off or to stand down from her position leading the investigation. From his own experience Webber knew both of these decisions were a mistake. But she was a stubborn woman, and a strong, committed officer. She had lost her marriage because of the job. He could see in her eyes the desperation not to lose anything else to it.

When she handed a file to Maria she held her gaze for a few moments. Webber watched the two of them, both unable to stop history colouring their judgement of each other.

When she was done she made her way to the front of the room.

"Ok, lets get started, and let's not tread on egg-shells around me either. So far as Operation Blackarrow was concerned, we were duped. There is no other way of describing it. We had to give it a try because it was a valid way of potentially drawing him out, but we were had. We couldn't have known it at the time, but the whole sorry process was an intricate diversion tactic designed to do one thing: Gain him access to my daughter". She broke off, trying to hold her composure.

Webber stepped in. "Sally McMullen was abducted shortly after we left Chelsea Bridge. We don't know how long after, but it would have happened quickly. She was last seen leaving a lecture at 12.30pm that afternoon. She wasn't in her halls of residence that night"

He put a hand on McMullen's shoulder, not so much as a comfort but more as a gentle persuader to sit down.

He gestured to the two officers who were sitting impassively to the side of the room. "These gents are officers from British Transport Police. The lady next to them is from Transport for London. They are here this morning to discuss the possibility of searching underground stations for suspicious activity. OK, you could argue it's a punt, but so was yesterday, and so was the raid on Andrew Garner's flat. At some point we have to get lucky on something".

He turned to the white board, now grown extensively from its humble beginnings with the body at Farringdon.

"The earliest indication of location that we had came from the sound analysis of the first DVD. The engineers were not particularly specific but they indicated that it was likely to be trains, or perhaps aeroplanes, in the background given the frequency of the noises picked up. We never ruled out the airport issue and continued looking at possible locations, but I think, to be honest, the information gained from Cathy Norris yesterday draws an end to that line of enquiry. She describes partly escaping from her captor for a few moments, and coming out of the room she was being held in into a dusty corridor in which she could hardly see anything. She is specific about the dust. She was bare-footed, and she describes it as sand-like. She could see steps, and she says she could hear what she thought was a train".

He turned back toward the team. "Admittedly, you don't have to be genius to work out she was probably somewhere in a disused underground station, but the point is this: Did he really lose control of her for that short period, or did he *let* her experience this so that she could bring it back to us. He did, after all, let her go. She was only free for those few moments because he was in the process of transporting her to the waste ground where she was ultimately found".

He turned back to the board, pointing at the pictures of the Tesseras that had been received. "Material analysis on the necklace items, what Maria says he refers to as *Tessera* showed they are most likely London clay. That might be nothing more than a co-incidence but the testimony of Cathy Norris backs up the theory that other victims might also have been held in an underground station, especially when coupled with the post-mortem analysis on the gritty material found under their fingernails and in their stomachs".

"There is also the location of the bodies when found" added one of the team. "Circle Line station areas".

"Exactly" said Webber. "But we have to be sure about this, because if we fuck this up we will be accused of everything from incompetence to wasting resources. It will be disruptive if we try and search areas underground, and it will take a lot of manpower. It will also give away the position quite publicly because even if we do it under the radar and without any mention in a press conference, some bright spark is going to pick it up. We are giving away a lot here for potentially very little".

"But we don't have any other options" said the same team member.

Webber nodded. "There's one extra thing I want to factor in though. He *let* Cathy Norris go. He knew what she would tell us. For a man who was also pretty meticulous about making sure his victims didn't carry any of his own DNA or prints on them, he was pretty laid back about the state of their hands and what that might show. The necklaces themselves are all of the same material, the suggestion being they are all from the same place. It's like he *wants* us down there. We could very easily be accepting another false reality here, another Chelsea Bridge moment".

Maria interjected. "The necklace was always designed to be an invitation. Of course he wants you down there. He wants *me* down there. This is why I am sent the same things. Whether or not we feel he has engineered it, I do not think you have an option".

Webber turned to the team. "Well? Do we stand or fall on it?"

The verdict was unanimous.

He turned to the officers from British Transport Police. "Over to you then, gents" he said.

The larger of the two officers made his way to the front. "Good Morning everyone. I am Sergeant Brian Goodman of British Transport Police. My colleague there is Sergeant Gary Mann. Yesterday we received a request for certain information which we have managed to scrape together, even though it was a bit of a hasty job. It's a list of disused London Underground Stations with a brief feasibility study of whether a person could be held in one without being found. Before we get into the nitty-gritty of what's what, this lady here is probably the best placed to give some background". He stepped to one side and gestured to the woman at the side of the room.

She stood up from her seat, but didn't move to the front. She held a clipboard in her hand and looked nervous. "I haven't spoken in front of so many police officers before" she said, clearing her throat and attempting to smile. "I am Lesley Downing, and I work for London Underground, reporting directly to the Chief Executive of Transport for London. I am Head of Safety and Authorisation and I am responsible for developing and maintaining the company's publicly available document known as the London Underground Safety Certification and Authorisation Document". She glanced down at her clipboard. "I received a request yesterday relating to the underground network, and which authority or authorities have control over disused stations. If I could just give a little background I think it would help everyone understand how an extensive underground search might best be done". She looked down at her clipboard again. "Basically, London Underground, as a company, is the hub through which everyone else who is connected with the network passes. We liaise with the three companies who run the tube lines, being Metronet Rail BCV Holdings Limited, Metronet Rail Sub-Surface Holdings Limited and Tube Lines Limited. The first two companies went into liquidation a few years ago but have since been absorbed into London Underground, although we still refer to them as separate trading entities because, legally, they are. Different assets, be they track, signals, stock etcetera, are managed and maintained by separate companies, be they train operating companies, station operating companies or perhaps rail franchisees. With regard to disused stations there is also the Transport for London Property division to take into account, as, following on from the creation of the role of Mayor of London, London Underground became, effectively, a division of Transport for London, with senior personnel in the former reporting directly to senior personnel in the latter".

"Fucking Hell" murmured one of the officers. "No wonder it's a fucking shambles".

The woman looked over to Webber for re-assurance. He nodded.

"Well, anyway, basically, we are going to have to get a lot of permissions from various different people in order to do what is proposed, depending on which stations we are talking about".

She sat down quickly, staring at her clipboard.

Sergeant Goodman took over. "So we have a large amount of administrative procedures and people to inform in order to co-ordinate such a thing and without someone like Lesley it would never happen". His attempt to support her did not go unnoticed, but still she stared at her clipboard.

"In the files in front of you" he continued "is our list of disused stations. You would be surprised, I think, that no-one can agree on the number of stations that are actually disused. Much seems to depend on what the station is actually used for now. Disused can simply mean no trains stop there but that it is still office space or storage space, or even used for maintenance. For the purposes of this investigation we are having to centre on stations that have minimal or no activity of whatever nature, save for the usual inspections under Health and Safety legislation by the various Landlord companies Lesley has mentioned, although, to be frank, given the wide spread of companies with different responsibilities for each, records and actual inspections in that regard appear to be sporadic or even non-existent".

He pulled a large display pad toward him and turned over the top page. "The best way to do this I think is to put the stations into three columns". At the top of the page he wrote "Yes", "No" and "Maybe".

"With my knowledge of the system as it stands, Lesley's records and the information set out in the files, we should be able to make a best guess at each one. Let's start first with the list produced by Lesley as it's shorter"

They rifled through the various papers, each locating the London Underground list.

"Starting with the Central Line. The old British Museum station. This has no surface entrance and the only way to get to it is via the track. It's a deep level site, so it would lend itself to sound containment, but you'd have to be well connected within the railway to be able to get access".

"We haven't yet ruled out whether or not the man we are looking for is a railway employee" said Webber, "or even whether he has help from an employee. We have already raided one possible suspect who, ironically, turned out to be a victim, but that doesn't mean that the work being done on that won't reveal more names".

Goodman nodded. "Ok. We will include access by employees as one of the criteria, which makes the British Museum site a good candidate. Deep Level, easy access via a maintenance train, possible accomplice".

"The only other one on the Central Line is Wood Lane. I would rule this one out. It's been extensively re-developed at surface level, it is still used piecemeal by several companies at sub-level, and it is classed as a sub-surface station as opposed to deep level. Too many service personnel pass through it to make it a safe option".

"Moving on to the District Line. Mark Lane, situated west of Tower Hill. If you are a London Underground employee you would have surface level access to this site, but it's not deep level. For now, it's a maybe I think".

"The only other disused station on the District Line, according to this public list, is St Mary's, situated between Aldgate East and Whitechapel. Not much between this and Mark Lane to be honest. Surface level access is possible if you know the right people, but it's sub-surface. I am working on the basis that if anyone is held for any length of time then it would have to be at deep level to make it viable. Otherwise, the risk of being disturbed is increased unless it is genuinely a never visited or never inspected station".

He added it to the "Maybe" section.

"So far as the Metropolitan Line is concerned, we have three disused stations, all of which are adjacent to each other. If you were brave enough you could use them interchangeably. They are Lords, Marlborough Road and Swiss Cottage, all situated between Baker Street and Finchley Road. There is no surface access to these, but maintenance trains could access them, and their close proximity to each other makes them of some interest".

One of the team interjected. "It says here though that they are all sub-surface, not deep level".

"I know" said Goodman. "For now, let's place all three in the "maybe's".

"Moving on to the Northern Line…" he scanned his list, and looked over at Lesley. "Lesley, your list shows Angel as disused. It's not though is it?"

Lesley cleared her throat. "Technically it was closed but was refurbished. The new version is a vastly more developed service area which is why we consider the old one to be closed".

He frowned and wrote "Angel" in the "No" column.

He turned to face them. "Now, City Road, on the Northern Line between Angel and Old Street. Access from the street here is possible, and the site was also used as a bomb shelter during the war. It is deep level and not overly visited". As he spoke, he wrote it in the "yes" column without waiting for approval.

He passed over the next station on the list, Euston, writing it in the "No" column. "Same reasons as for Angel" he said as he wrote.

"Bull and Bush, between Hampstead and Belsize Park. Let's look at this for a moment. It has street level access, and from the information I have put in the file you can see it has acres of space underground. It's deep-level, and, apart from being used as a potential evacuation point for the Underground in emergencies, it is not widely visited".

He added it to the "yes" column.

"Last one on the Northern Line according to the LUL list is South Kentish Town, between Kentish Town and Camden Town. This has to be a yes due to the access points and the deep-level underground layout".

"Lastly, on to the Piccadilly Line". He scanned down the remainder of the list. "I think we can rule out Aldwych, especially the Holburn side of it. From a service personnel point of view it is like Piccadilly Circus down there if you'll pardon the pun. Down Street, between Green Park and Hyde Park Corner is a difficult one. It was used during the war as a bomb shelter. There is plenty of space. It was also used by Winston Churchill briefly until the War Rooms themselves were built. You have to have balls to do down there the sort of thing he's doing, but then again, like Bull and Bush, save for the potential use of an exit during deep-level emergency, it is not overly visited. I would have to say yes to that one".

He added the latest names to the relevant columns. "And that leaves Brompton Road, between Knightsbridge and South Kensington, and York Road, between King's Cross and Caledonian Road, both of which are deep-level, both of which have the sort of layout that might of use, and both of which have track access".

He added them to the "yes" column.

Having reached the end of the list he turned his attention to the additional list that British Transport Police had put forward. "If you look at our list which follows on you can see that most of the stations double-up. However, there are some areas that are not mentioned in the LUL list that I think we should consider. Moorgate, on the Northern Line, is a deep-level site, and it has rat-runs within it the like of which you wouldn't believe until you get down there. It is visited on occasion for various engineering and service reasons, and part of its tunnel complex has been re-used for other Northern Line passenger services and cross-overs, however, that doesn't mean it is not possible to conduct things out of sight down there if you have the right access".

He added Moorgate to the "yes" column.

"Most of the other places I think can safely be left out of the picture. Somewhere like King William Street for instance has some appeal, but it's accessed these days only via a basement door in a commercial building and most of the tunnels are used for I.T cabling so there are regular visits down there by a wide variety of people. Holloway Road has a disused section that might be of interest, but to be honest, almost every section of the underground has a disused section in some way or another and we have to start somewhere".

"Plus" added Webber, "the bodies of the victims have always been left on display. Keeping someone against their will might be his style for the covert side of what he does, but he would not be minded to hide away the victims when the time came. For some reason, the public display is part of it".

"How many of these stations are on the Circle Line?" asked one of the team. "If all the bodies are left on the Circle Line then surely he needs to be holed up in a Circle Line Station somewhere?"

Goodman frowned. "None of the stations are on the Circle Line, not officially anyway". He scanned down the list. "Mark Lane is on the section of the District Line that doubles up as Circle Line. That's all".

"Then maybe we should move Mark Lane from the possibles to the yes column".

Goodman looked at Webber for comment, but Webber simply shrugged.

He made the necessary change.

"Anyone else?" he asked, but there was nothing more.

He looked over at Webber, the session complete.

"Right then" said Webber, getting to his feet. "Based on that analysis we have nine possible locations that will need to be searched. Sergeant Goodman will arrange the necessary manpower. Lesley will do what is necessary via Transport for London to get us timings and the necessary consents, and also the necessary line shut-downs where needed. For reasons of minimising disruption it is likely that the searches will be carried out simultaneously at night, and they have the rest of today to make sure the search can go ahead tonight. Is that right?" He directed his question at Lesley who nodded.

"Ok, then. All we have to do is hope for a stroke of luck".

July 10th

31

12.58am

**Bull & Bush Search Team (Northern Line)
Lead Officer: Sergeant Brian Goodman, British Transport Police**

Goodman checked his watch. Two minutes to go. In order to try and maintain an element of surprise the teams would enter their allotted stations at exactly the same time. 1am. It was the least disruptive time for passenger use and if there was an outside chance of apprehending someone it was probably best done by a simultaneous search operation so that no single search affected the others by giving a suspect an early warning.

He had his doubts about this particular part, but in the end it was academic. If the man they were looking for had the kind of understanding of the system that Goodman thought he did, then he would already be able to tell something was wrong as soon as the normal night-run timetable ceased. Shutting down certain lines was the only way the teams could access some of the areas on the search list. Anyone with a basic understanding of the network would immediately know something was planned just by the lack of trains running.

He made one last check of the team and equipment gathered outside the white block building on the corner of

North End and Wildwood Terrace. Bull & Bush had never had a surface station built, but the disused station doubled up as an emergency exit from the tube system itself and remained of strategic importance.

He watched the final seconds ticking down on the watchface, and then opened up the large metal door. The officers moved steadily inside. The stairs down were narrow. High concrete walls either side of them made the descent feel as if it were being made through solid rock. In single file, torchlight piercing through the amber haze, they zig-zagged their way down the shaft. With nearly two-hundred steps this was the deepest part of the underground system.

Officers searched the occasional storage space that branched off the stairwell in places. Lift engine equipment and disused lift parts, all covered in a thick layer of grey dust, were all that the darkness revealed.

At the bottom of the shaft they made their way through a narrow corridor, the amber lighting stronger in some places than others, and the tunnel eventually opened out and became wider, allowing them to walk alongside each other. Eventually they reached the track and what would have been the platforms. A small toilet area, set-back from the corridor, revealed nothing. There was silence amongst the team members as they moved through the corridors and empty spaces. Three officers broke away from the main group and into a second entranceway that branched off from the southbound platform. The stairs ran up into darkness. One officer waited at the foot of the stairs as the other two edged up the steps. The glow of their searchlight receded as they disappeared into the corridor at the top. Several minutes passed before they re-emerged. "It heads off in the northbound direction" said one of the officers, "back towards where we came in, but it's a dead end. Never got finished I suppose".

They met up with the main group.

"Anything?" said Goodman.

"Sod all" said one of the officers.

Goodman glanced around the empty space, nodding. "Bull & Bush clear" he said, for the benefit of the live feed.

Down Street Search Team (Piccadilly Line)
Lead Officer: DCI Claire McMullen

"The lift was removed over thirty years ago" said McMullen's colleague in response to her frowning at the taught metal spiral staircase that twisted down into the depths of the disused station. "And I wouldn't worry about the newsagent next door either. He may have never seen this access door open for as long he can remember but he's been served with a notice regarding essential engineer access. He won't think twice come the morning".

"Well". She said resignedly, "the only way to do it is to do it".

She led the team single file, clanking down the staircase, searchlights moving in all directions.

The stairs whirlpooled downwards, encased in a black metal grille. The sideways movement was relentless as they walked in what seemed like an endless left turn.

Two thirds of the way down, McMullen checked her map. "Right. This is the old second entrance to the room complex down below. The back four can take this stairwell, and we'll meet you at the bottom"

She moved the group on to allow the rear officers the space to take their alternative route.

As they made their way down they searched the rooms that came off the stairwell. Some were old toilet facilities, and one housed a metal bath.

"It was Churchill's" said one of the officers.

"Fuck off, was it" said someone in reply.

"No, seriously. Down Street was used by alot of committees during the war, including the government. Churchill used to have Cabinet meetings here".

They continued on into the depths of the station, stopping at the junction where the second half of the team were exiting through a small doorway from the alternative entrance above. "It's clear, Guv", said the first officer to emerge.

They crossed over the small bridge that spanned the east bound Piccadilly Line, and descended a small staircase into the platform area. The platform section had been bricked up, and some of the officers moved along the partition, examining the wall with their searchlights.

McMullen moved down along the eastbound corridor. She came across a small doorway and didn't wait for another officer before going in. She shone her searchlight around the grey interior. Battleship grey, everything the same colour. Even the light bulbs had been painted. She backed slowly out, shaking her head as another officer looked expectantly at her.

Carrying on toward the Eastbound platforms they came across a series of rooms. Nothing was revealed by the search and eventually they gathered in the base of the old lift shaft.

McMullen shone her searchlight up into the vast space above them. "I guess we consider this a clear search" she said, the desperation evident in her tone. "Let's just hope to Christ the other teams are having better luck".

South Kentish Town Search Team
Lead Officer: Sergeant Gary Mann, British Transport Police

Inside the station building, the lighting hardly made a difference. Before Gary Mann and his team could make any progress they organised themselves into two groups, Mann taking the lead group off the main corridor whilst the second group descended the circular lift shaft staircase.

The tiled walls showed the age and neglect of the station. Large areas of bare stone and brick could be seen and the commonplace grey dust coated everything. Sergeant Mann paused at one of the large former lift doors. Now blocked by a large steel-bar gate he fumbled around on the key ring for the right key and eventually pulled it open. He shone the searchlight down into the old lift shaft. The circular metal girders formed a perfect descending ring pattern down into the darkness and when his equipment lit up the floor of the shaft there was nothing out of the ordinary.

"We could climb down" said his colleague, shining his searchlight on the metal rings. "The girders are close together and look like they have decent grip".

"No need" he said, backing them up and locking the gate. "There's nothing down there".

They made their way through a tunnel, the metal sides gnarled with rivet heads, checking the walls for doorways, openings or anything that looked like it might be accessible.

Eventually, when they arrived at the track, they saw the rest of the team picking their way through the metal debris left along the space where the platform would once have stood, a soft amber hue bathing them from the walls opposite. The track curled away into the tunnel and Sergeant Mann made his way over to his colleagues.

"Nothing", said his colleague as he approached.

British Museum Search Team (Central Line)
Lead Officer: DS Rajinder Shah

The officers made their way along the track from Holburn. Access to the British Museum station from the surface was impossible as the original entrance had long since been built over. The only way to get to the labyrinth of disused corridors that made up the former station was to walk from the nearest operational one, Holburn.

DS Shah adjusted the shoulder harness that carried the camera and the live feed to the control room.

"I take it you're getting all this" he said, feeling distinctly uneasy in the darkness of the underground tunnel. Their searchlights danced swiftly in all directions as they advanced down the line, carving out a world from their blindness.

The voice in his ear piece was muffled, but audible. "We can see everything Raz, but try and keep the light steady, okay?"

He cursed under his breath. Walking a narrow track in pitch darkness, with a live rail only a stumble away and nothing but a torch and some verbal instructions to guide him was not his idea of a night out. It was a considerable relief to see the walls of the tunnel finally open out and for the officers to enter the amber glow of the track lights on one side of the tunnel opposite where the platform would once have been.

"Great" said one of the officers, sarcastically. "How the fuck are we supposed to get up there?"

Raz made his way over to the doorway that lead away from the track, set at head height from where they were standing. "Most of the disused tube stations have all had their platforms removed" he said. "We have to do it the old fashioned way".

He slung his torch onto his belt and cupped his hands together to make a step for his colleague's foot. "Come on dick-brain, ladies first".

One by one they hoisted themselves up into the doorway. The floor of the corridor was covered in a thick layer of grey dust, and their boots left imprints in their wake as they continued on. Posters still adorned the walls, some decades old, and despite the powerful searchlights they carried, too many corners remained in darkness.

"Christ, this is fucking eerie" said Raz. "It's like a ghost town".

They made their way through the corridors, checking the deserted spaces and feeding the live pictures back to the control room at Chelsea. Maria watched the screens but said nothing. Live feed was coming in from the other search teams, each assigned to a different controller, all feeds being recorded as they progressed.

"Look at this", said Raz, positioning the camera and searchlights to show a brick wall.

"The picture isn't all that clear, Raz" said the controller. "What are we looking at?"

"We're at the end of the eastbound platform. This is the old passenger exit. It's bricked up".

"Nothing wrong with that. It's what we were told to expect".

"I know", said Raz. "But look here". His hand came into the shot, his finger moving in a circular motion over some breize blocks. "This is new brick work".

He pulled at some of the loose bricks around the newer, darker area. As he managed to find a weak point he stepped back and began to kick at the loose stone. Eventually he managed to make a whole big enough to get the searchlight into.

And from the darkness, lying on its' side, eyes wide but lifeless, was the garish false smile of a young female corpse, head shaved and naked, reaching out toward him.

Moorgate Search Team (Northern Line)
Lead Officer: DI Joseph Webber

"This place is a fucking rats cage", said Webber, adjusting his shoulder harness to angle the map torch downwards. He turned the station diagram the right way up and directed part of the team toward the Metropolitan line end of the station. "You will have to go through these corridors here, and then it will branch off. This used to be part of the Northern City line as well as the Northern Line so there are several lift shafts and 10 platforms overall. I want this done quickly, you understand? I don't want this fucker legging it if he really is down here. Let's go"

The team dispersed and Webber led his section through the dust-coated corridor to a T-junction. One way lead to a lift shaft, and the other curved away toward a flight of stairs. The team heading for the Metropolitan Line area could already be seen disappearing over the crest of the steps, their searchlights fading with them.

"You two check out the lift shaft down there. Me and Eddie will head on down this way. Use your map. I am not coming back for you. The quicker we get out of this shithole the better".

As they made their way through the corridor, Webber checked his map again. He was staring at a small passage that seemed to lead off to ventilation windows. "It must be the old Northern Line lift shafts", said his colleague. Webber was shaking his head. "Who knows. All we need to do is get into it".

They edged through the darkness of the small corridor and up to the steel-bars across the lift shaft ventilation ducts. Webber gripped the covering and rattled it to test how robust it might be. It came away in his hand. He glanced over at his colleague. "Did you see that?"

He leaned into the gap as far as he could and peered first up, then down, the shaft. He could see the searchlights of other team members further down. He shouted down to them, and one emerged on the floor of the shaft confirming that the area was clear.

He pulled himself back from the edge and left the metal grille on the floor where it fell.

In the outer corridor they made their way down several flights of steps, checking the small storage spaces that branched off every few hundred yards. Eventually Webber saw the Platform 10 sign. "This is the farthest end" he said. "If we work our way back in that direction we should meet up with the others".

He folded away the map and adjusted the camera on his shoulder.

The corridor that lead from platform 10 through to platform 9 was littered with engineering cast-offs. Pieces of machinery, old cable rolls, lighting equipment, all of it covered in the thick grey dust and soot of the underground. At the end of the corridor, and across the non-existent platform, they came across the emergency stairs.

"They're blocked off at surface level, but the map showed that half way down there's a corridor that used to lead to the Metropolitan Line". He shone the searchlight up into the darkness.

Then he heard shouting. The sound of people running.

"Where the fuck is that coming from?" he said, but then held up a hand to his colleague to stop him answering whilst he turned his head slightly to listen.

"Up there!" He ran to the foot of the steps and started to climb as quickly as the tight, narrow, circular metal stairway would allow.

Half-way up he leapt from the stairs into the corridor that linked the station to one of the old lift shafts. Several of the officers had already gathered around what looked like a doorway. As he reached the group they finally managed to wrench a metal grille from a large opening in the wall leading in to the lift shaft.

He gripped the edge of the opening with one hand and peered down the shaft into the white searchlight that was being shone onto the shaft floor.

The live feed fed everything back to the Control Room, and the disbelieving, tear-filled eyes of Maria.

The body was lying on its' back, arms spread out in a Christ-like pose. The dark lesions on her arms where her wrists had been cut stood out like black chains against her pale, blood drained, skin. Her empty eyes stared up at the camera feed, her torn lips revealing the skull-like grimace they had come to know so well.

Maria wanted to speak, to say something, anything, but when she opened her mouth to say it, nothing came.

**City Road Search Team (Northern Line)
Lead Officer: Sergeant Keely Adams, British Transport Police**

    She paused momentarily, the key hovering millimetres from the lock. She had been entrusted with the City Road search team command because she was good at her job and she knew it, but nevertheless the doubts were already seeping in through the walls of her usually unshakeable confidence. She had been briefed as to what they might expect, and what (or who) they were looking for, and it had all seemed surreal in the briefing room as they put on their kit and tested their equipment; but here, in the dead of night, grouped together on the junction of City Road and Moreland Street, opening up a lift shaft door that hadn't been opened for forty years, she suddenly felt the weight of what it meant to be lead officer. To be the one who made the decisions and who went in first, no matter what was down there.
    "Sergeant Keely Adams, entering the lift shaft door now". She said it for the record, for the live feed that was being recorded, but she also said it to spur herself forward. To make sure she didn't falter.
    The heavy metal door opened inwards, and she was greeted by a dull orange glow of lights that spiralled downwards on the walls of the emergency stairs. She pushed the door as far open as it would allow and without hesitating she led the eight officer team down the concrete steps. Perception was everything. Confidence was everything.

She felt the cold metal of the handrail against her skin, the other hand darting the searchlight around the walls and steps beneath her. The large, vacuous space that once held the lift, now echoed to the sound of the intruders, and every few seconds they felt the rush of a warm air flow passing over them, smelling of fuel and dirt, as night-train activity somewhere in the tube network pushed the stale air up through any open space available.

The journey to the floor of the lift shaft only took a few minutes, and those few minutes represented the full extent of Sergeant Keely Adams' command. At the foot of the stairs she screamed, fell back against the officer behind her as she recoiled at the horror, and then hunched against the wall as the contents of her stomach forced themselves into her mouth. The officer behind detached the camera from Adams' shoulder harness, and Maria stood transfixed at the sight on the screen, the only commentary to it being the sound of an officer sobbing and vomiting.

Hanging upside down, suspended by the feet, was a naked corpse, the pallid alabaster skin bright white in the glare of the spotlights.

Brompton Road Search Team (Piccadilly Line)
Lead Officer: Sergeant Jagdar Ranu, British Transport Police

The service train stopped at 1am at the station of Brompton Road. There was no other way to access the site.

DS Ranu and the team stepped down from the train onto the trackside and made their way into the deserted station areas.

The access area lead through a long service tunnel, tiled and still displaying the name Brompton Road. The walls were covered in thick layers of dust, and the tiles were chipped and fading, most dating back to the original construction.

The team passed through a series of partitioned walls, each one identical to the former, their searchlights seeking the truth from each dark corner but revealing nothing.

One of the officers came across a locked gate. Ranu checked his notes and confirmed this was expected. The M.O.D. controlled half the site. They were concerned only by the current operational half. A dead half was not their concern.

They continued on back toward the main staircase. Two large pieces of machinery, both covered in thick grey dust, blocked the pathway. Ranu and the team shifted the smaller of the two, what appeared to be a large ventilator fan, and they began their assent of the stairs, and the climb to the surface.

"Wherever he is" said Ranu into the live feed, "he's not here".

York Road Search Team (Piccadilly Line)
Lead Officer: Frankie Lammora, British Transport Police

Everyone loved Frankie, It was an unwritten rule amongst the officers: You could rip the piss out of who you wanted, but Frankie was off limits. The reason Frankie was off limits was because he went down the stairs on the seventh of July during the Kings Cross disaster when everyone else was fighting to come up. He had subsequently developed a reputation for being the one guy you could guarantee would be going the wrong way at the wrong time and that meant that if you could count on anyone you could count on Frankie.

So when he said they were best off climbing down the old lift shaft at surface level on the York Road site, everyone just shrugged and nodded.

The circular metal rings made for good climbing grip, and, searchlights dangling like flailing optic nerves, they descended quickly to the old platform level.

"Ok, we'll take the track area, and the storage rooms. You lot make your way up the stairs and check the ventilator shafts".

Frankie adjusted his camera harness and directed the searchlight out onto the track. They made their way slowly along the trackside, picking their way through the dust and the debris. At the end of the Northbound platform, just before the track disappeared into the large circular tunnel that stretched before him, Frankie shone the searchlight up a small flight of steps, only four or five in all, and a small metal handrail that separated them from the track. As he walked up the steps he focused on the closed panelled door at the top. Taking the handle, he pulled at the door but it didn't open. He pulled it harder.

The scream that launched itself from his lungs upon opening the door reached even those officers at surface level.

All those in the near vicinity turned to run toward him, flashlights flicking wildly over the end of the platform where Frankie Lammora was pushing a rag-doll corpse off him and scrambling to his feet.

"Jesus Christ!" he screamed. "Jesus H Christ! Get the fucking thing away from me!"

Mark Lane Search Team (Circle & District Lines)
Lead Officer: Sergeant Steve Lader, British Transport Police

Sergeant Lader led the team into the pedestrian subway entrance from the main thoroughfare. At the end of the subway he opened up the security access door and they filed in, turning on searchlights as they went.

The stairs were narrow and dated, and the walls still bore posters from engineering works decades before. The stairs took them down to track level. There were no rooms or storage spaces running off the main descent. Just a vast open disused space that echoed to the sound of their intrusion.

They walked along the eastbound platform, moving in and out of the corridors and passageways that branched off. Other officers made their way along the two additional platforms, all eventually meeting back at the foot of the stairs.

Lader ran one last searchlight trail over the walls and track before declaring the area clear.

Maria stared at the grainy images on the screen. Mark Lane was the last station to declare the result of its' search.

She sat down heavily, fingers picking ferociously at the skin around her nails.

He was everywhere now. In her head. In her heart. In her Life.

"That should have been me" she said softly to herself, fingernails finally drawing blood from her own hands. "That should have been me".

She made her way out of the control room and back up to Webber's desk. Biting nervously at her fingernails she turned the images over in her head. Over and over with the sight of the CCTV horror-feed.

She had surrendered herself into Police protection because she thought she was helping to move matters forward. But the more she saw of the investigation the more she felt she was walking back toward the centre of the destruction, when she should really be walking in the opposite direction entirely.

But these are the things we cannot avoid: Attraction to the bad; A magnetic pull toward that which is wrong; A capacity for self-destruction that is second to none.

What separates the fire-fighter's run into the blaze to save another from the addict's swift descent back into addiction? Both run toward their possible death, and yet we exhalt one and condemn the other. Is this because one saves a life, whilst the other destroys one? Does this mean we should therefore judge the result of our actions on the basis of what saves a life or what destroys one? And what if that life is our own? Do we have the right to destroy our own life? Should we have that right? If something is ours to throw away, does the basis on which we throw that away really matter?

She wondered whether this made her damned, or whether it made her blessed. If she could save Sally, that would be a selfless act, but in leaving Police protection and making herself a loose cannon on deck, was she waiving her right to be saved? Was she crossing the line into destruction of life, throwing hers away without an attempt to save it? Was she damning herself to Hell….?

Why hadn't they found him tonight? Why did he win again? This was how he won last time – with so many pre-set bullets which he had fired at them. He had moulded them on degrees of disaster. He had distracted them by dropping bombs at the key moments to destroy their decision making processes.

And the way they all were now was the price they had all paid for that.

And so she let his words from before seep into her mind now. She let the way it used to be become the way it is now; the way it has to be now.

From the darkness that sits in the very bottom of my soul, I promise you I will bring you Atonement.

From the darkness that sits in the very bottom of my soul I promise you I will bring you Narcosis.

From the darkness that sits in the very bottom of my soul I promise you I will bring you Enmity.

From the darkness that sits in the very bottom of my soul I promise you I will bring you Vitality.

From the darkness that sits in the very bottom of my soul I promise you I will bring you Insight.

From the darkness that sits in the very bottom of my soul I promise you I will bring you Light.

From the darkness that sits in the very bottom of my soul I promise you I will bring you Solace.

From the darkness that sits in the very bottom of my soul I promise you I will bring you Immortality.

From the darkness that sits in the very bottom of my soul I promise you I will bring you Cleansing.

From the darkness that sits in the very bottom of my soul I promise you I will bring you Kenosis.

From the darkness that sits in the very bottom of my soul I promise you I will bring you Nothingness.

From the darkness that sits in the very bottom of my soul I promise you I will bring you Escape

From the darkness that sits in the very bottom of my soul I promise you I will bring you Silence

From the darkness that sits in the very bottom of my soul I promise you I will bring you Sterility

And as she finished the rant that she had created for him she recalled the last thing he had said to her: "Remember this, Maria. Remember that ultimately it began exactly where it ended"

"…… *ultimately it began exactly where it ended"*

And Cathy Norris had brought that message too.

She looked down at the small desk clock next to Webber's phone, and saw the date.

And it was from there that she knew what she had to do now.

She pulled a blank piece of paper from under Webber's in-tray, and began to write.

32

4.07am

Joe,

I was writing this letter to say sorry for what I am about to do, but the more I thought about it, the more I realised I was not sorry about it. I am sorry that you will think I have let you down, by not trusting you, but I am not sorry that I am going it alone. You and Claire must do whatever you need to do, but from the moment he took Claire's daughter I knew it was happening again: He was moving ahead – a long way ahead of where we are and what we are doing.

Look at the damage he has done tonight. He was down there. He is still down there, I am sure of it, but all we have done is shown his dominance. He still has control. He still has his hold over me, the same way he always did. It should have been over tonight Joe. Tonight we should have found something. Not just body after body. Not just women who could have, who should have, been me.

That is how I felt – that it should have been me. That is how I felt when you pulled up one, then two and then more women who had died like I should have. Why did he let me go, Joe? It wasn't because he wanted me in place of those he had taken. It wasn't because he was coming for me again. I was a smoke screen, like everything else he has done.

I should be happy, I guess. Happy that he has moved on and that now he has Claire's daughter, which was what he really wanted, then I may have a chance, finally, to live.

But I do not feel like I can live. Not now. Not ever. He will kill Sally. You know that. He will kill her and disappear again, the same way he disappeared last time.

Tonight was our chance, Joe. Tonight was the closest we had come. We were in his face. In his domain. But there was nothing with these bodies. Nothing that showed they had been held there. Nothing like the things I told you about, the things that Cathy Norris told you about. That's because they weren't held there, Joe. They were placed there. He knew we were coming, the same way he always knows we are coming. It was the same last time, and it is the same now.

I can't do it any more. I can't sit here and see him walk again. I can't sit here day after day seeing the same clueless looks on the faces of people the same way I saw them before.

When I was abducted, I lost a year of my life. For some reason he didn't kill me but he should have – because even after I was released, I couldn't live properly. Those twelve months changed everything for me. That date, 13th July, the date when I was first taken, it is only days away now, and you know what he said to me on the phone on the bridge. You know what he told Cathy Norris to say to me. It ends exactly where it began.

So I am going back there Joe. Back to where I was abducted. Same date, same place. He may be there, he may not. I will be, though. I am putting faith in the message. I have to heed the message because all the while I stay here I feel strangled – strangled by the inevitability of him disappearing again. I shall leave it up to you as to whether you want to be there. Whether you think it is worth it.

I'm sorry Joe. I'm sorry because you might have to pull my body from somewhere and you will think there was more that you could have done. Please understand that there was nothing more you could have done. I have to finish his hold over me, and I have to do it my way.

You see, the thing is, I should have died last time. I never really lived again after he let me go. I never found a way to. Nothing I tried ever worked because I knew he was always still out there, somewhere, and I can't go back to that, Joe. I can't go back to a life where he has escaped again. I will kill myself if that happens. Plain and simple. There is only so much a person can take.

If he walks away from this and you never catch him, I will never be able to live. I won't want to live, not then. It would be too much for me to know he was free a second time – that he was clever enough and dominant enough to do it all twice and still walk away.

And I can't face the fact that he will walk away a second time, which is why I have to go it alone and take my chances out there on my own. In many ways it doesn't matter any more, because I am already dead. I feel like I am already dead.

Goodbye, Joe. Thank you for trying.

Maria

She folded the letter in half. Wrote the name *'Joe'* on the outside, and placed it face down under the telephone on the desk.

33

9.45am

"I know you can't be specific, Doctor Vanner" said McMullen, "but you know the situation. Anything you can give us, even from just an initial inspection, would help".

The pathologist stood at the end of the room, still working on the last body to have been brought in. "You know I will do whatever I can Detective Chief Inspector. I appreciate the awful position you are in". It wasn't a specific reference to her daughter but she could tell from the direct look he gave her that he knew.

She wondered, too, whether the relief on her face that Sally was not one of the four bodies in front of them also showed. Instead, she simply refused to answer. She wasn't here for sympathy. She was here for something she could use.

"As I understand it", began Vanner, "there was not a great deal of blood at the locations where each body was found?"

"That's right", said McMullen. "Like all the previous victims, the killing must have taken place elsewhere".

"And yet you are still convinced that the victims are being held somewhere in the underground system? Despite the fact that the bodies are clearly killed elsewhere?"

Webber interjected. "The problem, Doctor, is that for this man to have even gotten these bodies in to the places where they were found he would have needed some extensive knowledge of the underground. Just because they were not killed where they were eventually found does not mean they were not killed somewhere else in the system and then taken there. He knows the underground system extremely well, and he must have had help moving the bodies around the system. It just isn't something you can do alone".

Dr Vanner completed the visual examination of the last body and pulled the green body-sheet over the woman's face. "Well, the obvious thing to start with is that they are all definitely of the same M.O. They have all had their lips and head-hair removed, and they have all died through blood loss, three of them slowly through the wrists being cut, but one of them", he pointed to the second body, "much faster through the jugular vein being severed. They all carry the same three symbols tattooed on their upper left thigh, and each of them are numbered. In roman numerals we have ten, eleven, twelve and thirteen". He pointed to each body as he said the words.

"So, an initial inspection can really only confirm that they are definitely the work of your man, but I would need to conduct full toxicology and perform the full autopsy to tell you if there was anything out of the ordinary".

"I appreciate that, Doctor", said McMullen, "but have you got any idea how old these bodies are? How long have they been down there?"

He drew a deep breath and considered each body as he exhaled slowly. "Well, it is hard to say precisely, but the key point here is that we still have relatively good skin condition on each one. Yes, the degradation is bad but we can still make out the tattoo markings, and the appearance of the face still has the strange mannequin appearance. I would say we are looking at victims who have died no more than about three or four weeks ago, but the state of degradation is similar for each, so I would say that we do not have a series of killings here which happened in succession. I think these victims were killed concurrently".

"All together?" said Webber, incredulously.

"Possibly".

McMullen stared at the faces of the corpses that were still visible, and walked slowly from one to the other, pulling up the green body-sheets until the three remaining faces were covered.

"It is possible" she said solemnly. "It is possible that perhaps he killed them all in some ritualistic communal slaughter". She leant against the wall at the far end of the room and folded her arms. "He had the benefit of preparation time. He had year after year to plan and think about how his resurgence would happen. If these women were killed more than three weeks ago then they pre-date the first body we found in early July at High Street Kensington tube station".

Webber frowned. "But if they pre-date what we believe to be the first killing this time round then it means he has killed out of sequence".

McMullen pursed her lips.

"And if he killed out of sequence" continued Webber…

"Then he planned the effect in advance" said McMullen, finishing the sentence.

There was a brief silence as both officers considered the meaning of what lay before them.

"So it's the number of bodies", said Webber, "rather than the sequence that matters".

McMullen nodded. "Maybe this is why he was banging on about number fifteen in the DVD".

"Limited time because of all this moon cycle, Metonic cycle shit. Twenty seven days to do whatever it is he's planning to do before he disappears again. I think you're right. It wasn't the sequence. It was the number".

Webber didn't want to press the point any more. They both knew who was potentially number fifteen.

"A day of wrath is that day", began McMullen as she took out her rosary. "A day of distress and anguish, a day of ruin and disaster, a day of darkness and gloom".

She looked down at her palm as she moved the beads, one by one, along the thread.

34

11.03am

They drove back to the station in silence. Every now and then, when he came to a junction and had cause to look to his left, he stole a glance at her, trying to gauge her mood, grasping for something to say.

Her expression didn't change as mile rolled into mile and they passed through the London traffic. The images of the victims, hauled up from the dirt and the dust of abandoned spaces, haunted them both.

He stared ahead as he drove, watching the sunlight turn the backs of his hands from light to shade, and back again, endlessly mimicking the *click-clack-click-click* of McMullen's rosary. The rhythmic motion, lashing and unlashing the back of her hand, hypnotised her. Both punishing and comforting all in one imperceptible flick of her wrist.

"I know how it hurts" he said, eventually.

"What?"

She was lost in her own thoughts. His words didn't mean anything to her. She hardly heard them amongst the clash of guilt and desperation in her own head.

"I know how it hurts" he said again. "Having Sally out there, and not finding her".

She wrapped the rosary into her palm and closed her fist around it.

"We will find her, Claire" he said, looking over at her. "Whatever it takes".

She stared down at the rosary. "That's the problem" she said quietly. "None of us know what it will take". She looked out of the passenger window, turning her face away from him. "Look at what we have just done", she said. "The full extent of resources available to us, running like rats through tunnels in the ground, and for what? No matter what we do we never get close".

"There will be evidence from those bodies, Claire", he said, trying to put some belief into his voice for her benefit if not his own. "There will be something at the locations. We have to believe that. And we know we are pushing the boundaries back against him now. He knows we are coming. We have been down in his world for fuck's sake. He can't move as freely now. He can't risk it. Regardless of what we think, he will be feeling it after tonight. He will make a mistake. Something will give him away".

She pushed the rosary beads around in her hand. "The DSI will stand me down, won't he" she said. It was more of a statement than a question.

"I don't know. I guess it depends on what you want".

"I want to find Sally"

"Then tell the DSI to shove it. Look him in the eye and say you are going to run the whole operation until your daughter is home and the man who's taken her is behind bars. He won't stand you down if he knows you've got it under control".

She pursed her lips. "What should I do, Joe? What would you do?"

He shook his head. "I don't know. We are beyond what looks good for our careers now. I was beyond that a long time ago".

The mobile rang and flashed up brightly from the dashboard displaying the word *"Station"*. Webber touched the screen and the call came over the speakers.

"DS Webber" he said, pulling the car over.

"Joe. It's Raz"

"Hi mate. Problem?"

"Yes. A pretty fucking big one".

Webber stopped the car and met McMullen's eyes. "What is it?"

"It's Maria. She's gone".

"What?"

"CCTV at the front desk shows her walking out about 5am this morning"

"How the fucking hell did that happen?" said McMullen.

Joe was already pulling out into the road, blue lights flashing.

35

Midday

McMullen stared at the frozen image of Maria on the CCTV screen. They had re-wound it and viewed it several times, noting down what she was wearing, what she was carrying, and circulating the description to those units in the immediate vicinity; but the lasting image for McMullen was Maria's frozen face, staring up at the camera, staring into McMullen's eyes.

"She could be anywhere by now" said McMullen, not taking her eyes from the screen.

Webber sipped tea from a plastic cup, staring at DS Shah who sat opposite him.

"Don't look at me like that" said DS Shah defensively. "You know what she's like. She's like willow the fucking wisp. She goes where she wants when she wants. She had the run of the station for fuck's sake. I couldn't be watching her all the time. Christ, we were pulling bodies out of the underground like we were picking fucking strawberries. It's no wonder she freaked out".

"You were supposed to be watching her" said Webber flatly.

"Yeah, well. You want to try babysitting her. Then you'll know what I'm talking about".

"It doesn't matter now" said McMullen, turning away from the screen but leaving the grainy image staring at them.

She sat down at the table with them, pulling her tea towards her. "Did she say anything before she left?"

Raz shifted uncomfortably in his seat. "Not that I remember. She spent most of her time in the control room with me, listening to the various teams reporting in. Every now and then she would come up here, to the M.I.T room, talking to the team, watching them as they collated the information coming in". He glanced over at a plastic white board that had been hastily erected with a map of central London pasted on a board next to it. The underground stations were listed with information of each victim set out beneath. The map was criss-crossed with markings as the team sought to identify patterns or a catchment area, or anything that would suggest relevant movement or location".

Webber sipped his tea. "So nothing gave her away? Nothing suggested she was about to walk?"

"You said it was no wonder she freaked out" added McMullen.

"Everybody was freaked out, they just hid it well. It's not exactly everyday stuff is it?"

"No-one's having a go, Raz" said Webber.

"Well it feels like it" he said, getting to his feet. "She was in and out of the control room, that's all I can say. She was jumpy, but we all were. She didn't say much to anyone. Just kept watching and listening. That was about it. After the search was over she just sat at the Guv's desk. I checked on her but she said she just wanted to be alone for a bit, and as I had plenty to do anyway I just left her to get on with it. Next thing I know she's not there, and I'm running round the fucking station like a lunatic trying to find her".

"By which time she was already gone" said McMullen.

"Pretty much. Yeah. I checked CCTV for the exits as a last resort and there she was. Which was when I phoned you".

"What the fuck were the front desk doing?"

"Cigarette break" said Raz. "Not them. Her. That's what she told them".

"She knows, and so do they, to use the yard for that".

Raz shrugged. "It's easy to be wise after the event".

"So my desk was the last place she was seen before she left" said McMullen crossing the office floor.

"Yes" said DS Shah, collecting their plastic cups and throwing them into the bin.

McMullen sat down slowly, scanning the desk. She opened the top drawer on her left, and then the one on the right. She moved the papers that sat right in front of her. "Well, there's nothing here" she said, slumping back in her chair.

"Just when we thought things couldn't any worse" added Webber, rubbing his eyes.

July 11th

36

9.30am

The following morning they were back in the incident room.

"You look like you haven't slept" said Webber.

"That's because I haven't" replied McMullen, pushing the papers away from her and rubbing her eyes.

"You need to go home and get some rest. You've had no sleep in the last two days. We can cover things here. The investigation will still move forward without you".

"No way" she said. "I am staying here, on the job, sleeping at my desk if I have to, until Sally is found. And I think we are closer to that now than we were yesterday".

"How?" said Webber, sitting down at his desk opposite her, take-away coffee in hand.

"When we raided Andrew Garner's flat we found him dead".

"Murdered, you mean" corrected Webber.

"Yes. Murdered. The killer had gotten to him first".

"We thought we were raiding the killer's flat", said Webber, "but he was one step ahead of us and decided to leave us a little message explaining how wrong we were".

"Wrong in a spectacular fashion".

"No arguments on that score" said Webber. "So what's your point?"

"What if we weren't wrong?" said McMullen.

Webber scoffed. "How do you work that one out?"

"Look back at the bridge incident. That was a smoke screen".

"So what?"

"What if this guy was a smoke screen as well?"

"I don't think I am following what you are saying. Why don't you just go home and get some rest first. Let me pick up from wherever you think you are, and you come back when you are fresh".

She pulled the papers toward her, shaking her head. "We were duped on the bridge and we were duped at the flat. The minute we raided Andrew Garner's flat and found him slaughtered we put him in the victim category".

"That's because the man who killed him knew we were there and took great delight in telling us. He set us up, Claire. He fed us evidence that led us there just so he could make a point".

"But did he?" she questioned. "I have been over it and over it. That evidence was the same evidence that led us to search the disused stations. It wasn't spurious evidence. We were looking for a railway worker, and there was a reason why we were doing that".

"Because we had enough evidence to suggest that a railway employee may be a suspect. He knew we would think that from the evidence we would inevitably gather, so he picked a hapless no-mark with no family who fitted the profile and killed him ready for us to find".

"But how did he know we would centre on Andrew Garner? We could have pursued someone else. He couldn't kill all the employees who had a pattern of absence. Why him?"

"Claire, there weren't that many with that particular pattern at that particular time. There were only a handful of possibles, and they all checked out. Apart from this guy. There was nothing special about Garner. The killer could easily just have topped one of the others instead. It wouldn't have mattered. It would have achieved the same effect. It would have achieved the same effect because we were contacting them all. It wouldn't have mattered who it was he topped in advance of us being there. He would still have had his moment".

She fell silent.

His phone rang. "Yes?"

There was a brief exchange of words. He opened one drawer, then another trying to find a pen. He scribbled down a name and number on the back of an A4 sheet protruding from under the phone. "Yes" he said. "OK".

"Who was that?" said McMullen.

"DS Shah. Dr Vanner rang. He wants you to call him. Do you want the number?"

"No. I've got it over here".

"Fine" he said, scrunching up the piece of paper and dropping it into the bin next to him. "Go home Claire", he said. "Please, for Sally's sake. You are no use to her all burned out".

"He knew him" she said, staring down at the papers spread across her desk.

"What?"

"He knew him" she said, looking up at Webber. She pushed a sheet of A4 toward him where she had ringed a small paragraph in red. "Look there, Joe" she said, tapping the paper.

He took the statement from her. Next to a paragraph describing the state of the flat on the day of the raid she had written *No Forced Entry* and underlined it in red.

He looked down the page, and then took another sheet from her. She passed him another statement, and another.

"We went after Garner in the first place because we thought he was a suspect. When we found him murdered we immediately assumed that we were wrong and that he was a victim – that we had been duped and that we had the wrong man".

She got up and moved closer to him, perching herself on the front edge of her desk. "But there was no forced entry" she said. "He didn't have to break in. And we all know the general rule that most people are killed by someone they know. I don't think we were wrong to raid Garner as a suspect. I think where we went wrong was to assume we had the wrong man and just bag up his things like he was a victim. Whether he was or not is still in doubt, because I think he let his killer in, and with no signs of forced entry that can only mean invitation. And look.."

She reached behind her. "This is the statement of condition from the place where David Sachs and his lover where attacked. The front door has surface damage on the front and the back, meaning he kicked an already open door. The internal walls of the hallway have brush marks and scrape marks". She passed him the statement. "There is none of that here. Andrew Garner let his killer in, and that can only mean one thing. He knew him".

She sat back down at her desk. "We have been coming at this from totally the wrong angle. I want all the evidence looked at again from the point of view that Garner knew the killer. And, until we can rule it out, Garner is to be treated as a possible accomplice".

Webber was shaking his head. "Nothing we have points to there being an accomplice. Maria would have known. Cathy Norris would have known. We are looking for a single killer. There was no outside help".

"Maybe. But that doesn't explain why the scene of Garner's murder showed a degree of trust between killer and victim. There had to be trust in order for him to get in without force. And the flat itself showed no signs of struggle".

Webber looked down reluctantly at the statements he held in his hands. "Back to square one, then".

*   *   *

"Tell me about his friends" said McMullen, doing her best not to sound impatient with the elderly woman.

"I told you when you first came here" said the woman. "I only ever made him frozen shepherds pie, and he would give me a half bottle of whiskey. I never had nothing to do with him much apart from that".

Webber was standing at the window of the woman's flat, looking down into the small concreted space that led to Andrew Garner's front door. The railings at the top of the steps still had crime scene tape blocking off any access to it. "But you knew he worked for London Underground" he said, putting on his best user-friendly smile.

"It was a bit hard not to notice that" said the woman. "He practically lived in his bright orange vest". She sipped her whiskey. "Terrible business though, what happened to him. I hardly go out these days, you know. Not that I went out much before anyway".

McMullen stifled a frustrated sigh. "So you never saw anyone coming in and out of his flat, and didn't notice anything different about him in the weeks leading up to his murder".

"Nope" said the woman. "So far as I knew he was working. Sometimes I wouldn't see him for a few weeks, you know, due to the nightshift patterns and stuff".

"Did he ever talk about anyone? A girlfriend?" asked McMullen

"Not to me"

"A boyfriend?" said Webber, smiling.

"He never talked about nothing like that. He just came up here. Moaned about how hard he worked and how little he got paid for it. He would hand over the whiskey and I give him a pie or two and it was all smiles till the next time".

"Neighbourly, but nothing more" said McMullen.

"You said it" said the woman.

"Well, we've taken up enough of your time" said Webber. "We shall leave you in peace".

On their way down the steps McMullen couldn't contain her frustration. "For fuck's sake" she said under breath. "No wonder we never get anywhere. You'd think half the population were fucking blind. I bet if I dropped a tenner on the pavement she'd fucking notice that".

"Take it easy", said Webber, as they ducked under the crime scene tape.

DS Shah nodded in their direction as they entered the basement flat.

"Anything?" asked McMullen hopefully.

37

1.37pm

Webber gathered together the papers in front of him and placed them back in the file. He sat back in his chair, let his head fall forwards, and began to rub the back of his neck. As he closed his eyes the sensation on his skin dragged the memory of his daughter back to his mind's eye. Her tiny fingers. The way she would place one hand around his shoulders when he carried her, the other hanging casually at her side as she perused the world, safe in her Daddy's arms.

He stopped rubbing his neck and pushed the image away, replacing it with the sight of the next file on the pile to his left.

He glanced up at his computer screen as the bleep announced the arrival of an email.

"*Dear Detective Inspector Webber*

Account Number: -------.

In accordance with your Production Order I attach the last six months bank statements of customer name Andrew Garner. If I can be of any further assistance please do not hesitate to contact me".

He forwarded the message to McMullen, then printed off the attachments.

His phone rang.

"Webber" he said, recognising the mobile number of DS Shah on the caller ID.

"Raz and I are on our way back" said McMullen. "You didn't miss much by not staying".

"You didn't find anything then?" he said distractedly as he stapled each individual month's bank statements together.

"It was like he didn't really live there. A second search was pointless. We'll have to go over the initial search report and the lists when I get back".

"OK" he said.

"What are you working on right now?" she asked.

"Bank statements. Garner's bank manager has come up with the goods".

"What about the phone records?"

"I've already been through those again. We didn't miss anything. The number that comes up several times still can't be traced. Hopefully the phone company will come up with something shortly. Whoever he phoned on that number it was pay-as-you-go. No obvious trail".

"Bollocks" said McMullen. "What about the credit cards?"

"Nothing out of the ordinary. Nothing that doesn't match his lifestyle or his likely movements".

"OK. Well, usual rules apply and all that. We just have to keep looking".

"Seems that way".

She rang off. He sat back in his chair again, running his finger down the first set of bank statement entries, placing a mark next to anything that he thought worth looking at further.

By the time he had finished the third statement he decided he needed a break. On the way down to the coffee machine his mobile rang. He froze on the stairs, fumbling in his pocket. He stared at the words on the screen.
Number Witheld.

He accepted the call, but the caller rang off.

When he selected number re-dial the ringing tone continued but wasn't answered. It didn't even switch to voicemail.

He put the phone back into his pocket, his first thought being that he had possibly missed a call from Maria.

He got himself a coffee from the machine on the lower floor, and made his way back to his desk. Part of him wanted her back in the station. Part of him didn't. He didn't blame her for the way she felt. He just wished that she had never clouded her motivations. Running away was one thing. Running away to die was something else.

Halfway down the fourth bank statement he was beginning to establish a pattern. It wasn't obvious at first, just a few recurring payments showing up on a regular basis, but it was the size of them which first drew his attention. The payments were to the same bank. A savings account maybe? Each payment went out at the same time each month to the same account number held by the same bank and appeared to be in Garner's name. Why hadn't the bank manager sent him statements for that account number as well? It was, after all, the same bank, and he had specifically requested details of all current accounts and savings accounts.

He finished going through the remaining statements. The same recurring monthly payment showed on each.

He began typing a return email to the bank manager who had supplied the copies. And then, as he typed, the realisation dawned.

"No" he said to himself slowly. "It can't be".

He turned back to the bank statements, cross-referencing one with another and placing a mark against all of the direct debits.

"Fuck, fuck, fuck" he said to himself as the realisation of what they might have missed began to crawl toward him out of the black and white numbers on the page.

He scrolled hurriedly down the email from the bank manager searching for the direct dial telephone number he was sure he remembered seeing at the bottom of the message.

"Thank Christ" he said as he punched the numbers into the phone.

38

9.07pm

The receptionist smiled as she passed the guest information card across the desk to Maria. It was an innocent comment but it carried so much history.
"If you could just fill out your details, please"
Fill out your details.
She stared at the card.
Name.
Such a simple thing. Jane Lister. Maria Blakemore. Someone else?
How many times had she struggled in the past when she had first taken on her new identity? How many times had she almost given the wrong name as her witness protection programme had kicked in. How many times recently had she wished she was anyone other than who she really was.
She had told Webber that she could not live anymore if they failed to catch him a second time round. She had meant every word. In many ways, she was already dead. She felt as dead as those cold corpses they had pulled out from the underground, and she felt that way because one of those should have been her.
But he let me go.
Yes, he let me go. And now I am going back.
She wrote a name at random on the guest card, and filled out the rest with fictitious details. Paying in cash and not

needing to use a credit card she was booked in within a few minutes, and made her way up to her room.

The branded hotel, with every room in every building in every location always being the same, was a comfort. It gave her anonymity. It gave her what she had always craved: Normality. A chance to blend into the background and be unremarkable. It was being remarkable in some way which had been her downfall in the beginning. If it hadn't been for her beauty, and her ambition, he would never have happened across her. Life could have been so different.

Life.

There was no room for that now. Life was over.

She emptied out her jean pockets on the dresser. Just over three thousand pounds in cash, a driver's licence and passport in the name of Jane Lister, and a mobile phone. This was what she amounted to now. Nearly thirty-nine years old, and these things represented the sum total of what she had become. And they didn't even amount to that – not in reality. The ID was not her. The ID was a made-up her; made-up in order to defy a killer who simply walked straight back into her life despite everything. If she took those items away she was Maria Blakemore, unable to prove to the world that such was her real name, and good only for three thousand pounds, taken from a bank account in the name of Jane Lister when she closed it down earlier that day. The ID, at least, had been good for that if nothing else.

She stared at herself in the mirror above the dresser. The irony of her false identity now being her *only* identity was not lost on her. Her parents were dead. She had no brothers or sisters. The only ID she had to prove who she was sat before her in a false name created by the authorities who had failed to make her safe.

"He is the only person who knows me for who I really am" she said softly into her reflection.

And with that, she set about piecing together the geography of where he had once abducted her, and where he must surely therefore collect her from now.

July 12th

39

9.38am

McMullen paced up and down in front of the white boards. "How the fuck did we miss it?" she snapped.

"Because we weren't looking for it" said Webber. "We had his flat, where all of his records showed he lived. It was his main residence so far as we, and anyone else, knew".

McMullen didn't respond. The *click-clack* of her rosary matched the pace of her strides.

"They're faxing through a redemption statement" now added Webber. "It will tell us all we need to know. Address. Account Number. Length of time he's owned it. Raz is getting on to the Land Registry for copies of the Land Register. It may show us something we don't already know".

"Like what?"

"Other mortgages secured on it. Secured loans could lead us to other accounts, other income. It might even show a co-owner. We may even get another lead out of it".

She stopped pacing up and down and stared at the computer screen. "How long?" she asked.

"They can't send it by email" he said. "They're faxing it. Fifteen minutes they said".

She thrashed the rosary back and forth over her hand. "We go straight there when we get the address. I don't want any local bodies on it. Not until I can gauge what we might have".

Webber frowned. "We don't even know where it is, yet" he protested. "All we know is that it's a mortgage account. It could be anywhere, and we don't have time or resources to go it alone".

"I know what I'm doing" she said, fixing her eyes on him. "If it's within our reach without too much time lost then we're going it alone".

Webber made his way over to the fax machine. There was nothing he could say. *Your daughter* he thought to himself *so that makes it your call.*

McMullen drew a long arc from Andrew Garner's picture on the white board to a blank space in the bottom right hand corner. He watched her write the words "second property" before she looked backed expectantly at him.

It was several minutes before the fax machine suddenly whirred into action. As the first page came through Webber snatched it from the tray. He scanned down the page.

"Brighton" he said. "It's a flat in Brighton".

He read aloud the address and McMullen wrote quickly.

"Right then" she said snatching up her jacket. "Let's get down there".

40

Midday

They parked several hundred meters down the road from the flat. McMullen killed the engine and checked her rear view mirror. DS Shah and another member of the team pulled up behind her.

"Don't get your hopes up over this one Claire" said Webber.

She bowed her head, her straight blonde hair falling around her face, creating a mask through which he could not see. She realised she was dressed all in black. That hadn't been a conscious decision. "If I thought for one moment she was in there, Joe, I would have done this the formal way and contacted Sussex HQ". She lifted her head. "But I don't think she's in there. In fact, it is precisely because I think she is somewhere else that I am doing all this covertly. We shouldn't be here without Sussex knowing, but I haven't got time to involve another force and its' hierarchy, and its' politics and its' procedures. I need to get a result on this quickly".

"Even at the cost of problems with evidence?"

"There won't be any problems with evidence" she said. "We will search the flat, do it properly, bag and catalogue everything and then I will let Sussex know. They can send their own forensics in. At worst they'll be pissed off but I need to ride the wave here. I need to get everywhere first and not let my daughter die because of politics, pen-pushing, admin and protocol. I don't want her to be the last thing on the fucking clipboard tick-box".

Webber nodded. "Fair enough".

The two other officers followed them as they approached the flat. It was accessed by a small flight of steps. There was no way of seeing into the flat. The curtains were drawn. There was no other visual access. She turned to Webber. "This is how we play it. We say we knocked but no-one answered, even though we all know we didn't knock".

"We don't have a warrant".

"We don't need one if we found the door already forced"

"If there is someone inside we're fucked".

"This flat is owned by a man who is now dead, If there *is* someone inside then *they* will be fucked, not us".

No-one else said anything.

She took one final look around and then Webber forced the door.

There was no sign of life inside. They moved quickly through the small flat – bedroom, bathroom, kitchen, lounge. Nothing. There was a door to the rear of the kitchen, but it led down another small set of steps and into an alleyway.

They set about searching the rooms. Drawers, cupboards, anything that looked like it held a compartment. They searched through papers, some boxes they found in a small utility area off the kitchen. There was nothing that gave them anything they could use.

The pictures in the lounge were of aeroplanes. Military, not civilian. There were more aeroplane pictures in the bedroom and from the ceiling hung several model air-fix 'planes. On the dresser to the side there was a large World War II bomber model. Webber took a closer look. "This has seen better days" he said, running his finger over an area of the wing that someone had coloured with a crayon to try and make it look like fire damage. "I used to do that" he said. "Try and make the thing look like it had flown through a few missions, only I used to use a lighter on the front of the wings to get the burn effect. I nearly set the place on fire once. Never heard the last of it". And then he was suddenly overtaken by the joys of childhood, and his daughter's voice and smile came to him.

No. Not here. Don't bring them into this world.

He turned away and began searching another cupboard, pulling a box toward him. Inside were programmes and trinkets from various RAF public events. "No porn" he said out loud to McMullen, still trying to centre himself.

"What the fuck does that have to do with anything?" she said.

"If this guy is to be treated as a possible accomplice to crimes involving the abduction of women, I would have expected him to have god knows what in his flat so far as offensive material goes".

"We have nothing that suggests a sexual element to these killings so far" she said. "No-one has been sexually assaulted despite opportunity".

Webber shrugged. "Even so, this is a guy who never married and who lives on his own. He's got no family, and his London life consisted of working all hours in the absence of evidence to the contrary. What did he do for female fun?"

"Abduct and torture women" she said flatly.

"That's my point" said Webber. "If he really was capable of that we would have seen some sort of connection through pornography or images or stuff he wants kept away from view, instead of...." He waved his hand almost disapprovingly, "aeroplanes. Christ. Most of us grow out of that shit and those who don't are generally not your serial killer types".

"You know the score" said McMullen. "Rule nothing in. Rule nothing out".

They took out a bundle of evidence bags and began to bag up items they thought of use. They were working in the dark so far as relevance was concerned. McMullen was taking pictures of each room when they were interrupted.

"What are you doing?"

A petite young woman stood in the doorway, staring apprehensively at them.

Webber froze. The first thing that hit him was the thought: *No Warrant.*

"Who are you?" asked McMullen.

"I want to know who you lot are first" she said, looking around, her nervousness seeping through into her voice. "And what's he doing?" she asked, pointing at Webber. "Why is he taking Andy's stuff?"

"Do you know Andrew Garner?" said McMullen.

"Andrew? No-one calls him Andrew, he hates it. Are you Police?"

Fuck thought Webber. *Fuck Fuck Fuck.*

"Not exactly" said McMullen.

What?! Webber couldn't help himself. He picked up the box and made for the car.

McMullen took the woman through to the lounge and asked her to sit down. "We work with Andy. I know I called him Andrew but that's because I couldn't be sure who you were". She smiled. "Whether you were friend or foe". She re-inforced the smile.

"Is Andy in trouble?" she said. "I've tried calling him so many times but this last week he hasn't answered".

McMullen thought back to the phone records. There had been no obvious repeat patterns, no regular numbers. Some re-occurred, but there was no evidence of heavy use of any one number. "Sorry, I didn't ask your name. My name is Claire. I am Andy's supervisor at work".

"I'm Paula Jackson. I'm, well…was, Andy's girlfriend… sort of. We're neighbours. I live in the flat below. I haven't heard movement up here for ages. I thought maybe he was back. You didn't answer my question though. Why are you here and not Andy? What's happened to him?"

Webber walked back to hear McMullen say "Andy hasn't been into work for a while and he isn't at his flat in London where he usually stays. We have explained everything to the Police but because he's a grown lad and everything they don't seem to be doing much. So we thought if we all came down here on our day off we might be able to find him here. But we didn't and now we don't know what to do".

Paula eyed them reservedly, still not sure what to make of them. "Well, he hasn't called me. If you see him tell him to let me know that he's OK. Ever since he's started to spend more time in London he's changed, you know. He used to be alright. But not so much these days".

"Why's that?" asked McMullen. "Is that our fault?". She said it jokingly, still smiling.

"No. The friend he had who caused all the problems wasn't from work. He was from the City. At least that's what he said. You could never know whether that guy ever told you the truth or not".

Webber sat down at the edge of the room, trying to minimise his impact and not disturb the woman's rhythm.

"What was his name?" asked McMullen.

She shook her head. "I don't know. But he was the reason Andy and I grew apart. At first Andy was always home from London, every chance he got. Then he stopped coming back and I had to look after his flat for him. You know, pop in and pull the curtains and stuff so it looked lived in. Then, when he did start coming back again every now and then, he had his friend with him. He never told me his name. They just used to call each other "Bro" and that was when I knew I was fucked. When two guys who aren't brothers start calling each other Bro it's cos they got something between themselves, or at least that's how I look at it. So I let myself drop out, you know? I still had a thing for him, the stupid bastard, not that he'd ever know it but he had a new friend and a new world".

"A new world?", said McMullen

"That's the reason why Andy and I finally stopped seeing each other. Infinity. It's a lap-dancing club down the other end of town. I told him if he wanted to do that shit he could keep it in London, but he said his friend had an image to keep up in London which is why he came down here to do it".

"Do what?"

"I don't know and neither do I want to know". She checked her watch. "Look, I got to go to work shortly". She picked up a pen from the table in front of them and wrote her number down on the back of an unopened letter. "If you do see him, tell him to give me a call about the flat. I want to give him my keys back, but I don't want to just shove them through the letter box., you know? I'm not that heartless".

McMullen took the number from her. "Thank you" she said. "I will".

The woman got up and left, acknowledging Webber with a polite nod on the way out.

He leapt over to the seat in front of McMullen where the woman had been sitting. "What the *fuck* are you doing!" he hissed.

McMullen fixed him with a hard stare. "What choice did we have? I haven't got time to piss about Joe, and you *know* no-one ever talks to the Police like that. I had to lie to her. If I had done it the formal way and told her we were Met officers, and that Andy was dead we would have got fuck-all out of her. We would have Sussex Constabulary swarming the place all pissed off and unco-operative and Sally would be that much closer to death. Fuck procedure, and fuck doing it right. This is my daughter we are talking about for fuck's sake".

He raised his hands. "Alright, alright, I understand, you know I do, and I will back you up, but you have got to start getting some proper procedure behind this because if you don't, and we do find something down here that we need to prosecute this fucker, you will have been the root cause of letting him off on a technicality. We don't have these procedures so one of us can act like Dirty Fucking Harry, we have these procedures so that when we drop the evidence on the CPS desk they can go in and get a fucking conviction where there needs to be one. Please don't screw that up, for Sally's sake if no-one else's".

She took a deep breath. "I know. I know you're right, but we have got to get something to go on. We just have to".

"Well, the first thing you need to do is to get the fuck out of here and back up to London".

"What? You heard what she said. We have to follow up that lead before we go anywhere".

"Did you not hear what I just said about procedure? You need to get back to London and square what happened here this afternoon with Sussex hierarchy. What she just said to you is evidence and we need it taken formally, and she needs to know the truth before we lose all goodwill and end up with a hostile witness. The second thing you need to do is go back to Andy's employer and his work colleagues and see if anyone knows whether that guy was close to anyone, whether it was through work or through something else".

"So what are you going to do?"

He took out his warrant card and handed it to McMullen. "I am going to trust you with that, because if I stay down here and find out what I can for you, and for Sally, then I can't be a police officer whilst I am doing it. You may not have gotten much right here this morning, but one thing you did get right is that people don't talk to the Police, least of all the people in the places where I am clearly going to have to go now. I will feed back to you what I get, but it will be up to you to clear the tracks for these things to be done formally through the Sussex force. I am happy to do it the way you want it done, but I will not carry the can for inadmissible evidence when we get to trial. I can get you what you need from here, unofficially, but you will have to find a way to make it official, and you can only do that from your rank, and from London, not here".

She took his warrant card from him. "Thank you, Joe" she said. "Not just for this, but for, you know".

For talking to the team when I was too choked to do it; For organising the station search when I was too clouded to do it; For taking the pain of my missing daughter when yours is already gone; For letting me hang myself on procedure in my desperation and yet pull me back up again....

"I know", he said.

41

1.38pm

Maria opened up the left-luggage box and placed the small plastic bag inside. The bag contained the driver's licence and passport in the name of Jane Lister, and a letter she had written to whoever might ultimately open the box. She locked it, and placed the key inside her jean pocket. There was only one thing left to do now: To check out.

On the journey back to the hotel she ran through the old sequence of events in her mind. When she had been found, when he released her at the end of her suffering, she was unconscious and naked on the street at Brompton Road…. But the disused station at Brompton Road had been searched during the investigation and found to be empty. Despite that, it remained in her opinion a place that he was familiar with, and a place that linked the two of them. She had no more of an idea where this man was than the Police had, but she knew the most effective place to start would be were it all ended last time. Maybe he wouldn't care. Maybe she would wander endlessly these London streets waiting to fall back into Hell. Maybe Sally was already dead, but none of it mattered anymore. She could not live this way, and if her fate was to end up lost and penniless, who would care? Until he was caught she would never have the chance to live, so what did death matter?

The nearest operational station to Brompton Road was South Kensington. The first body to be found three weeks ago was on the small stretch of tube over-ground line between Gloucester Road and South Kensington. Was this the sign? Is this part of the ritualistic smoke screen that forms the message? Does the horror always restart in the same place it last happened? Is this the law of the universe? Is this how she will be set free? People say that ghosts only walk the earth because their energy is imprinted upon the place they last suffered. Perhaps she can only achieve her freedom by walking the place she almost died? She felt frozen in time, and had never been able to move on. Going back to Brompton Road was something she had never done. Maybe this was overdue. Maybe closure, of sorts, was what this was all about for her.

So, yes. Brompton Road first, just to see, but then on to where the horror really first began. The place she was taken from.

At the hotel she took one last look around her room. Apart from the cash which she pushed into her pockets, there was nothing left of hers in the small space. She glanced at the bed, perhaps the last one she would ever sleep in, and picked up her jacket from the back of the chair.

At the reception desk she returned her key, and walked out onto the street with a sense of relief. She was free now. By going back, she had unchained her wrists.

She headed off in the direction of South Kensington tube station. She thought, briefly, about calling Webber, just to say that everything was fine, but in retrospect she didn't think he would be impressed with her or what she had done.

And to be honest, given that she had spent years faking herself and finally now felt as if she no longer had to, she didn't care what anyone thought of her. None of it mattered now.

And this left her with a nothingness. It made no difference what history said, she was only beholden now to the things she allowed into her personal space. And perhaps this was the problem: He was so endemic inside her now that she didn't know where she ended and where he began.

42

9.48pm

Webber spent the next two hours in a pub on the edge of town, before making his way down to the beachfront, taking in the freedom. He found himself a cheap hotel, paid in cash, then made his way into the main part of town where he settled in a bar and drank until he reckoned the underworld where stretching their drug-starved limbs and blinking bloodshot eyes into the early part of a late night.

He was more at peace here amongst the drinkers and the stag-parties and the screaming hen-night revellers than he had been anywhere else for many months. Even though he knew he could never escape his duty and that he was always a copper regardless of what his ID said, the freedom of not having his warrant card was more liberating than he had anticipated.

And that was because he was finally accepting a truth he had sought to deny since they died. He blamed the job for the fact that he wasn't there. He blamed the job for taking him half way across London, so far away that all he could do whilst they burned alive in the car was sit, dumbstruck, in the passenger seat of the area car, the blues and twos screaming in his ears, wondering why the people of London, those he sort to serve and protect every single day, would not now clear the road in front of him so that he could, at least, get to his *own* people before they were gone forever.

But he had been too late. And now they were irretrievably lost. And he blamed the Metropolitan Police for that. He and Maria had more in common than he had first thought.

And yet, the more the gin went down, the more he clenched his fists at the deeper truth that crept out of his darker recesses. It was him. He was the one he really hated. He was the one who had decided that they should make that particular trip themselves because he had wanted to keep back as much leave as he could, so they could finally make that family holiday of a lifetime.

He dug his fingernails into the palm of his clenched fist. Was it him? Or was it the job? Or was it both?

Or was it just Life with a Capital "L"? Was it just the shitty end of an inevitable destiny that befalls us all – we cannot control when or how death comes for us.

He left the bar, slipping his jacket on as he went. The evening had been warm but now, approaching midnight, there was an edge to the air that made him wear his jacket rather than carry it. He arrived at the front entrance to Infinity, and took his place in the short queue. Men joked with each other, strangely subdued he thought, as they stood before the small stretch of red carpet that spilled out onto the pavement. Two pairs of gold standposts with red rope hanging between them guided clients into the lobby, and two bouncers guarded the doorway, frisking the men before they entered.

Inside the lobby he paid the entrance fee, and made his way up the stairs. The music was loud but not so loud that conversation couldn't be heard. He was shown to a table and he ordered a beer. By the time it arrived he had already been "introduced" by one friendly dancer to her other friends, and he couldn't help but respond. Regardless of the nature of the place he was in, and the job he was here to do, he fell for the warmth and the hospitality. It didn't matter how many times he had been behind the scenes in the sex-trade in London during his career, picking up the pieces of the human cost that always haunted him, the illusion of attraction and the acceptability of money in amongst the lie, seemed to create a truth all of its' own. And suddenly he was in the machine, being greeted and encouraged and flirted with, and then, led by the hand to the private area he had asked for. It didn't matter which girl it was. He had to start somewhere.

In the half-light, drowned in a purple-hue, he sat back as she danced for him. After a few minutes she asked "Can I go on?" and he reached into his pocket taking out the fee for the service so far, a picture of Andrew Garner, and a fifty pound note.

"If you can tell me who this guy is, you won't have to dance for the extra money".

She frowned at him and stood bolt upright, the spell immediately broken.

"Before you shout for your manager, or reach for your baseball bat, I am a private investigator, hired by the man's wife to find him. You, this club, my presence here, none of it will ever be mentioned. I just want to know if you recognise him. He was local to the town, and he would have come in with a friend each time".

She started to put her clothes back on, and then sat down next to him, taking the photograph from him.

"No. I don't know him" she said.

He didn't object when she took the fifty pound note from him. "Do you know anyone else I could ask, or could you ask the other girls, backstage for me, perhaps?"

She considered him. "I guess you are a little too good looking to be a copper" she said.

"Thanks. Is that a yes?"

She nodded. "Regardless of what people might think of us, we are a good bunch at this club. We stick together. We get our fair share of dipsticks, but we also know what's what long term, you know what I mean? Provided there are no names, I'll ask".

"Thank you" he said.

They got up. "You will have to wait in the bar" she said.

She strode off, long slender legs seeming to glide her body across the floor despite the three-inch heels.

He went back to the bar area and bought another drink, turning to watch the pole-dancer performing on the impossibly small stage.

After fifteen minutes or so of being approached by beautiful girls and politely declining them, one of the bouncers came toward him.

"This way, Sir. Please".

"Why?"

"Club business" he said flatly, taking Webber by the arm.

He was led through to the back of the bar and then through a side door into a small, dimly light room. Another bouncer was scanning TV screens displaying the CCTV from the private area, the bar area, and the front entrance.

A tall, thin, dark-haired man smoking a cigarette entered the room. He smiled and extended his hand.

"I am David Laine" he said crisply. "I am the owner of the Infinity Club. I take great care of those who work for me, and even greater care of those who show an interest in them. Now, before I ask you your name I do sincerely hope that you will not claim to be from the Police. I have a very good working relationship with both the

Commissioner and the Local Authority and our place in this community is by way of mutual consent. That requires trust, constant attention to detail, and a hefty degree of openness. So if the Police were sending someone tonight, I would have known about it. This means that you are in the very last category of things I have to be aware of, and that is an acute awareness of the trigger points that fuck-up my delicate equilibrium".

He stepped in closer. "And you, my friend, look to me like a definite trigger point". He looked Webber up and down. "Miss R says you are a private investigator, looking for this man". He held up the photograph of Andrew Garner. "You have been hired by his wife to find him because he has disappeared. Do you wish to add anything to that?"

Webber shook his head.

"When did he disappear?" said the club owner.

"Three months ago"

"Last seen where?"

"Piccadilly Station". It was the first thing that came into his head.

"What's his wife's name?"

"Ann. Ann Garner"

"Children?"

"No"

"Tube or Main Line?"

"What?"

"Last seen in Piccadilly. Tube or Main Line"

"Ah… tube, why?"

"You said he was local"

"Yes"

"Address?"

"I am not at liberty to say"

He repeated the words. "Not at liberty to say, and yet you expect my female colleague, and her friends, to cough every last bit of information for a mere fifty pounds".

Webber didn't say anything.

"Tell me, Mr Investigator, what is your name?"

"James Lawrence"

"Of what agency?"

"Lawrence & Co"

"Do you have ID?"

"No"

He nodded at the bouncer who asked him to spread his arms and his legs whilst he was searched again. The club owner turned to a computer and googled the names he had been given.

He turned back to face Webber. "Nothing about you checks out Mr Lawrence. But I will tell you this. Your name, your presence here, and your questions will all be passed onto Sussex Police when I have my weekly meeting with them. We get a lot of people like you in here Mr Lawrence".

He paused. "But something troubles me".

He nodded to the bouncer who stepped aside and the club owner guided Webber to a small sofa where they both sat down.

"Miss R mentioned something to me that I shall be raising with the Police. However, on the basis that you are ballsy enough to come in here and put yourself on the line in such a manner I will tell you too. You mentioned that this man came to this bar with a friend. One of the colleagues of Miss R has already spoken to the Police about the man I think you are looking for, so I would imagine that you are already one step behind. However, this friend was seeking some rather, shall we say *bespoke* services, and whilst we do not encourage men to seek sex from our girls or others, we cannot avoid the fact that many men who visit us either ask our girls for sex or ask our girls where they can find sex. We are not as enlightened here as some of the other cities whether it be in England or on the Continent, but, ordinarily, a man should, if he wishes, have the option of full sex after the *appertif* of the lap-dance, don't you agree? Anyway, as offering such a service is a step too far for my own tastes, we do nevertheless pass on details, where we consider the man to be genuine, to others in the sex trade who may be able to help".

"What are you saying?" he asked, not following what the man was trying to tell him.

"If you go to this address and say that David Laine from Infinity sent you, then I think you will find a lady there called Marianne who will be worth talking to".

"And how do I know you aren't sending me to a beating, just to teach me a lesson".

He eyed Webber through a frown. "I think the man you are looking for Mr Lawrence is a rapist, with a deep hatred of women. Leaving people like that active in my sort of industry does not make for good business. Marianne is a brave and yet difficult woman. She caters for many, and she has an ability to weed out those who are genuine from those who are not. I think the Police already know about all of this, and your behaviour tonight suggests to me that you cannot be from the Police because you are coming across as absolutely bloody clueless. But I cannot rule out the fact that you might be genuine, and as I am a man of the community, and the gentleman in this picture is part of my community, I will give you a break. If anyone in this industry is going to know where your man is, it will be Marianne. And if it is true that you have been instructed by this man's wife, and this man is now missing, I can only suggest that she, and you, prepare for the worst, based on the company he was keeping".

43

11.31pm

Webber left the club at his own pace, grateful to avoid the ignominy of being physically thrown out, but even as he put distance between himself and the queue of men on the pavement, he knew he was still being watched by the bouncers on the door as he walked away up the hill and out of town.

He felt tired now. He also felt under threat and exposed. He wasn't used to operating without the full force of the Met behind him, and he certainly wasn't used to operating without the due process of law. McMullen was right. The Police might always get there in the end, because the weight of the law and the persistent plea-bargaining and all the other pressures of being out in the light come into play… eventually. But here, here in the dark, here on the streets in the early hours of the morning, without a warrant card, an area car or the hope of salvation in sight, people *talk*. And they exercise power too. The power struggles between the serving officers and those who they seek to apprehend are one thing. But the power struggles that go on under the radar between those that are being traced is quite different.

And here he was. In the no-mans land of civilian life. Trying to extract information without a badge and without any credibility, and the only thing that had gotten him anything tonight was the pity of an underworld club owner who considered him clueless.

I won't be fucking clueless when I'm back raiding your red-fucking carpet establishment for drugs and prostitution and taking your house and car under the Proceeds of Crime Act, you arrogant shit...

….. And yet even in his weakened state, full of too much gin and full of too much anger at not being able to pull rank in the club and radio for back-up, he knew that wasn't how it all worked. Everyone was inter-linked. We scratch their back, they scratch ours.

Business is business.

Christ, the fucking club owner knew more than he did about a man they had been chasing for the last three weeks – a man the Met *lost* first time round.

He looked down at the map on his i-phone, the flashing blue pintop, and turned into the street that the phone told him was his destination.

Yeah, that's right Joe, wander around the back streets, clearly pissed with your i-phone on show.

He checked the address under a street-light, then against the nearest doorway, and then crossed the road to the odd numbers, weaving his way down to two-hundred-and-one.

It was an innocuous looking façade. Much like all the other houses in the street. It could just as well have housed a family of four, rushing out every morning, jumping into the car for work and school.

Only it didn't.

Fuck knows what it housed.

He walked up the small run of steps to the black and white frontage. He pressed the doorbell. He looked around the small, discreetly lit enclosure, created by an archway above and semi closed sides at the top of the stairs.

The intercom came alive. "Yes?"

"My name is James Lawrence" he said. "David Laine from the Infinity club sent me".

He heard nothing more until the door buzzer rang out. He pushed it. It was much heavier than he anticipated. *Steel?* And went inside.

The interior was brightly lit. A black and white marble mosaic on the floor stretched from one end to the other and three rooms, doors closed, branched off from the main lobby. A spiral staircase, marble steps and a black handrail, swirled up and round to the first floor. A chandelier lit the entrance lobby and there was a small, wrought iron occasional table inside the door, with an old fashioned antique phone on it and a note pad.

He wasn't sure what to do, so he stood there, waiting, taking in his surroundings.

A well built man, late twenties or early thirties, emerged from one of the rooms. He was dressed in a dinner suit, as if he had just exited from an evening party.

"Mr Lawrence" he said in assured tones. "May I take your jacket?"

Joe offered up his jacket, eyes darting from closed door to closed door.

"May I get you a drink?" asked the man.

"Gin. Straight"

"Of course. If you would like to take a seat in the waiting room, Marianne will be down to see you shortly".

He turned the handle of the door he was ushered toward, still expecting to be met with the official beating he was sure was coming.

Inside was an old fashioned study, complete with floor to ceiling bookshelves, all fully stocked, and the old fashioned ladder-runner that slides from one end to the other allowing access for books at the top level.

He sat sown on the leather sofa. Classical music was playing. There was a fire-place, unlit, in front of him and the ceiling boasted two chandeliers.

The man entered the room with a glass of gin on a silver tray, placing it on the table beside him. He glanced down at it. No half-measures here, he thought. And then, from behind the man with the tray came a tall, slender dark-haired woman. He guessed she was in her late-forties, but still boasting an hour-glass figure, and youthful looks. She had thick, jet-black hair, hanging around her shoulders in large heavy ringlets. She wore a black bodice that gripped her waist, making it look unusually small, and yet bolstered her breasts making them look disproportionally large for her body. She wore fish-net stockings, black high-heels, and had a black and gold silk dressing gown on, with a dragon design on the back and sleeves. As she held out her hand, saying in deep, engaging tones, "I am Marianne", he looked straight into clear blue eyes that unnerved him.

"Hi. I'm James Lawrence"

Marianne sat down next to him. "It's OK, James", she said, smiling. "I know that is not who you are".

He picked up his drink. "Why does everyone keep telling me I am not who I say I am?" he said, jovially, trying to lighten the mood. Marianne had a heavy presence and he felt intimidated by it. It was as if he had entered another world. One where he could do anything and yet could still walk back out into the street as if nothing had happened.

She laughed, a restrained, deceptive laugh. Warm, but yet somehow detached. "We are all different people at different times" she said. "What matters is only who we are right here, right now".

She turned to face him. "I am expecting a client in a few minutes" she said "and I will be engaged then for several hours, probably until dawn. David considers it safe to talk to you, and therefore I am happy to do so".

"Thank you" he said.

He took out the picture of Andrew Garner. "Do you know this man?" he said.

She didn't turn to look at the picture. "David has told me who you are calling about" she said coldly. "We do not have to dance around the subject".

He put the picture away. "Would you be kind enough to tell me what you know?" he said.

She smiled at him and reached forward, putting her hand on his knee. "You seem like a fish out of water, Mr Lawrence" she said. "I will tell you what I know, which is no more than what I told the Police, and then we can both be on our way".

She sat back. "The man you seek spent a lot of time at the Infinity club. When I say a lot of time I mean he became known as a weekend regular. Most of the clients that pass through Infinity are transient. Brighton is a popular place for stags and hens and it is, to a small degree, a party town, even though there is far more to it than that. But, for better or worse, it has developed this reputation amongst some. So it is rare to find the same faces back in every weekend because it is really only brothels who have regulars. Lap-dancing is an expensive past-time if you do it every week. Your friend would have to have had money and lots of it, and the girls there figured the money was not coming from the man in your picture, but from the friend he brought along each time".

"And were they right?" he said

She considered him for a moment. "Why do the Police not know about you asking these questions, Mr Lawrence?"

He shrugged. "David Laine called me clueless. Maybe that explains it".

She continued to stare at him. "Well, anyway", she continued, "he asked the girls for sex every time he was there despite the management being clear about their policy on that. Then, one night, he freaked one of the girls out saying that he wanted to fuck her like it was rape, but that it wouldn't be, he just wanted to know what it was like to rape someone"

Webber felt his guts churn.

"That sort of thing has no place anywhere. Do you understand that? Regardless of what we do and what we are, from the most casual of student lap-dancers trying to pay for college through to people like me who cater for the more bizarre, we do not tolerate blatant attacks be they verbal or physical".

"What happened?" said Webber.

"David had him in. The man said that he was from the City, that he had gotten carried away and that he really didn't mean it and he offered David money. The guy had plenty of cash on him, more than you would expect even from City boys. David didn't believe a word of it, and it was clear the man had no remorse".

She got up and crossed to the unlit fireplace. "I am not always proud of my history" she said, "but one thing I have learned is that I am what I am, and I cannot ever leave that behind me. This is why I still do what I do. I have always been this way, and even when I try and leave it behind I cannot. My history and involvement with prostitution is like a scar that I cannot ever heal or remove. So I decided to make it work for me. To build up a reputation for the bizarre but to have only clients with money who had a lot to lose themselves so we could ensure mutual anonymity. On that basis, David sent him to me".

She turned to face him. "At first, the man was crestfallen. He said that his childhood had been a difficult one and that whilst he was successful in what he did for a living, he could never forget that he was an orphan and, because of that, he always questioned whether people truly loved him or not, which he claimed explained his lap-dancing addiction and his outburst that night at Infinity".

"What did you tell him?"

"I told him that if he was looking for love then he was looking in the wrong place whether it be here or whether it be Infinity".

"What happened then?"

"He said he just wanted someone to love him, and that he would pay handsomely for it. I told him what my main clientele wanted, and that I would provide that, and, indeed, had provided far more than that in the past, and I gave him my price and he agreed to it. We then embarked on a long client-escort sexual relationship where he would call in advance, arrange a time, when he arrived we would talk, like you and I are now, then we would have sex, and then I would not see him for maybe a week or two, but it was never more than two weeks. And I don't mind telling you, Mr Lawrence, I am expensive. I am expensive because of what I am asked to provide – total anonymity in a high class and under-the-radar environment".

"So what went wrong?"

"Over time, his requirements changed. I won't bore you with the details, but the price went up and up"

"I need to know what it was the man was after. It might explain where I will find him, or where I will find this man". He held up Andrew Garner's picture.

She sat down heavily in a single seater, high-backed leather chair and crossed her legs and her arms. "He beat me. That's the bottom line. He asked me to simulate rape, just like he asked the girl at Infinity. Like I said, I am not proud of what I have been, but I vowed a long time ago I would make it work for me, and I did. But this man…. He made me feel damned in the end. There was no price I could put on what he wanted that he couldn't afford to pay, and for the first time since I was first dragged into this trade…." She broke off and stood up, composing herself quickly. "… I lost control. For the first time in ages the one thing I said would never happen again happened. He was the one in control, despite all this". She waved her hand at the décor, the building, the situation.

"How bad was it?" asked Webber.

She turned away. "Bad" she said firmly. "Pretty. Fucking. Bad".

"What did you do?"

"I broke the covenant and went to the Police".

"And what did they say?"

"They said they needed to catch him at it. And they wanted his name. Neither of which I could give them. I believed for a while that if I gave him up, regardless of what that would mean for me, then he would find me and kill me. Plus I didn't ever know his name. He just insisted on having no name".

She sat back down, finally regaining herself. "And that, Mr Lawrence, is the story of your friend's friend. After I told him that he was not welcome here anymore and that if I ever saw him again I had CCTV recordings available for the Police, he stopped calling. It was as if he had never been part of my professional life"

"Did that surprise you, given how scared you were?"

"I made a mistake, Mr Lawrence" she said, engaging his eyes. "I made the mistake many of us make".

"Which was?"

"Just because the client is paying for the service, doesn't mean that he can abuse it. There is a price for everything, I understand that, and I also understand that I am the backstop for such things, often accepting the backstop in return for money. But money cannot buy you everything, Mr Lawrence. And we all know what happens when your money cannot get you what you want".

"What's that?"

"If you want it badly enough, you just take it. By force if you have to"

He finished the rest of his drink. "Is there anything else you can remember about this man that might help me find him, or find the guy in the picture? I think that if I find the man who hurt you, I might just find the man I was asked to trace".

She smiled. "I told you, I didn't know his name, and all I know is that he was from London. He always paid me in cash and I never phoned him – he always phoned me".

"I see. Were there any physical markings on his body? Moles, scars, birthmarks, tattoos, or similar?"

She bowed her head. "There was a tattoo. I remember that" she said. "It was a pair of snakes, entwined together, with wings and a crown on top"

"Can you draw it for me?" he asked

"I will draw it for you, Mr Invistigator, but only on the basis that the business between you and I is over, and that you do not come back here again. Is this agreed?"

"Yes," said Webber. "Agreed"

July 13th

44

12.23pm

Maria stood on the opposite side of the street to the wine bar. The wine bar which had once been the mecca for anyone of any gravitas within the model industry. But that was a long time ago. Nineteen years in the life of a trendy café bar is enough for it to change beyond all recognition – nothing but a reflection of passing fashion. The trends which once exhalted it, ultimately, are the trends which bring about its' downfall.

She took a deep breath. In her left hand she clutched the mobile that she prayed would ring. Why hadn't Webber called? Why hadn't he let her know he would be there, with the full force of the Met just a radio message away? Had McMullen refused to sanction the call? Was her exit from Police custody considered inglorious and petulant? Was this her punishment? To be left alone to go it alone because that is all that is deserved? Perhaps it was better this way – better that she didn't know. Better that she walked in, believing herself to be alone and operating outside of the Met Machine, so that when he looked into her eyes he saw that she was telling the truth – that she really was afraid that no-one was coming for her.

So why do it? She thought. *Why go in there. Why go in there and answer the message. Why go in and say 'Yes, I understand that it will end exactly where it began'.* It was *because she had no choice. It was because she had to bring it to an end. Maybe the Police would succeed this time where last time they failed. But what if they don't? What if he disappears the way he disappeared last time. What then? How will she live then?*

She bent down and touched the back of her calf, checking the position of the hunting knife taped to her leg, covered by her jeans. Seconds was all he needed to disable her, but seconds were all she needed to pull the knife. Serrated edges. Doing damage on the way in, and more damage on the way out.

She made her way across the street, keeping her eyes on the large glass frontage of the bar, watching for someone sitting alone, someone with no real reason to be there. As she reached the door she looked up and down the street, eyes darting from one face to another as London went about its' business. In anyone else's world, just another day. In hers, an historical anniversary that served to remind her that free will doesn't always last. Sometimes Life leaves us only one option.

She went into the bar and walked slowly over to a table in the window. As she sat down she scanned the faces of the customers within. Mostly couples, some groups of friends. No-one alone.

The waitress came over. Maria ordered a glass of wine, nothing else, and she sat back in her seat, her right foot gently touching the back of her left calf for reassurance.

Was this madness? Had she got it all wrong? If she was wrong, then what was the point of the message. What was the point of being told that things will end exactly where they began?

The waitress yelped as she bumped into a man heading toward the table from a different direction. There was an exchange of apologies, the contents of the tray almost having fallen, and then she placed the wine on the table, smiling as she moved swiftly away.

And there he was.

She took a sharp intake of breath.

"Hello, Maria"

He was around six feet tall, jet black hair, greying at the sides, wearing black T-shirt and black jeans. He looked slim, sinewy. She thought of the strength that there must be in his arms to pin down, to restrain. To hurt. And then there were the piercing blue eyes.

Cold eyes. Dead eyes...

...And the scar that ran from under his right eye down to his jawbone in one continuous arc.

He sat down opposite her. The waitress returned quickly. He ordered a glass of Merlot, but didn't take his eyes from Maria as he placed his order. It was as if the waitress was not there.

There was a silence as they stared at each other. She kept her hands under the table, resting on her knees, not just because it was closer proximity to the knife, but because she didn't want the shaking to give her away. Eventually, she managed to get the words out, hoping to God that her voice didn't break as she spoke.

"What you have done is very stupid. The Police have me under surveillance. Say what you have to say. You only have a matter of minutes, and then you will be banged up where you belong you sick bastard".

"You lie so well, Maria".

She held his gaze.

The waitress put his wine glass in front of him saying, "stay sitting down" as she did do. She was smiling. "You're safer there than moving about".

He smiled back at her. "My apologies" he said, handing her a twenty pound note to cover their bill. "I expect I was blinded by beauty".

She rolled her eyes at Maria and made her way back to the bar to get on with her job.

He took hold of his glass, touching it gently against Maria's. "A toast to old friends?" he said, still staring at her.

"Fuck you" she said softly.

She drew one hand from her knee and picked up her glass, sipping it slowly. "You don't know I'm lying. Being here is as good as turning yourself in".

He savoured the taste of his wine, and looked out of the window. He spoke matter-of-factly, as if reciting something old and boring to him. "The building has two entrances and exits. The front, which is too obvious, and the rear, which is accessible in a hurry through the arch behind the bar and the kitchen, provided the element of surprise prevents the staff from intervening. There is also a small unbarred window in the men's toilets which leads out into a passageway to the side of the building, and the same within the women's toilets, although that window leads out into the rear yard, a few feet from the back door. Deliveries come and go through the side passageway because the traffic wardens turn a blind eye to the brief obstruction caused by the vehicles. If the Police were here to seal the exits there would be obvious signs at all these exit points. There are none. And the final confirmation I needed was the look in your eyes when I sat down. If the Police really were here to arrest me, they would not risk you being harmed should I fail to escape, so there would have been a plain clothes officer somewhere in here, and you would never have resisted glancing over at them every now and then from the second I sat down".

He turned his attention back to her. "And you haven't".

He watched her take a bigger sip of wine. "Your hand shakes slightly" he continued, "which explains why you hid your hands when I first sat down, but you are drinking with your left hand, which is odd because I know you are right handed. This must mean that you need to keep your right hand free for some reason. This suggests a concealed weapon, probably a knife, as the heat of the July sun makes jackets too suspicious, and you have no handbag with you, so whatever you have it most likely isn't a gun. Although I would not have thought it beyond you to acquire one, you are not that stupid. You may want me dead, but you do not want to have come here to meet with me, having left behind all Police protection, carrying a gun, because that, in anyone's analysis, is pre-meditated murder, and you have motive Maria, in bucket loads, and I know you don't want to go to jail for me because that would mean…" he leaned in close to her "that would mean I won".

He sat back in his chair and sipped his wine.

Noticing her glass was almost empty the waitress came over but Maria ushered her away before she could speak.

Why the fuck isn't Webber here….

"Think what you want" she said. "I am here because I want this to be over. I want to end the way you taunt me". Suddenly she felt weak, exposed. "I want you to stop".

He laughed. "It does not stop, Maria. Not for you, not for me, not for anyone. It cannot stop. It is…. inevitable that this goes on. It is part of the natural cycle. Don't you understand? There are millions of people out there who are all sick but they do not know it. My work, Maria, is never-ending".

She was starting to feel sick and she didn't know why. She could feel a bead of sweat running down her neck, but the café was air-conditioned. She looked down at her hands, which had stopped shaking, but they were blurring around the edges. She blinked away the tear-fluid, but the vision was worse.

She looked up at him, frowning, as if struggling to find something to say. She was struggling to think.

She watched him sip his wine.

The wine....

She looked down at the empty glass. The waitress glided between the tables.

Before he sat down... the collision with the waitress... the tray....

The wine...

She looked up at him, her heart-racing and her breathing becoming laboured. "You fucking..." she leant forward to draw the knife but her left side lost all strength and she fell from her chair toward the floor. People gasped as he leapt forward to catch her, and then he hauled her to her feet. She tried to speak but her words were indecipherable and she couldn't fight the haze that was slowly engulfing her ability to move.

Oh God... No...

He waved away assistance, making light of his companions condition. Everyone agreed that fresh air was best and that it was probably the heat of the day that had caused the problem.

People care, but they don't want the burden of caring. They are always happy to let someone else take the responsibility. And in that simple example of human group behaviour, the only people that could have stopped Maria's abduction simply sat back and watched her drinking partner taking her away, ignorant of the truth of what they were seeing.

45

2.32pm

"But there was no sexual element to these crimes" protested McMullen. "You are going up a blind alley".

Webber was rubbing his head, ear pressed to his mobile, sitting in his hotel room, hand cradling a cup of black coffee.

"I know there is no sexual element. That wasn't what I was saying. I was just telling you what the woman said. Did you get my photo-message?"

The previous night, *or was it early that morning*, he had taken a picture of the hand sketched tattoo from Marianne and sent it to McMullen. For the last six hours she had been trying to find a match.

"Yes" she said. "I got your message at 9am. What the fuck were you doing until 9am? Anyway, we got a match, eventually, earlier this afternoon. The best guess based on what the woman drew is that it represents the badge of the Royal Air Force Paramedic Unit".

He sat upright and stared at himself in the mirror. "The model fucking aeroplanes" he said.

"Yes. I have requested a list of the current, and ex, MOD employees of that unit country-wide".

"Andrew wasn't RAF. He was straight as a die electrician born and bred".

"Yes, but we're not looking for him though, are we. He's a statistic now".

"Did you have any luck with Sussex over the club owner?"

"Apart from the fact that they will take your face from CCTV and ask why the Met are sending officers for lap-dancing training?"

"I was on leave, if you remember. I just got carried away. Isn't that the story?"

"I know. Initial indications are that they did have a report logged that matched what you described but that it wasn't taken any further. For them to get involved there has to be a crime and apart from prostitution – for which they were never going to arrest her because they consider she keeps a lot of stuff off the streets that otherwise they would have to deal with - there was no crime, well, apart from alleged GBH, but for that to have gone any further she would have had to have co-operated, and she didn't. So it was nothing more than another log on an ever-increasing log of miscellaneous misdemeanors from a faceless public".

"She seemed genuinely frightened by the guy" he said.

"Not frightened enough to have him taken off the streets".

"Nature of the beast, I guess" he said. "As long as he was off her patch he was someone else's problem".

"I take it you're on the next train back to London" she said.

"This afternoon, why?"

"Because if those bastards at the MOD don't have a list available by the time you get here, we are going down there mob handed. You've got two hours".

He glanced down at his watch. "We are not going to get there today" he said, wincing at the pain in his head.

"Just get back here" she said curtly.

July 14th

46

9.03am

She awoke to cold and to darkness. She could feel the harsh cutting of metal against her wrists and ankles. Her head was throbbing and she felt pain almost everywhere. Not the stabbing type of the first attack all those years ago, but a dull pain, a new pain, pulsating within her body.

As her eyes adjusted she could still see nothing more than the dark around her. There were no shapes, no structures that she could make out. Just a vast blackness.

"Hello?" she said, tentatively, but the word sounded hollow and simply rang out in the nothingness before her.

She felt around with her hands and as she moved she heard that awful sound of chains on stone. "Oh, God" she whispered. "No…"

But it was what you wanted. You wanted this.

Metal bands clasped her wrist and ankles, each one attached to a chain. She used her fingers to feel along the length of one attached to her wrist. It ended like it had done before: at a metal ring driven into the tiled wall behind her.

She wept as she felt her way along each of the chains. Each one ended in the same way.

She slumped to the ground and sobbed. It was only then, as she drew her knees to her chest and wrapped her arms around them, that she realised she was naked.

She cried aloud. Her sobs disappeared into the void. She buried her head in her arms, hugging herself. She had lost her chance to end it. He had won now. She was back where she had been nineteen years before, and this time she was not going to be set free.

Then she heard the door open. She looked up and forced herself to her feet. There were footsteps, and then a searing light hit her. She raised her arms to shield her eyes, turning her face away.

She didn't hear anything more. Just the low hum of the generator that powered the spotlights. She could feel their heat on her skin, exposing every last inch of her naked body.

She tried to see in front of her, holding her hands to her eyes. "Show yourself you bastard!" she shouted. "You have me now, so show yourself!"

There was only silence.

"Taking a good look, I hope?" she spat. "Well it will be your last, you sick fuck."

"Ssshhhh….", he said.

She heard more footsteps and the jangle of keys.

Then his voice came again. "You are recovering from a large dose of Rohypnol and Heroin. Drink the water in the bottle beside you".

With her head bowed against the light and her arms still raised to shield her eyes, she glanced around her. Her back was pressed up against the stone wall, but a few feet away to her right she saw it. A plastic unmarked bottle.

"Why should I!" she screeched. "It's probably fucking poison!"

"That is all" he said flatly.

She heard the keys. "NO!" she screamed. "Don't leave me here you bastard! Don't you fucking leave me here!"

The lights went out and she heard the door slam and the locks turn methodically one by one.

"NO!" she screamed, sinking to her knees, sobbing. "NO!"

47

9.57am

McMullen took the steps of the MOD building two at a time, striding into the spacious reception area and showing her warrant card.

"Yesterday I requested a list of RAF Paramedic Personnel. The request was part of an ongoing and urgent Police operation. I need to speak immediately please to the people compiling that list".

The woman at the reception desk was as polite as she could be. "May I take your name".

"Detective Chief Inspector Claire McMullen. This is Detective Inspector Joseph Webber"

"And with whom were you dealing in respect of the request please. There are obviously many departments".

McMullen stared at her. "Flight Squadron Leader Philip Baker" she said, not taking her eyes off the woman.

"Thank you. If you would like to wait for a few moments I shall see who is available to see you".

McMullen pursed her lips but refused to move. Webber took her arm. "Why don't we wait over here" he said in hushed tones. "Pissing everyone off and making a scene won't get us any closer. You know what the MOD is like to deal with. It's all three week waits and funny handshakes".

She let herself be drawn back toward the entrance, but still stood facing the front desk.

"We haven't got time to be pissed around, Joe" she said.

"And we aren't being pissed around. Jesus, we requested a personnel list only a few hours ago. If we had the same request directed at us it would take the same amount of time. They don't just dish out this stuff to order, you know".

After several minutes a small but muscular man in an RAF uniform appeared. "Detective Chief Inspector" he said, extending his hand. "Flight Squadron Leader Phil Baker. Perhaps you and your colleague would care to come this way?"

He was gracious in an obvious attempt to put them at ease. Webber made a point of catching McMullen's eye to re-inforce the *stay-calm* approach.

They were led through a series of corridors before taking the lift to the fourth floor. Once inside the offices of the Squadron Leader McMullen pressed her point home.

"I am sorry to badger you in this manner" she said, "but there are a number of issues I cannot really discuss openly at present, all of which hang on how quickly we can have that list of RAF Paramedic employees"

Baker sat down and gestured to the two of them to do the same. "The list is under preparation Detective Chief Inspector, I assure you, but I think I am also entitled to know whether one of the serving officers might be under suspicion of something? There is, of course, also the issue of the Military Police, whom I suspect you have not yet contacted".

She shifted in her seat. "There wasn't time" she said. "Which is why I went straight to you".

"And I understand that" said Baker. "But I can only respond quickly if I have full co-operation". He was smiling as he said it. He knew full well that he had them over a barrel.

She relayed the full story to him, leaving out exactly how they came to know about the tattoo but confirming nevertheless that it was more than likely their main suspect carried the tattoo described.

"You know that the list, once we have completed it, will only show current and ex-serving officers who served in that particular role, don't you? It is not standard practice for all RAF paramedic staff to tattoo themselves with the regimental wings"

"I understand that" said McMullen. "But we have to start somewhere".

"Very well" concluded Baker. "If you would like to take a seat in the waiting area outside I shall contact you as soon as the list is available. I would not expect to wait much more than another hour or so. We are aware of the urgency of the request".

"Thank you" said McMullen, getting to her feet.

They took their seats in the waiting area. Webber drew two plastic tumblers of water from the cooler and handed her one. "I don't know about you but my throat's as dry as a bone".

"That's because you've been on the piss all night" she said, disparagingly.

"Maybe, but it got us here didn't it? And that's a damn sight farther than we had gotten ourselves so far".

She stared out of the window at London passing by below. "Sally is out there somewhere" she said. "Probably wondering whether she is going to live or die".

"We'll get her back, and we'll get him along the way. You have to believe that".

"Maria didn't believe it" she said. "Maria called time on us and on the investigation and went her own way".

"She had her reasons. For the record, I think they were the wrong reasons, but you know how things are. We all have to make our own way in life. She had a lot to live with after what happened to her, and then suddenly there it all was again, happening right before her eyes. Anyone in that position would freak out. It was not a judgement on us".

"Wasn't it?" said McMullen, still staring out the window. "We've been all through the likely underground locations and we can't find him anywhere. He's got to be close because the time between Cathy Norris' release and the abduction of my daughter were so tight that he had to have held her under our noses somewhere here in London. And yet, despite everything she gave us as to where she had been held, we got fuck all from Operation Honeycomb".

He scrunched up his plastic cup and threw it in the bin. "We are closer now Claire than we have ever been. If we get nothing immediate from the lists we at least have an indentifying mark and, thanks to the Brighton leads, a description of the killer. Somehow, somewhere, Andrew Garner is linked to the guy not just because he knows him, but because of some link to the RAF. Look at the memorabilia and the model aeroplanes. We are close now Claire, we have to be. We just have to keep plugging away".

Eventually, Flight Squadron Leader Baker emerged from his office with a sealed brown envelope.

McMullen nearly tore his hand off when she took it from him.

48

11.42pm

She didn't know how long she had been there before he came back. It could have been a day. It could have been more. She rapidly lost the concept of time. There was no day. No night. Just the never ending darkness and her fitful sleep in amongst the tears. She resisted the water initially. Why should she preserve herself just for his purpose? But then thirst got the better of her, and, perhaps, a survival instinct. Ridiculous, she thought, that her instinct should be to survive. Survival amid futility. The irony of life.

She was laying on the ground, cold and shivering when he returned. She didn't get up at the sound of the key. This was an act of defiance. If he would not show his face then she would not perform for him.

The lights came on and she didn't move. Her hands were already covering her face. Her own touch brought her comfort.

She heard his footsteps, the heat of the lights, and nothing else only that low hum of the generator.

For a while there was just silence. She tried to see what was happening through the slits between her fingers but the lights were too bright. Instead she listened, intently, for sounds of movement, for clues as to what might become of her now.

"At last" he said, loudly. "The two become one".

His voice was strong, bold. Not as deep as before, and he sounded more agitated this time.

She didn't reply. She just lay there, waiting.

"I thought you may have something to say to me, Maria. Something pertinent. It has been so long".

"Fuck you" she said quietly.

He laughed. "Yes, of course. Ever the spirited one, aren't we? You know, I had to admire you back then when we were last together, Maria. You always believed that you would live, didn't you? You fought so hard mentally against the gradual, inevitable decline of your mind".

She said nothing.

"Captivity is such a strange thing, isn't it? A mental battle, rather than a physical one. To have control over one's mind is so admirable. Darkness, a deprivation of the senses, a shutting down of the physical body, all these things lead us to our final destination – our mind. It is our mind that makes us who we are, Maria, not our body. Our bodies are a distraction. They make others misread us. They make other people form assumptions which really are just not correct. And then when we speak, Maria, we have to unpick all the mistaken beliefs that the other person has formulated by simply looking at us".

There were more footsteps. "First impressions last, it seems, Maria".

"I thought you were a sick-fuck the first time and I still thing you are a sick-fuck now".

"You see!" he said, as if he had proven some essential point. "That is exactly what I mean".

"You are insane!" she shouted. She was getting angry, and frightened. She didn't want this. She didn't want to engage with him. She didn't want him inside her head like he had been before. She would not be able to end it that way. He would defeat her if she let him inside that deeply.

She forced herself to her feet, shielding her eyes all the while. " I never thought about what happened to me after I escaped, you know" she said. "After I was gone from your prison, you were also gone from my mind. After I was free, you ceased to exist. You were nothing. You were exactly what you said you were in the letters: The wind, blowing past me and totally irrelevant".

He stepped out from behind the spotlights. "Then perhaps it is time you were reminded of that relevance" he said. "We are not alone here, Maria".

She struggled to see his face but she could only make out the shape of him with so much light behind him. "What do you mean?" she said, wary now she could see his presence.

"I have another guest here" he said. "But she is not faring as well as you".

He moved back behind the lights, and then said, "By the way, Maria. You did not escape last time. I released you. There is a world of difference between the two".

He turned off the lights and she was plunged into darkness. She heard the three locks being turned and then silence. Just the dying heat of the lights against her skin.

49

2.48pm

The team assembled in the incident room, each with a list of names in front of them from certain sections of the alphabet.

"This list" began McMullen, "is every serving officer, both male and female, both current and ex, who has ever served in the role of paramedic in the RAF".

She pointed to the tattoo picture, now a full blown life-size artwork taken from MOD records. It showed the twin snakes with the RAF wings set behind them and the Royal Crown sitting above them. "The reason why we are pursuing this as a legitimate lead is because the suspect clearly has knowledge of human anatomy and also of drug use, be it combinational use of drugs or how to administer them. There must be some basic medical training sitting behind this. Look at how David Sachs and his lover were first attacked. The physical aspect of that attack would not be a bad fit for military training. David Sachs is six-feet tall and yet his attacker disabled him and controlled him quickly enough to get a syringe administered to him".

She turned to the pictures of the items taken from Andrew Garner's flat. "Look at the items taken from the flat in Brighton. Sussex Police are still concluding their forensics" she glanced momentarily at Webber, "but we already know that he was an RAF nut. What connects him to our suspect? Why did our suspect have to kill the man who was essentially his accomplice? Some have even described them as friends. What strikes me about all of this is that we haven't seen a body – save for those recovered during the disused station search – since Garner was found killed. Garner was numbered fourteen. We still haven't seen number fifteen. Is this because he can no longer get access to the tunnels without Garner? All of this needs to be in the back of our minds as we work through the list".

She turned to face the team. "We are looking for anyone resident in London. Anyone who has left the service recently, but who was also part of the service nineteen years ago. Just keep an open mind".

They all set about their tasks whilst she seated herself next to Webber. "There are fucking hundreds" she said to him.

Webber nodded. "Some are UK resident, some have gone abroad. Some are in the NHS for fuck's sake. How easy would it be to miss him? What if he has jumped ship and we should be looking at NHS personnel instead?"

She shook her head. "We can only work with what we've got".

"I know. But even with this list we haven't got jack shit. What do you think they're going to find? Like the guy at the MOD says. Even if we find a list of potentials in there that doesn't mean each one of them carry the tattoo".

"All the time we fuck about on this, Joe, the less time Sally has to live".

He frowned. "I am trying to think about resources. Being busy doesn't always mean we are actually getting anywhere does it?"

"Meaning?"

"Meaning we have a list of potential suspects now that is ridiculously long and even if we shave it down we will spend the next few days and weeks running all over London or God-knows-where trying to remove as many from the equation as possible until we get a hard core, by which time Maria will be long gone, so will our man, and…"

"So will Sally" said McMullen finishing his sentence. They both sat in silence for a while scanning their lists.

"So what do you suggest?" said McMullen.

"We only made some in-roads into this investigation when we stopped treating Andrew Garner as a victim and started treating him as a suspect", said Webber. "That was the turning point. After that, we got to where we are now in a pretty short space of time. On that basis, we should be looking at how these two are linked. We should be looking at why Garner and our man were ever together in the first place"

"Convenience" said McMullen. "He needed Garner because without him he could never get in the tunnels".

"And that tells us that he cannot have been a railway employee. Garner was the key to the tunnels because he was the railway employee. You said it yourself up there just now – we haven't seen any killings since Garner was taken out of the picture. I don't think he can get to the tunnels without him, which is why he had to let Cathy Norris go and why her release was such a shambles with her seeing everything she shouldn't have seen, like trains and tunnels and steps".

"But why not just kill her?"

"That's my point. If he killed her, with Garner gone he couldn't get her out. Not to the Circle Line locations anyway".

McMullen frowned. "This means Sally isn't held in the tunnels"

"Which is why we didn't find her in the underground search. It's the link between Garner and the suspect that we need to be looking at, I'm sure of it".

"What is that link though? The only thing that links them is a fondness for lap-dancing bars, and model aeroplanes".

Webber sat in silence for a while, meticulously making a paper aeroplane from the sheet in front of him. "When I was in the flat, I said to you that I used to make model aeroplanes when I was a kid. I used to burn them with my dad's lighter to make them look like they had flown dangerous sorties and come back alive".

"I don't remember. I was too busy trying to diffuse the bomb that was Paula Jackson, the neighbour from hell".

"Well, as I was talking I remember looking at the state of that Bomber model, and the crayon colouring on it".

"What's your point?"

"My point is that model aeroplanes are a kid's thing. Ok, you get some adults doing it, but in the main you make model aeroplanes when you are kid. And that aeroplane, for whatever reason, meant something to Andrew Garner, which was why it was at "home" in Brighton instead of in London, which is why it was on display instead of hung from the ceiling like the others, and why it was in his bedroom where he would see it every morning when he woke up".

Webber sat up, having finished the paper aeroplane. "I reckon he had kept that thing since he was a kid, and how many things did you keep from childhood?"

McMullen shrugged. "Nothing. Nothing I can think of"

"Exactly" said Webber, "and certainly nothing that you would put on your dresser so you saw it every morning you woke up – unless of course it meant something to you".

"And here we are trawling lists of men who made it into the RAF as a paramedic…" said McMullen

"And investigating the death of a man who didn't", said Webber, waiting for the penny to drop.

"They were childhood friends" said McMullen.

"They must have been" said Webber. "That model aircraft on that man's dresser has been moved around from place to place, and taken care of in every move, and looked after even to the point where it can still be displayed today and that only means one thing".

"It meant something to him" said McMullen.

"And this guy, according to his neighbour from hell who was also his girlfriend and whom we have no reason to disbelieve, was an orphan".

"We should be checking lists of children's homes where Andrew Garner stayed as a kid" said McMullen.

"And cross referencing everyone we find on those lists with the list we have here".

"And that will give us a name".

"I reckon so" said Webber, casting his paper aeroplane into the air across the office and finally seeing it fly.

50

9.12pm

Through the darkness she could hear voices. A woman pleading. Then she heard the locks snap open.

The lights came on almost immediately and a woman fell to the ground in front of them. He stood behind her and took her by the hair pulling her up into a kneeling position.

She was sobbing loudly, her wrists and ankles bound with what looked like some type of wire. She screamed when she saw Maria but he jerked her head back shouting: "SILENCE!" as he did so.

Her naked body heaved under her own sobs as she tried to stifle her crying.

"Oh God!" screamed Maria as she stared at the woman. "What are you doing?"

He pulled the woman closer to Maria. Now he was away from the lights she could see his face more clearly, his cold blue eyes boring into her. The scar on his face seemed more prominent in the shadows cast by the lights.

"It is time for you to remember, Maria. To remember the relevance".

And then she saw he was wearing surgical gloves. "What are you going to do?" she said, heart pounding in her chest, arms still raised to try and shut out the lights.

He took out a syringe from his back pocket and plunged it into the neck of the woman who screamed. She continued screaming as he held her by the hair, fighting against her restraints, trying to scramble to her feet. Slowly her resistance became weaker, until her eyes rolled and she became limp. He held her still for a few moments looking at her. "Sssshhhhh, Sally" he said. Then he dropped her, and her body slumped to the ground.

"Sally?", said Maria.

He looked at Maria coldly. "This is your fault" he said calmly. "She will die because of you".

"No you sick-fuck!" she spat. "If she is to die it will be because of you!"

He walked towards her and she drew back against the wall. He looked at her intently, studying her. He reached out towards her face and she moved quickly away. "Don't you fucking touch me!" she screeched. "You stay away from me you sick mother-fucker!".

He didn't pursue her. He just continued staring at her, intently. Looking at her face, her hair. Then he stepped towards her and reached out again. She was straining at the chains. She couldn't go anywhere but back the other way and he blocked her path.

She began to weep as he touched her hair gently. He stroked it, cupped it in his hands, looked at it as if it was something he had never seen before. Then his hand moved to her cheek and his thumb touched her lips. She could smell the rubber of the surgical glove, feel the stickiness of it against her skin.

He circled his thumb over and over her lips getting harder and harder until it hurt and she winced. As she twisted her head away he seemed to wake up, to remember himself, and pulled his hand away swiftly.

"She will die because of you" he said quickly, turning and walking toward the woman.

"What are you doing?" she said, trying to control her breathing and her heaving chest. "What have you given her?"

"She has had a large dose of Rohypnol and pure heroin. She will be unconscious for a while. When she wakes up she will be dazed and confused. She will also be in considerable pain which will pass with another injection of the same mixture. Provided she does as I ask when she comes round she will be given her injection quickly before I purify her. I will release her mind in order to purify her body".

He turned to face Maria. "It is a mercy", he said.

"Purify? What do you mean, purify?"

"You will know soon enough, Maria" he said.

He moved to the back of the room and when he returned he held a cordless gun shaped box. He bent down and straightened out the woman's body. Then he switched on the machine and began to tattoo her. He was crouched over her, the vibrating sound of the cordless tattoo gun permeating the air.

"Don't kill her" she said. She blurted out the words, as if they were not hers. "I am the one you wanted, so you say. Let her go. Kill me instead".

The buzzing stopped and he leant back, kneeling now at the side of the body. She could see the first symbol on her leg. The moon cycle.

"Your time will come. This woman's time is now".

"Why?" she said hastily. "Why her? Why must she be first?"

He looked at her quizzically. "Because you seem to have forgotten the relevance of this. I am doing this for you and yet you show me no gratitude. You don't understand do you? What happened to you was not chance. It was an inevitability. Other men would not have let you go, Maria.

They would have stolen your beauty and fucked you until you couldn't face living and then they would have beaten the life out of you anyway whilst you begged them to stop".

Then he looked at her again with that sudden look of realisation that had come over his face when he had been touching her. He looked confused for a moment. Then he switched the tattoo gun back on and pushed it against the woman's skin.

"I don't understand" she said. "What are you talking about? Why was what happened to me inevitable?"

"It does not matter at the moment" he said, hunched over the woman's body.

"Please" she said. "You stole my life from me. It isn't true that after you released me I forgot everything. Christ, I have never been able to forget it. Do you think a person forgets something like that? I may as well have been killed for all the good it did me being released. I didn't have a life after that. My family disintegrated, my trust went, my whole fucking life disappeared and I never built another one".

He stopped what he was doing and put the tattoo gun down on the floor. As he stepped away she saw the second symbol on the woman's leg. Purification.

He walked over to her and she tensed. "I let you go" he said, curtly. "I gave you life. Do you not understand me? I gave you your life back so you could live it. So you could know what evil is out there, around you, be aware of it. I gave you your life back".

"Gave it back?" she said, incredulously. "How was I supposed to have any sort of life after that?"

His hand shot up and grabbed her throat. She choked against his grip, her hands on his wrist but she had no strength. "You lived well and you lived safely" he said looking straight into her eyes. "That is the best way to live". He stepped in close, his face almost touching hers. "Tell me, Maria, did you ever paint yourself a face again? Did you ever walk out at night with your dark curls crashing over your low cut top and your curves? Did you ever smile at a man whom you had never met and let him take you places you had never been? Did you ever walk a street, day or night, without being aware who was behind you? Who was watching you? Did you!"

He was shouting now. He squeezed her neck until she couldn't breathe. "Please.." she managed to whisper. He continued staring at her and then screwed up his face in a look of disgust as he threw her to one side, letting her go.

She fell against the wall, cutting her arm. She screamed as the stone tore her skin. It was a deep laceration and the blood came freely, dripping onto her torso and legs. She began to sob as she sank to the floor, cradling her arm, the chains pulling at her all the while.

He went back to the woman and started up the tattoo gun again.

"If that is the life you gave me" she sobbed, "then I don't want it. You can take it back. I won't live the way you dictate I will live. I will never show you gratitude for what you did to me, for what you have done to these women. There is nothing in what you have done that makes you anything other than a sick, twisted, freak".

He stood back from the body. The third symbol complete.

"Do you see the relevance now?" he said, standing over her. "No, of course you don't".

He crouched down next to her, grabbing her hair in his fist. His voice had changed. He was almost hissing his words now. There was pure hatred in his eyes. "After I shave this bitch's head and carve her lips off her pretty face she will come round. She will come round screaming in pain and disbelief at the marks I have carved onto her body. She will come to understand why she is here and she will say your name, like all the others had to say your name before they died. Only this time it won't be for the camera because you are here, with me, so I can show you in person what it means to kill for you".

"No!" she screamed. "No, please. Don't do this. Don't do it. You have me. You have me. It wasn't all for this… everything you have done was not for this. It can't have been. I have seen what you have made these women do. I have seen them trying to say my name, trying to reach me. And now you have reached me. You have me. What was the point of it all? Tell me! What was the point of it all?"

He stood up, saying nothing.

"I don't know what kind of fucking insanity you are in, but I will not go back to what I was. I don't know what you think you did for me but you did nothing". She was sobbing loudly now, struggling to get the words out. "You did nothing but destroy everything I had, everything I lived for. I had no life after you took me, and no life after you let me go. Do you understand? I am already dead, you mother-fucker. I am already dead!"

She forced herself to her feet. Blood from her arm smeared all over her left side. She put her arms out in a Christ-like gesture. "Release me" she said. "Put me out of my fucking misery. I don't care what you do or don't do with her. Just finish it for me, please. Just stick me with the fucking needle and let me go. Let me out of my prison. Let me free, do you hear me? Let me go free!"

He stared at her and she could see his chest heaving. He was almost panting, like he couldn't breathe. He looked at the blood on her body and back at her face. It was like he was suffocating on the spot.

Her arms dropped to her sides and the sobs enveloped her body. She sank to her knees. "Let me go free" she said, crying into her hands. "Just let me go free".

She sat there, hunched up in a ball, crying, and he stood there staring at her for what seemed like an age.

He didn't say anything, and she had nothing left to say.

Eventually he picked up the woman's body under the arms and pulled her out of the room.

She watched him leave, the woman's head lolling from side to side. Then the lights went out, the locks tripped, and she was alone in the darkness again.

51

10.14pm

"I need his date of birth" said McMullen, sitting at the computer and typing in the details.

He passed her the printout from the file records.

"What's that?" said Webber, looking at the internet address displayed on the screen.

"It's a link the Child Protection Squad gave to me. Unlike the MOD they, at least, appreciate the need for urgency in an investigation. It gives us access to their intranet via a VPN account and therefore to their own internal records without us having to ask them to do it for us. It will get us into the records of children's homes and related fostering organisations for any year provided they are computerised now and also provided they are in England or Wales".

"And if Andy and our man spent their time in a Scottish children's home?"

"Then we're fucked" said McMullen.

She typed in his date of birth and waited for the information to come back to her.

"Jesus" she said. "The poor bastard was moved around a lot".

"Maybe" said Webber. "The question is, who was moved about with him, and when".

She printed off the first list and they ran through the institutions. "He enters care there" said McMullen, pointing to the date of the first entry, "and leaves it at age sixteen. It doesn't say where he went".

"It makes no odds where he went" said Webber, he was outside the system by that point. He counted up the number of institutions that Andrew Garner had been resident in. "Seven overall" he said.

"That's a hell of a lot of moves between the age of eight and sixteen" said McMullen. "Pretty much a move every year".

"No-one ever said the system was fit for purpose, even now" added Webber.

She typed in the names of the homes one by one, printing off the list of children's names for each year as she went.

When they were done they trawled through each home for each year, making a list of all those children who were housed in the same place as Andy more than once.

Then they cross referenced those who had been housed with him more than once with those who had been with him more frequently in the early years.

"This child here, Sotto Morelli, was at the home for two years before Andy arrived. Then when Andy was moved a year later, they were moved together".

"So they met when Andy was eight and Sotto was six".

"Yes, and stayed together until Andy was thirteen and Sotto was eleven".

"Dangerous ages" said Webber. "Like brothers by that point, probably, assuming they were friends in the first place".

"The records don't say why, but after being apart for a year, they were re-united the following year. Andy was fourteen and was Sotto was twelve, and that's how it stayed until Andy left. Basically they were together for the whole of their time, wherever they were moved, save for that year in the middle. There is no-one else who matches that frequency or that level of contact".

Webber was already scanning down the MOD list.

When he saw it, his blood ran cold.

July 15th

52

6am

She lay on the cold stone floor, hunched in the foetal position. She was trying to work out what had happened when he was here, what had affected him so much. Somewhere in amongst the madness there may be a way out. Somewhere inside his mind.

He hadn't tattooed a number on the woman. He had completed the symbols but amid the arguing he had stopped, and never finished.

She tried to remember what it was she had been saying to him. She could remember telling him she wanted to be released, to go free and if that had to be by death then so be it.

But the way he kept staring at her prayed on her mind. It was as if he kept slipping away momentarily, into some other place, only to jerk back into the moment. He almost seemed angry when he did so.

And that gloved hand on her lips…. What was it about the lips? And the hair. All these bodies had been found in the same way. No lips. No hair. And what had he said about beauty?

God has given you one face and you paint yourselves another?

"And the speech about having given me back my life…" she thought *"he honestly seemed to believe that he had done. He believed that in letting me go he had saved me.*

And yet I had not been wrapped up in his purification. That was by way of death only, it seemed".

She fell in and out of sleep, her mind turning his words over and over.

"Did I walk down the street without looking behind me? Did I paint my face now? Did my dark curls hang around my body? He was talking about beauty. He was talking about what made me attractive. Make-up, lips, hair, my body.

What was he purifying?

She pictured Sally's face when he had first dragged her in. Eyes wide with fear and confusion. Shaking. Crying. Unable to understand what had brought her here. What she had done that had let her fall through the cracks of normal society and end up here, locked away from the world, helpless at the hands of a madman.

"But even in her fear she was beautiful. Blonde hair. High cheek bones and grey/blue eyes. She had looked after herself. She was slim. Yes, beautiful.

It was beauty. He was cutting off beauty.

But why me? Why would he do that to get to me? And yet he wasn't doing it to get to me because he had been doing it long before I was abducted. I was number seven. Six others had died before me.

What was it about me that caused him to let me go".

She pushed herself up and got to her feet, feeling around in the darkness for the bottle of water.

She sipped it slowly, forcing herself to focus. She tried to remember how she used to feel when she was counselling people. How she used to let herself become them. How she used to try and feel their pain, imagine herself as them. It had always been cathartic for her, a release from herself even, to work in that way. She pictured his face, scarred and back once again in the killing cycle he ended so long ago.

"Other men would not have let you go, Maria. They would have stolen your beauty and fucked you until you couldn't face living and then they would have beaten the life out of you anyway whilst you begged them to stop"

"What was he talking about? It was so specific. It wasn't just that other people would have killed me. He was saying other people would have raped me. Then they would have beaten me, probably to death".

She forced herself to focus on his face. On his eyes as they spat hate.

"After I shave this bitch's head and carve her lips off her pretty face she will come round. She will come round screaming in pain and disbelief at the marks I have carved onto her body. She will come to understand why she is here and she will say your name, like all the others had to say your name before they died. Only this time it won't be for the camera because you are here, with me, so I can show you in person what it means to kill for you".

……what it means to kill for you.

"Why would he be killing for me? I had never asked for this. I had never been a party to it other than the forced abduction, the fear, the torture, but that was as victim not as perpetrator. He can't have been talking about me. He must have been talking
about someone else".

"Maybe that's it", she said to herself in a whisper, water bottle frozen half way to her lips. "Maybe he thinks I am someone else".

And yet they are forced to say my name. They are forced to say my name.

She laid back down, her mind churning everything over and over.

She had to work out what had stopped him in his tracks. Her life depended on it.

53

9.13am

She made her way quickly to the front of the room. "Alright, listen up. We've got a suspect. More watertight than before so we need to give it full resources".

She took out a marker pen and wrote the name "*Sotto Morelli*" on the board.

"This guy was in a care home from the age of six. He befriended our first suspect Andrew Garner in the same home when Andrew arrived aged eight. Apart from a brief spell in separate homes at age thirteen they were close friends for the whole of their time together".

She turned to face them. "We are now working on the basis that the connection between these two is what made the whole process work, and that the connection was made early on. By that I mean in childhood, which is why it has survived. The killer needed Andrew to get to the tunnels, and after he killed Andrew he was unable to function in the tunnels in the same way. This is because Andrew was the link to the railways, being the employee. Our man is not a railway employee. Our man is, or rather was, a paramedic in the RAF". She scanned down her list to double check her details. "He's a retired paramedic having quit by his own choice two years ago to teach at the University of London Air Squadron".

"Guv, with all due respect, it doesn't make any sense for him to have killed the only guy who was facilitating what he was doing. Do we have any leads on that?"

"Not yet. Maybe it was because he was finished, maybe it was because he had no choice".

"Maybe" interrupted Webber, "we were closer than we ever thought in the early days and he had no choice other than to cut that line. Don't forget we were treating Andrew Garner as a victim at that point as opposed to a suspect. Maybe that was his point"

"Either way", continued McMullen, "this is the best lead we have, and his appearance on the MOD list, when we factor in the tattoo, means we are now looking at a substantial lead".

She passed the details of the home address given for the suspect on the MOD list to DS Shah. "Raz, it's down to you now. Get as many bodies as you can down to this address. If you feel you need a warrant when you get there call it in. I want this bastard water tight evidentially".

Webber was on the internet. "Guv, I think you need to look at this".

She hurried over to where he sat. She studied the screen. "You are fucking shitting me" she said.

"I wish I was" said Webber.

She sat down at her own computer and pulled up the files for the various filed reports from the underground search operation. The handwritten paper statements from the members of the various search teams had long since been scanned in and added to the growing electronic databank of the case so far.

"Jesus" she said "there were five members of that team. This could take hours. The search teams will be at the address before we're done".

"Split it" said Webber.

They passed out the five statements of the Brompton Road search team individually to members of the team including themselves.

"According to internet information, and I admit we have yet to verify this but we certainly have no reason to doubt it, the University of London Air Squadron is on Brompton Road. It is therefore possible, when we look back at the search team reports of Brompton Road disused tube station, that something was missed because we didn't have this information then. If this guy teaches at that institution, and therefore had access to the site in some way, he may not even have needed Andrew Garner" and then it hit her, and she turned to Webber. "And therefore he may not need him now"

"Which means that she might be down there still".

She turned back to the team. "Let's get to it".

They trawled the individual team member reports. Each report was around ten handwritten pages, and aside from the difficulties of reading another person's handwriting, they weren't entirely sure what they were looking for.

And then, from the corner of the room, someone said. "Guv, can I read you this?"

"Go on" said McMullen, looking up from what she was doing.

"It's from one of the British Transport Officers allocated to the Brompton Tube Station search:

"Part of the station was inaccessible due to a locked iron gate at the only doorway that led into the unsearched section. Upon questioning of the Transport For London personnel present, and also following comment from the senior officer present from the British Transport Police it was considered that this area would be outside of our search remit for the following reasons: (a) it is MOD owned and occupied so the likelihood of use for the

harbouring of abductees is minimal if not impossible; (b) it is outside of our jurisdiction, and (c) It is totally inaccessible to anyone other than military personnel"

McMullen held her nerve. "The report mentions the senior officer present from the British Transport Police. Who was he and what does his report say?" She turned her attention to the rest of the team. "Come on, we can all access it. What does it say?"

The same officer had already cross referenced it.

"It's here Guv" she said "The lead officer was Sergeant Jagdar Ranu, British Transport Police".

"During the course of the search a junior officer asked me about the locked gate he had found. The gate itself divides that half of Brompton Road Station which is within civilian control with that half of the station which is within military control. From my knowledge of the station, which extends back over several decades, I am aware that the Brompton Road entrance that is under the control of the MOD is sealed off, and further evidence of this fact is given by the well documented attempt at intrusion from a member of the public several years ago which resulted in the unfortunate death of the intruder. There is no access from ground level on the MOD side to the deep-level rooms at Brompton Road Station. The only access is via an old disused lift shaft which has been stripped out, resulting in a sheer drop of several hundred feet. I therefore advised the officer that the area was within MOD control, accessible only to Military Personnel (albeit unlikely) and, in any event, outside of our jurisdiction".

She looked up at McMullen. "That's it, Guv"

"We may have searched Brompton Road Tube Station", said McMullen, "but we searched the wrong half".

"Guv?" said the team member.

Webber spoke up. "We have half the Met out there raiding the last known address of an ex-MOD employee who now teaches at the University of London Air Squadron on Brompton Road, which means he is at that location every single day, and our own records show that we have spent the whole of our investigation directing our energies underground only to find fuck all".

"Because we were searching the wrong half of Brompton Road station" said McMullen.

July 16th

54

4.12am

"The Police know where I am. They will work this out" she said.

She said it like a statement. As if it had some gravity.

He stood behind the lights, saying nothing.

"Sally. What happened to her? Where is she?"

"I am still thinking about her" he said from the darkness. "When the time is right I shall help her out of her hell".

When the time is right.

"Where is the moon now?" she asked. A throw away comment. She was as casual with it as she could be.

Silence.

"Why the moon?" she asked, continuing, despite not knowing how he might react, and what consequences that might have for her. Self-preservation seemed pointless now. If she was going to die then she was going to do so knowing the truth, at least, however insane it turned out to be.

Still no response.

"That reporter had the beginnings of catching you at the very start, didn't he? Is that why the killings stopped? Did you see him piecing together the cycles. The Moon. The Circle Line."

He started walking up and down behind the lights in the darkness. She held her arms to her face still, trying to be ready for when he showed himself. She was trying to control her breathing. Trying not to sound afraid. She was trying to remember her job, to distance herself. To be there and yet not there.

"The bible references", she continued, "the roman numerals. What was that for? Why use the bible? Why dress it all up? This is not a crusade. This is not God's work. This is the work of a madman, isn't it? Come on, show yourself. Tell me. If I am to die anyway why can't I know the truth? And why won't you show yourself? Why do you hide behind those lights? Why can't I see you?"

"Blessed is he who does not see and yet still believes", he said. His voice was devoid of emotion. Cautious, even.

"That's bollocks and you know it. You are not a God, Moon God or otherwise. You are not a crusader. You are not born of the greater good".

"No, Maria. I am not. Did you not read your letters? Did you not read the questions I asked you? I asked if you thought I would be defeated by the greater good".

He stepped out of the darkness and walked toward her. "Am I, Maria? Am I to be defeated by the greater good? No-one knows where you are. No-one is coming for you. Whether you live or die is under my control. That makes me a God, surely, or, at the very least, it makes me your God now".

"Is that what it is about? Control?"

He raised his finger to his lips in a 'be quiet' gesture. "So many questions, Maria. Why so many questions?"

"Because when you release me, when you let me die, I want to know why me. What was it that caused me to be sucked into this nightmare, sucked into your insanity. Where do I fit in? Tell me where I fit in".

He studied her for a moment. "What do you think about Time, Maria?"

"I don't know what you mean".

"Sachs was right to a certain degree, and, yes, if the truth be known I did like the identity the press built for me. It was apt. Why the moon? Because the moon is pure white, Maria. The moon is purity. When the sun shines on us we burn. We screw up our eyes. We do not see clearly. But when the Moon shines on us we see everything in a pure white. We see clearly, Maria, when the full moon shines on us…

"It tires me that I should explain myself. It is obvious to me. There is a need for purity among us. The moon is so much more to us than the sun. It controls the tides, the moods of people. It even affects your menstrual cycles. It is a greater influence on us than the sun could ever be. The sun simply gives us life. But what is life without meaning? It is the Moon which mothers us. The Moon nurtures us and brings us that greater depth".

"I don't understand" she said, trying to push him on now he had started talking.

"I don't expect you to, Maria. But I can say that purity is born of the Moon, and the waning moon takes the filth away. To be bled to death as the moon dies with you will render you pure, Maria. And David was half right, I will give him that. The number twenty-seven is of relevance, but only because the lunar month has twenty-seven days. The rest was a fortunate co-incidence. Why do you think the New Testament has twenty-seven books to it, or that the Circle Line, when it was first built, had twenty-seven stops within it? Perhaps, it is co-incidence. Or is it some deeper rooted psychological cycle that we are all locked in?

"The women are numbered Maria, because there will eventually be twenty seven deaths. In the same way I disappeared on the twenty-seventh of July in the last cycle.

After the twenty-seventh, my work is done, and during my lifetime I really only have three opportunities to conclude this great work. The first, when the Metonic cycle of the moon began, and now this year, when the nineteen year cycle is up, and what cannot be done now will wait another nineteen years. It is all cycles, Maria. Round and round. Round and round. Does History not repeat itself? Year after year, doing the same thing?

"We are part of a bigger picture, Maria. My work, if it isn't finished, will be taken up by someone else I am sure. The cycle will continue, despite our paltry efforts to end it".

He turned away from her. "The reason I asked you about time, Maria, is because I held you for a year. Do you remember? Twelve months, and then I released you. But a lunar year? If you go by the Moon, Maria, there would be thirteen months. Divide twenty-seven into three-hundred-and-sixty-five days of the year and you will come up with thirteen".

He turned back to face her. "There should be thirteen months, Maria. I was your thirteenth month. The one you never thought you would have".

She stared at him. She wanted to tell him he was insane, to spit in his face, to tell him that there was no place in society for his sick breed of fantasy....

13th July, Midday...

but she pressed her body hard against the stone wall and closed her eyes. *Focus, focus, focus.*

"Is that what the symbols mean?" she said. She opened her eyes and looked at him.

"In the first investigation the Police found the meanings of the symbols. They believe the three symbols mean purification of women by a moon god, probably through death. Were they right? Is that what they mean?".

"It is not hard to work that out, Maria".

"But why women? Why not men?"

"I have attacked a man in this cycle, Maria".

"One man, yes. The rest have all been women. Why do you hate them so much?".

He narrowed his eyes at her, but she held his gaze. "I do not hate them, Maria. I am saving them. I am saving them from themselves for they know not what they do. Men will ruin themselves by their baseness in any event. They are not my concern. All men are wretches who inevitably let themselves down and are generally beyond redemption. But women…", he stepped in close, "women have the chance, at least, at purity".

She bowed her head. An act of supplication and surrender. She was getting somewhere now.

55

9.34am

Webber opened up the email from SO19.

"They have nothing to add to the plans, Guv", he said, scanning the rest of the message as he spoke. "It looks as though the intention is to absail down the shaft. Armed officers and equipment first to secure to the area, then us".

The plans of the underground layout had been supplied by the MOD whose own officers had now been added to the numbers assigned to the search. The politics of it all did not go unnoticed by either side – civilian and military – with both claiming priority rights to lead the operation. In truth, McMullen didn't care who took the spoils, provided they got down there without wasting so much time, but the Met Machine was not ready to let any part of London slip from its' grasp, jurisdiction arguments or not.

"How many officers?" she asked.

"Seven armed. The rest is either Met or Military. Thirty in all".

"That should do it" she said putting on her jacket and securing her radio.

As they hurried down to the rear-yard and the waiting vehicles, Webber said "Why don't you stay on the surface? Just for safety's sake?"

She glanced disapprovingly at him as they exited the double doors into the searing brightness of the morning sun. "What, you think I'm going to compromise the operation?"

"You are already compromised" he said as they climbed into the area car.

"I don't give a shit, Joe. I know I'm compromised. I also know that if I sit back and let someone else go down there I will never forgive myself".

"Your call" he said dismissively. "I don't suppose we can make it any worse than it already is".

They travelled the rest of the way in silence, both listening to developments on the radio as SO19 reported progress in establishing a surface base. Reports came in co-ordinating equipment delivery. Disparaging comments on the involvement of the Military Police peppered every conversation. Eventually McMullen put word out to knock it on the head, at least as far as her own officers were concerned, and the criticism tailed off, but the resentment was clear.

As they approached the Brompton Road area they were met by the expected Police cordon. Yellow and Black *Police Line* tape blocked certain accessways, and as they made their way to the front of the station motorcycle officers moved their vehicles aside, only to reclose the barrier behind them, blue lights flashing silently against the sun.

Webber was the first out of the car, showing his badge to the nearest firearms officer.

McMullen joined him without saying a word. The frantic activity around them made her wonder whether they should move the Police Line back. They didn't need wide angle shots plastered over the Evening Standard if they could help it.

As they waited for the senior SO19 commander to brief them, Webber glanced around the sea of equipment and people preparing to descend the shaft.

This is it he thought to himself. *Come out, come out, wherever you are……*

56

10.31am

"Is that why you destroy their beauty?" she said, still looking at the ground.

He touched her hair, and her face, and she realised he wasn't wearing any gloves. She felt her heart jump. He was always strict about any contact. Normally, such an act would result in being hosed down against the wall in freezing water. She kept herself perfectly still. She did not want to show any form of aggression yet.

"A woman's beauty is a precious thing, Maria, but it is also a terrible thing".

"Why?" she said, her voice barely audible.

He stroked her hair again but said nothing.

She closed her eyes. *None of these women were found to have any sexual injuries* she thought to herself. *This is not about sex, at least, not for him.*

"So their lips and their hair" she said. "Why do you…" she struggled for the words, not even believing she would ever say them. "Why do you…. remove them?"

"So they may appear pure to those who find them. That is why. It strips them of their beauty. Without these things, without these tools of attraction, beauty does not compromise them. They are free of such a burden. They are pure. Their Scarlet Tesseras, their little hooks, are gone. They are free. And the Police will not find these things either. I burn them afterwards. It is part of the purification. Their spirits are then free. Free of the physical body which held them prisoner and polluted them".

"I had family" she said. "My parents loved me regardless of how I looked. They were proud of my beauty. That is why I moved to London. To become a model".

"They were fools" he said, dismissively. "They knew nothing".

"But they loved me. The point is that they loved me and they would have loved me whether I was ugly or beautiful. My looks were irrelevant".

He scoffed at this. "If you believe that then you are naive, Maria, and I know you are not naïve".

"Do you have family?" she asked, looking up at him.

He didn't answer her.

"A sister, or a Mothe – "

"Enough!" he shouted. "There is no point in this. You have asked me tell you what you wanted to know and I have told you. In answer to your first question, the woman you met is still alive, but I have decided that you will have your wish, Maria. If you wish to be released from what you call your prison then you will have that wish".

She ignored him. She needed to push him on his relationship with women. Despite what he said this had to be about women. All but one of the victims were women. The mutilation was directed toward their appearance. His motivation had to be tied to women.

"My greatest regret" she continued "is that I never had children. I never had the chance to have a family. I would have loved a daughter. I would have given anything to have a daughter. A little girl"

"Stop this!" he said curtly. "I gave you what you wanted".

"But if you had a daughter, if you had a little girl, would you feel the same then? Would you – "

He rushed toward her and grabbed her by the throat again. "If I had a bitch of a daughter" he hissed "then she would be purified. All women are the same. They cannot help themselves. They paint themselves up, make the most of themselves, show off whatever it is they think they have got and it results in one thing". He gripped her throat tighter. She started to choke. He pushed up and back and she fought against him but he was too strong. "Death" he said. "Do you hear me? Death! Yes if I had a daughter I would save her first. I would save her soul from the inevitable shit of life in amongst these fucking animals we call men. I would release her at the first opportunity and save her the heartache of what life would inevitably bring her!"

He let her go and she gasped for air, but she could not lose the moment. "Kill me like that, then" she said, her voice hoarse and interspersed with coughing. "Kill me like that. I want to die like I am one of your own. I want to die like I am your daughter. I want it to be intimate. I want it to be the way you always intended it. A release. A good thing. Something with a purpose, not just gratuitous violence for no reason".

And then he was staring at her with that vacuous stare again. She repeated her last words, but with a softer tone. "A release. A good thing. Not just gratuitous violence for no reason".

She was looking up at him as he stared down at her.

"Let me cut my own hair" she said gently. "Bring me a mirror, some scissors. Let me prepare myself, and then, when it is time, drug me so I don't feel it. Then release me".

He was still staring at her when she said "A good thing. Something with a purpose. Not just gratuitous violence for no reason".

He was breathing heavily again. She bowed her head, looked away.

"Yes" he said eventually. "Yes, that will be your way".

57

1.07pm

"We are wasting time" said McMullen, pacing up and down.

Mick Phillips, the SO19 Commander on site, stared impassively at her from across the small row of tables and laptops. He kept a close eye on the CCTV feed from the remote camera that was being lowered down the lift shaft as they spoke.

"My officers are not going to plummet to their deaths for want of a five minute recon" he said flatly. "The more information we have, the quicker we can get on with the task once we are down there".

"You've had the plans in advance" she insisted.

He looked up at her from the laptop screen. "For about five fucking minutes, yes". He looked backed at the screen and began discussing something with a fellow officer. The conversation, as far as he was concerned, was over.

Webber came alongside her. "Leave it" he said. "You know the score. It won't be long now".

She snorted. "Christ, most of the time they're being criticised for going in all guns blazing. What happened to shoot first and ask questions later?"

"Just leave it".

Within minutes the unit was satisfied and they started their final equipment check. Webber and McMullen stayed close as the officers made their way to the lift shaft and climbed into the absailing harnesses. "We've only got room for two at a time" said the equipment team leader.

With night vision goggles in place, the first two officers leaned back slowly and began the descent.

The inside of the shaft was littered with loose cables, old metal pipes and the ever-present thick grey dust of the underground system. The unmistakeable ridging of the metal rings that supported the concrete sectional construction served as useful footings as they went deeper into the void.

At the bottom they decamped quickly, weapons swinging into firing position. Their instructions were for reconnaissance only. To engage only if necessary. The Commander wanted the full unit in place before anyone went live. They took up position inside the double doors that enclosed the bottom of the lift-shaft. Slowly, quietly, one of the officers leaned into his radio and confirmed a clear area.

The next two officers began the descent.

Within a few minutes the full unit was crouched at the foot of the lift shaft.

"Jackson", began Phillips, "you stay here to oversee the incoming search team. The rest of us, we fan out from the bottom of the steps as planned. Recon only. There are two hostages and one target so far as we know but we need to verify that before we go to phase two".

The officers acknowledged the instructions.

"And for fuck's sake make sure you identify yourselves properly if you are going to engage a target. I don't want to be dragging either hostages or officers out of this shit-hole because someone didn't shout loud enough. Got it?"

The were nods from everyone.

"Okay, let's get to it".

The two lead officers got to their feet and pushed open the lift shaft doors, revealing a staircase of twenty or so steps. Slowly, with eyes close to the night-vision rifle sight, they made their way in.

58

1.12pm

When he came back he brought a safety razor, some scissors and something which made her blood run cold. It was the same mirror he had always had. A showgirl's mirror. Bare light bulbs all around the square edge, exposing every little flaw, encouraging attention to detail. Encouraging perfection.

It sat on top of a small cupboard, itself set up on wheels. The cupboard was red with gold edging around each of the doors. The paint was faded and chipped, as if it had been in use long before either of them had had cause to use it.

He set down the scissors and the razor. He said nothing, just looked at her with that vacant look.

A few minutes later he returned with a bowl of water and some shaving foam. Each time he left the room he was meticulous in locking the door. All three locks. No exceptions.

And yet she had not been hosed down like an animal after he had touched her. That was a regular occurrence the last time. He was always touching her. Her lips, her hair, her face, and then hosing her whilst she crouched, shivering against the wall.

When everything was in place he pushed the mirror nearer to her and handed her the scissors. "Begin" he said, coldly.

The chains were long enough for her to have just enough room to reach above her head. She took a deep breath, looked at herself in the mirror, and then started to cut her hair.

The black curls fell steadily at her feet, but she did it slowly. She needed time. She needed the time to get inside his head. The very thing she hated the thought of doing was now the only thing that was going to save her: To connect with him.

"Is there any particular way I should be doing this?" she said.

"No. I shall collect it all afterwards. It will all be burned anyway".

He stood watching her

"You are very cold about this" she said.

"It was your choice" he replied. "I am giving you what you wanted".

"And I am grateful" she said. "But I still wonder why me. I still wonder why you let me go, even though I was pleased that you did. I still wonder what made me…" she looked over at him as she cut off a large chunk of hair and dropped it purposefully to the floor, "…special".

He looked away. "You will be free soon, Maria. That is enough for you".

"Was it just that the moon cycle was up? Was it just that the Metonic cycle was over? Or was that happy co-incidence?"

She stopped cutting and turned to face him. "I am as good as dead, and content to be so because I know what you are saying to me now. I didn't realise before, but what you are doing is like something spiritual. Tell me I am wrong".

He stood at the far side of the room watching her. "No, Maria, you are not wrong. I am releasing you. I thought I made that clear".

She turned back to the mirror and started cutting again. Small chunks. *Snip. Snip.* Her chains pulling at her all the while.

"Yes, you have made it clear. I just never really saw it before, that's all".

He continued watching her.

She turned the cupboard slightly so she could see him in the mirror. "So are you a Christian?" she said. "Going back to the letters you wrote to me. Could I ask you the same question? Do you believe in God?".

"I have created my own religion, Maria. I used the bible because it is widely accepted in this country as relevant. I could just as easily have used something else. The point is that there is good and there is evil, and there is no defining line between the two other than what one person considers acceptable or unacceptable".

"There is no right or wrong but thinking makes it so" she said, smiling at him in the mirror. "I read that in your letters, too".

He uncrossed his arms and walked toward her. "Exactly" he said.

"Why are the other killings not like this?" she said, watching him closely as he stood over her.

"What do you mean?"

"Why do you think people don't see what I see. Why do you think it is such a fight with them?"

He smiled. "Because they do not understand, Maria. Plain and simple. But then, they have not talked to me the way you have. They have not talked to me the way you did back then. The first time".

"Is that why you let me go?" she asked.

"I told you why I let you go" he said. "To live your life. The life it seems that you no longer want".

"I no longer want it now I know what it means. It would be a half life. Better to be released properly. With dignity. I know what you mean about the female looks. I can see that now. It is what we do. You are right. We cannot help ourselves. In fact, we are proud of it".

He folded his arms, narrowed his eyes. "Why?" he said sharply. "Why would you be proud of it?"

She shrugged. "I don't know. It validates us in many ways"

"And yet you all hate that validation. You hate the attention it attracts unless it attracts the right attention".

"I guess so" she said, "but it is also about insecurities. Perhaps it is our equivalent of your male bravado. Front, if you like. Appearing real but not real".

"Tell me something, Maria" he said. "If I were to place a magnet in the middle of some iron filings, should the magnet object to the fact that the filings all move to the magnet?"

"I don't know what you mean" she said, still cutting slowly.

He stared at her intently. "If you painted your face and dressed your hair up and put on the things that excite men, do you lose the right to say no to a man's advances?"

She hesitated. "No" she said. "I do not give up the right to say no. What I give up is the right to anonymity". She left it at that. She was on raw ground now, she could see that.

He stared at her whilst she continued cutting. She was down to a bob now. The next stage would crop her hair close and then it would be almost too late.

"You are saying that I may know you, but I may not touch you. Is that what you are saying?"

"No". She stopped cutting. "You remember when you wrote to me that nothing is good or bad but thinking makes it so?"

He nodded.

"Well, it is the same type of thing. I am neither giving up my right to say no, nor am I not giving up my right to say no, but your thinking makes it so".

He stepped back from her. He kept his arms folded but after a few seconds he turned away. "Continue cutting" he said.

She did so, watching him intently. "Earlier, you said that men would always hang themselves by their own baseness. What did you mean by that?"

He paced up and down now. "That men are animals. Regardless of what they believe about themselves they are all the same. They are weak, governed by sex, and once there is alcohol inside them they are out of control".

She smiled. "I do not disagree with you there" she said. "I have spent too long avoiding such people in my life. It is true what they say. Do not feed the animals".

He turned to face her. "But you court them" he said. There was judgement in his tone. She started to panic.

"No. I did not. You set me free remember? You set me free to live in a way that was... how did you describe it?"

"I set you free to live safely" he said swiftly.

"Yes, yes. You set me free to live safely. And I didn't paint my face after that. I didn't trust anyone after that because I couldn't. I tried, I really did, but I couldn't. I wanted to make myself attractive but I couldn't. Every time I looked in the mirror I saw what you saw. You taught me". And then she made a move that had to come at some point whether she could bear it or not. She put the scissors down, turned to face him and held out her arms. "You taught me" she said, arms outstretched, chains scraping along the stone floor. "You taught me, and the sadness of it all is that it made no difference. You were right. The business of right and wrong is inside the millions of heads that are out there. That is why I never stood a chance".

He was frowning now, as if he were trying to work something out. "No. No" he said shaking his head. "I helped you".

"Of course you did" she said, arms still outstretched. "Of course you did".

He took a step toward her.

"You will have to touch me at some point" she said calmly. "You have already touched me, without gloves. And I will accept my punishment for that, so if you touch me now…."

"Continue cutting" he said.

She picked up the scissors again. "It was only when we talked about how you would deal with a daughter that I realised what the process itself meant. A good thing. Something that has meaning. Not just gratuitous violence".

She watched him in the mirror. He was becoming increasingly agitated. She had cropped her hair now to the scalp. All that was left was for her to shave her head. She didn't make any recourse to him. She just used her hands to wet her head, and then used the foam on a small part. She picked up the razor and began to shave.

"It is a good thing that we do now" she said, slowly. "And I understand what you say about a daughter. I can see that now. Perhaps the same for a mother too, or a sister. Any woman who is close to you".

His eyes widened and she tensed. Then he looked away. "There is no one close to me" he said without emotion. "No one who lives on the physical plane, at least. The Moon is my mother. The Moon is all our Mothers".

Her heart was racing. She tried to stop her hand from shaking but she couldn't do it.

She put the razor down. "I am sorry for that loss. I cannot continue. My arms are so sore, and the cut here" she pointed to her left arm, "it is getting so sore now. I want you to finish for me please".

He looked up at her. He said nothing at first. She thought he looked genuinely surprised but she didn't hold his gaze. She looked away.

He walked slowly toward her and then took her hands. He studied them for a moment, and then took out some keys from his pocket and unlocked the clasps around her wrists. "I do this" he said "because I want to, but understand that you will die tonight regardless of chains or otherwise. I have no wish to speak about my mother or anything else now. I am going to prepare the syringe and you will need to finish this yourself".

As he undid her wrists he also checked the clasps around her ankles. There was no way she was going anywhere.

She continued shaving her head. They didn't speak for several minutes and he stood at the side of the room preparing the syringe. Heroin and Rohypnol. "It is a massive dose" he said, matter-of-factly. "You will be dead within minutes, probably of a heart attack".

"Thank you" she said.

When he was finished he placed it in his back pocket, just as she had seen with the other woman.

"I am nearly done" she said, shaving the last side of her head. "You will need to do the back. I cannot see".

"If you try anything it will be over in minutes for you, do you understand?"

"I understand" she said.

He started to shave the back of her head. He was slow and methodical. She was guessing but there had to be a chance that she was the only victim to which he had done this whilst they were conscious. This was of value. Something out of the normal routine. It would weaken him.

"Thank you" she said as he worked.

He looked at her again with that vacuous stare.

"How did you lose your mother?" she asked, not looking at him. She was looking down as he shaved the back of her head.

"My mother was a showgirl" he said slowly. "A good woman. She was killed when I was a child. It is a simple fact. That is how I lost her". He gestured toward the mirror cabinet. "This mirror was hers. It is all I have of her now".

Her hands were shaking uncontrollably now. She tried to control her breathing. It was the position of submission that must have done it. She was naked, cut and bleeding, totally submissive, with head bowed whilst he held the razor and the power, and from all that had come the one thing she was looking for. She needed to personalise this to have any chance of escape. She needed to bring him out of the distance if she was to be set free. She wasn't sure what to say next. She sat in silence for a while. *Focus, focus, focus.*

"Killed?" she said.

He paused for a moment, looking down at her. She froze in position. Then he started scraping with the razor again. "She was attacked, that's all. She died of her injuries".

She gripped her hands together to stop them from shaking.

Pleasepleasepleaseplease.

"Were they caught?" she said closing her eyes tightly.

"No".

Her heart was pounding in her chest. She was sure he could see her shaking. He must see that. She wanted to cry but she fought to control it.

"I'm sorry for you" she said.

He didn't answer. He dipped the razor in the bowl of water and continued scraping the blade against her skin.

"I have lost both my parents" she said. "I know how it feels".

"Did you watch them die" he said flatly. Not a question. His tone had changed.

"I was at their bedside" she said "each time".

"A soft bed" he said. "A bed with people around it. A bed with nurses and doctors and people who had done all they could".

"Yes" she said.

"That is not watching them die, Maria. That is just sitting with them already dead. They died when everything that could have been done for them had been done for them. After that, everyone simply stood around waiting for the bed to be free so they could put the next person in it to wait for death".

She was crying, trying to hold herself still. "That's so cruel" she said, softly.

"Cruelty is watching someone die and being helpless to stop it".

She froze. The DVD's. Her name. They had been saying her name, as if she could bring them some salvation, and yet she had been powerless to help them. Powerless to stop it.

Her heart pounded in her chest. What was he saying?

"That is how I felt" she said. "When I saw the DVD's, each time, that is how I felt".

He didn't respond. She kept her head bowed. Listened to the razor being dipped in and out of the water.

"I felt powerless to stop it. I watched them die. I watched them die calling for me".

"This is why I let you go Maria. Only you would understand how it felt to truly hear a call of desperation and be powerless to stop the horror that followed. You would understand because you lived through it".

"I watched them die saying my name and I was powerless to stop it".

"You were in the shadows" he said. "You could not have stopped it".

But I did stop it, you sick fuck. I am here aren't I? I am here putting an end to it.

"I wanted to " she said. "I wanted to stop it so badly".

He stopped what he was doing. She wanted to look up, but she daren't. "I wanted to reach in to the television and put my hand on yours and stop you doing it" she said, her body shaking with fear, and shivering in the cold. "I wanted to. You will never know how much I wanted to". She started to cry more freely. She wiped her eyes.

"You were in the shadows" he said. "You could not have stopped it".

Is that where you were? In the shadows? Her mind was racing. *Oh God. She was saying your name wasn't she? You watched your mother die and she was saying your name. She was saying your name and there was nothing you could do.* She forced herself to think back over what he had been saying. She forced herself to remember.

"She was attacked, that's all. She died of her injuries..... This mirror was hers. It is all I have of her now"

"I didn't know what to do" she said. "When they were saying my name, I didn't know what to do".

"Take the pain" he said. "That is all you can do".

He knelt down beside her. She held herself in position, not looking at him. "When someone is being hurt" he said, "and you cannot help them, all you can do is watch. Watch and take the pain of it all. My mother was raped. She was pawed over by dogs of men whilst I watched them do it from the shadows. When someone is being hurt, Maria, and you cannot help them, all you can do is watch. Watch and take the pain".

He moved closer to her. "How did it feel, Maria? How did it feel to watch and take the pain?"

"That's why you let me go?" she said.

"Yes. That is why I let you go. So that you may understand what it means to live safely, and so that you might understand, eventually, what it means to watch and take the pain. We are all helpless in our own ways, Maria".

He stood up and scraped the razor steadily over the last of her scalp. He felt it with his hand.

She was sobbing heavily. She moved her feet and felt the weight of the chains against her ankles. It had to be now. There was no more time.

"When they said my name, on those things you left for me, it hurt. I was born Maria, but for the years after you let me go, that wasn't my name".

"But it was the name you recognised. It was your true name". He knelt down beside her. "A name is such a personal thing. You never forget your true name".

She turned her head slowly, and looked into his eyes. "What is your name?" she said.

He smiled. "My name is Death, but others have known me as Sotto. It is Italian. It means 'from beneath'

"Sotto la superficie" she said, quietly.

"Yes. Beneath the surface. Past the superficial. Seeing the truth, perhaps". He stood up. "It is time now" he said.

"M… May I have the towel?" she asked.

He handed it to her and she leant forward, leaning in toward the mirror and seemingly getting to her feet. She was rubbing her scalp vigorously, shaking the towel as she leaned forward. Under the motion she lifted the scissors from beneath the mirror. She continued to rub as she opened up the blades.

"I don't want the syringe anymore", she said from under the towel.

"What?" she heard him say.

She had to be swift. Her feet were chained and if she lost the distance she would not survive. She pulled the towel away, whipping it around her wrist as she did so.

"I don't want the syringe anymore you sick-fuck!" she whirled around with the open blades of the scissors and screamed as she plunged them deeply into the soft flesh of his neck. For a split second he did nothing, the surprise overtaking him. Blood seeped heavily, too heavily down the front of his body. She pulled the scissors out and ran for the wall. "I want you to beat me down the way those men beat your mother down! I want you to rape the fuck out of me the way they raped the fuck out of your pleading mother! I want you to hear me begging for my life because do you know what? I am the only one of these poor bitches who will die like your mother! That will be my way! Begging and pleading with you inside me! Fighting for my life, and shouting your name!"

He lashed out at her but she ducked and moved along the wall, the chains dragging behind her.

"That's right you sick pervert! That's right Mummy's Boy! Do your worst! Did you watch her die, little boy? Did you see mummy getting all fucked up? Getting all screwed and beaten to death?"

"You will fucking die for this!" He screeched, staggering toward her, grasping blindly for the syringe.

"Come on then, Mummy's Boy" she shrieked. "Come and beat the bad men! Come and cut my lips off and slit my wrists and bleed me to death. Come and throw my carcass over the wall for all to see! Because do you know what? This won't end for you! This won't end when the moon cycle completes! Do you want to know why it's only women?! Do you want to know why you only cut and bleed women?! It's because you were a little boy! A little tiny boy in the shadows who couldn't do anything when his mummy got fucked up! You couldn't hit the men then and you can't hit them now, can you! No, because you are still a little fucking boy! Blaming his mummy, blaming her lips, blaming her hair, blaming her face and her beauty and her dresses and all the things that made her proud to be a woman and you are blaming them because you are too fucking weak to take the fight to the men where it fucking should be! Oh, you make me sick! You are so pathetic!"

"Shut your fucking mouth!" he shouted. He was crying now, spittle coming from his nose and mouth as he shouted. Blood poured down the front of his body.

She had the towel wrapped around her left hand, and the scissors open bladed in her right. She opened her arms in a Christ-like pose. "Sotto!" she wailed. "Sotto! Help mummy. Sotto please help mummy! Please!"

She leapt back up to her full height, shrieking at him. "I am the only one who will die like your mother did so do it to me! Beat me down! Rape me! Kick me to death! See how that makes you feel!"

He screamed as he lunged for her, syringe held high in his right hand. He plunged it down at her, punching her in the face as he did so. She fell to the ground, holding the open bladed scissors above her, arm held rigid as the full weight of his body fell on her. She felt the scissors crunch into his chest, driven not by her but by the force with which he crashed down. She felt sharp pain everywhere as they both hit the floor, and she scrambled, scrambled, scrambled to her feet.

She pulled the scissors from his chest. Blood was covering the floor now. She couldn't tell if it was her own or his. She didn't need to think. She raised the scissors high in the air and drove them down hard, repeatedly, into his neck. She was crying now, sobbing uncontrollably as she pulled them out and drove them in again. "You bastard!" she screamed over and over. "You sick fucking bastard!"

And then, as he stopped moving and she fell back onto her knees, she felt something sharp in her shoulder.

She pulled at it and found she was looking at the syringe. The plunger had been pushed all the way down.

She dropped it to the floor. She had to get out before the cocktail kicked in. She searched his pockets for the keys, wiping her eyes as she rifled first one pocket, then the next, frantic now, his blood covering her as she searched. Eventually her fingers touched something metal. She pulled them free. He tried to grab her but he was directionless, choking sounds bubbling from his wounded neck, unable to breathe. She unlocked her feet from the chains and ran to the door.

She didn't know how long she had. Seconds maybe. She was already starting to feel dizzy. Her vision blurring. She struggled with the keys. One lock. Two locks. Three locks.

Outside she felt the sudden rush of hot but stale air, tinged with the stench of oil and diesel. There was barely any light. She glanced behind her to make sure he hadn't followed. *The other girl* she thought *Where is the other girl?*

She felt her way along the cold tiled wall, the sounds of the deserted underground space throwing up the distant whispers of unidentified voices and the deep rumble of distant tunnels and trains.

"Hello!" she shouted. "Is anyone here? Can anyone help me?! Anyone! Please!"

She could see a dull glow from a tunnel opening a few hundred metres down the disused platform. Her feet dragged through the thick grey dust as she forced herself to move faster against the pain.

She ran for maybe twenty metres or so before her legs went from under her. She was still calling for help, her voice growing weaker, as she crawled against the cold stone of the platform as far as she could. At some point between the ecstasy of release and the misery of not knowing where she was or how she could find help, the drugs took her over and she slumped into a darkened haze. As she lost consciousness she thought she heard shouting. She thought there were lights ahead of her, but it was too late.

She could never have known that the shouts were identifiers from the armed Met officers making their way toward her, and the light she feared was the saving grace of McMullen's torch as the Detective Chief Inspector defied all warnings and ran toward her screaming Sally's name.

Epilogue

Five years later

"Thank you for coming" she said, as he approached her.

He smiled. "Why wouldn't I come? It's been a long time, Maria".

"Maybe for you. For me it's the only free life I have ever known these last few years. I still feel like a child".

He smiled again. "I would have contacted you, but we don't really have the luxury of keeping in touch, do we? MIT is as full-on as it always was".

"So I'm a distant memory", she said, joking.

He frowned. "Hardly".

She got up to walk with him. She guessed he had no intention of taking a seat beside her; He seemed disinterested in the beauty around them, the vibrancy of Hyde Park where the City met the green heart – it's own in-built landscape of escape.

They walked slowly under the line of trees. Couples lay on the grass, talking, kissing, experiencing the peace of each other.

"Congratulations on your promotion" she said.

He bowed his head, hands in his pockets. "How did you know?"

"I look you up every now and then, on the net, just to see where you are these days. If it wasn't for you I would be dead".

"Be honest with yourself, Maria" he said. "You were pretty much hell-bent on putting yourself in danger come what may".

"I had my reasons, Detective Chief Inspector Webber".

"Don't mock us, Maria. A lot of good people put themselves in harm's way to help you. We did our job this time round where it wasn't done before".

"I know" she said. "It wasn't meant like that".

They walked on in silence for a while.

"So what was it you wanted to talk about?", he asked.

She stopped at the fountain, dipping her fingers into the cool water, squinting against the shimmering reflection of the July sun.

"I'm selling up. Moving away".

"From London?"

"From England". She turned to face him. "Through my NHS contacts I've got the chance to go to Australia. I've the got the right qualifications, enough money. It's far enough away for me to believe I can really start again".

He took out a pack of cigarettes. Lit one up.

"I'm pleased for you" he said. "I thought about doing something similar right after the dust settled over the Circle Line case".

"Why didn't you?"

"The only people I ever loved may be dead, but their spirit stays in London. To leave that behind seems wrong, somehow. Like I dishonour them. I still live in the same flat, still think about that day he broke in. I still think about those words *"Do you think they called out your name?"* and I realise now that it would have been impossible for them not to. Whether it was into a phone, or just the little one calling for me, it would have been impossible for them not to think of me in the last moments".

He broke off, stopping himself before he reached a point where he couldn't stop. That stuff was in a box now, tucked away. Gone but not forgotten.

"The point is" he said flatly "I belong here".

She touched his arm. "You are a good man, Joe. I knew that the moment I first met you. I thought maybe you were naive, because you believed in the strength of the Met in a way I didn't agree with, but that didn't change your heart".

"A broken heart" he said.

"It will mend" she said firmly. "Mine did"

He looked at her, brow furrowed as if he had been asked to answer a question to which there was no known answer. "Maybe" he said, not really believing it.

They walked on through the park. "When do you go?" he asked.

"Soon. I had to wait a long time for the Visa but that will be through this summer. After that, I will be gone".

"Do you want me to tell Claire?"

"I don't suppose she will be interested, do you?"

"Who knows. No-one has had any contact with her since she left. You know she never came back to work, don't you?"

"I didn't know for sure. I heard a few rumours".

"When we recovered Sally I think she decided right there and then, down in that shit-pit, that she was getting out of the force".

"I can't say I blame her".

"She had always said the job ruined her marriage. She wasn't going to let it take her daughter away as well". He glanced up at the July sun. "I envy her".

"What, you'd consider leaving the force?"

"No" he said coldly. "I envy her having the choice. I have no-one to leave it for, not now. To be honest, I am not sure I want it anyway. Once my family were gone, I was crystallised. With them gone, I only have the job".

"And you can't leave the job because you think they died for it".

He looked at her with that same quizzical look. "I guess so, yes".

She took his hands in hers. "Joe, you are a good man and a good police officer because you believe in what you do. Sometimes in life, all you have is what you believe in. Christ, I should know because for years and years I had nothing I believed in and I might as well have been dead. Because of you, I have something to believe in now: Freedom. True freedom. You gave me freedom from the fear that he was coming after me. Yes, I know everyone had a hand in it, but it was you who drove it forward. It was you who took up the reigns when Claire crumbled. Without you, I would still be faithless. So for that, I thank you. That's why I wanted to see you. I wanted to say thank you, before I was out of the country and gone forever".

He let her touch infuse through him, absorbing it.

"You could have gone any time. You could have made the run for Australia even when he was alive".

"But I wouldn't have been free" she said. "It would have been exactly what you just called it – a run. Thanks to you I don't have to run anymore. Wherever I go now I am free. I was free from the moment you dragged me out of Brompton Road because at that moment, when he was dead, it didn't matter where in the world I was, I was free because I was able to believe in something. With him gone, I was free to believe that living might at last be possible".

"Something to believe in" he said, smiling.

"Yes", she said softly. "Because sometimes that's all we've got".

He pulled his hands away and reached for his cigarettes. "I wish you well, Maria", he said, "I really do".

His mobile phone rang out from his jacket. "The office", he said, as he checked the screen. "I should…"

"You should take it" she said, smiling. "You are free to do what you want to do, Joe, and that's why you'll take that call". She kissed him quickly on the cheek. "It's what you believe in".